Acclaim for *Sweet Olive*

"Judy Christie writes small town fiction with big time charm! *Sweet Olive* is a tender, romantic tale loaded with faith, hope, and heart."

—LISA WINGATE, NATIONAL BEST-SELLING
AUTHOR OF *THE PRAYER BOX* AND *FIREFLY ISLAND*

"In *Sweet Olive*, Judy Christie invites us into a community of people who value beauty and prize authenticity, in life and in art. Her story draws readers into this community and makes us want—like the main character Camille—to put down roots."

—MARYBETH WHALEN, AUTHOR OF *THE MAILBOX*,
THE GUEST BOOK, AND *THE WISHING TREE* AND
DIRECTOR OF SHE READS, WWW.SHEREADS.ORG

"When Camille Gardner is sent to Sweet Olive, Louisiana, to wrap up an oil deal, she plans to get in, get it done, and get out. Distractions prevail—first the captivating and whimsical art of local craftsmen, and then the flying sparks from the handsome attorney who opposes her business plans. Soon Camille's assignment in Sweet Olive is completely, wonderfully derailed in the most unexpected way. Talented author Judy Christie delivers a page-turning tale of endearing characters set in charming small Louisiana towns."

—SUZANNE WOODS FISHER,
AWARD-WINNING AUTHOR OF
THE SEARCH AND *THE WAITING*

"Louisiana charm! With an endearing cast of characters, *Sweet Olive* is a heartfelt story with so many twists and turns I couldn't turn the pages fast enough. I can't wait to see what Judy Christie does next with the Trumpet and Vine series!"

—CARLA STEWART, AWARD-WINNING AUTHOR
OF *CHASING LILACS* AND *SWEET DREAMS*

"I enjoyed Judy Christie's *Sweet Olive* so much. We all loved her Green series, of course. But in *Sweet Olive* she turns up the heat and goes deep into the pain of the past then brings us into the hope of the future. Having lived in Louisiana for close to thirty years, I understood these characters and loved visiting with them. The story made me homesick but it also made me smile and cheer and sigh. I loved it from the first page and I think you will too. If you're looking for a good David vs. Goliath story with a little bit of Louisiana lagniappe, this is the book for you!"

—LENORA WORTH, AUTHOR
OF *SWEETHEART BRIDE*

MAGNOLIA
MARKET

A Trumpet and Vine Novel

Judy Christie

ZONDERVAN®

ZONDERVAN

Magnolia Market

Copyright © 2014 by Judy Christie

This title is also available as a Zondervan e-book.
Visit www.zondervan.com.

This title is also available as a Zondervan audiobook.
Visit www.zondervan.com.

Requests for information should be addressed to:
Zondervan, *Grand Rapids, Michigan 49546*

Library of Congress Cataloging-in-Publication Data

Christie, Judy Pace, 1956-
  Magnolia market / Judy Christie.
    pages cm.
  ISBN 978-0-310-33057-8 (trade paper)
  I. Title.
  PS3603.H7525M35 2014
  813'.6--dc23

                          2014011398

All Scripture quotations, unless otherwise indicated, are taken from The Holy Bible,
New International Version®, NIV®. Copyright © 1973, 1978, 1984, 2011 by Biblica, Inc™
Used by permission. All rights reserved worldwide.

Any Internet addresses (websites, blogs, etc.) and telephone numbers in this book are
offered as a resource. They are not intended in any way to be or imply an endorsement
by Zondervan, nor does Zondervan vouch for the content of these sites and numbers
for the life of this book.

Publisher's Note: This novel is a work of fiction. Names, characters, places, and
incidents are either products of the author's imagination or used fictitiously.
All characters are fictional, and any similarity to people living or dead is purely
coincidental.

Cover design & illustration: Wayne Brezinka
Cover photography or: IstockPhoto
Interior design: Mallory Perkins

Printed in the United States of America

14 15 16 17 18 19 20 / RRD / 20 19 18 17 16 15 14 13 12 11 10 9 8 7 6 5 4 3 2 1

For Paul

Chapter 1

$\mathcal{A}$very Broussard rearranged a stack of cashmere sweaters on the antique cypress table and straightened the lamp shade. The cozy glow settled her nerves on the gloomy Louisiana afternoon.

She moved behind the counter, then shuffled a stack of credit-card receipts, a small smile visiting her face. Devoted customers, undeterred by a steady January rain, had swooped in for the shipment of Mardi Gras gowns, extra profit flying through the stained-glass door. Only a couple of women had whispered loud enough for her to overhear, but today their snide words did not sting.

Last year had been tough, but the store was at its peak. Everything was in order.

She savored her long-buried happiness.

The tinkling of the bell on the front door snuffed her optimism, though, and she glanced down for a quick assessment of her appearance. The form-fitting knit dress and leather boots whispered style and competence. Her white-gold bracelet reminded her of what was at stake.

Prepared, she plastered on a smile—but balked before the practiced words of welcome escaped.

The guest was not who she expected.

A man, more than six feet tall, stood under the blue awning, just beyond the threshold. His khaki canvas jacket was soaked, and his short, dark hair—brown or black, it was hard to tell—glistened with rain.

Despite the blast of frigid air, warmth washed through Avery at his easy grin. When he stepped to the threshold, his presence infused the space with a dose of male energy that caused Avery's heart to thud.

He was as unlike the rare males who dashed in for a gift certificate as the boutique was from a Dollar Store.

The attraction fizzled when he stomped his boots, leaving a pile of mud at the entrance.

"Sorry for the mess." His attention didn't leave her as his deep voice, with a trace of southern drawl, preceded him into the store. "Your intercom out back isn't working."

He carried an olive-drab tool bag and looked vaguely familiar. He wasn't their regular deliveryman—and surely not a customer.

She straightened her shoulders.

Whoever he was, she wanted him on his way before Evangeline arrived.

He set his tools down and stood on the terra-cotta tile inside the door. "I'm here to start on the repairs. I'll add that intercom to the list."

She shook her head, hoping her smile would soften the words. "I'm afraid you've got the wrong address. This is Evangeline's Boutique."

His dark brown eyes narrowed, forming a tiny furrow between his brows.

"I'd be happy to take one of your business cards," she added. "I'll need to have a few repairs done in the spring."

The furrow deepened, and he glanced at his black sports watch. "I was sure we agreed on five." The grandfather clock in the corner punctuated his remark.

The five somber chimes caused Avery to draw in a breath. "I hate to send you back out into this weather, but I have a business meeting. Would you like to use the phone to—?"

The creak of the back entrance interrupted her, and she scurried past the sweaters to grab the guy by the arm. "I need to lock up now."

He looked at her hand on his arm, his eyes lingering before moving back to her face.

"Please," she whispered, trying to tug him toward the door.

But his work boots didn't budge as Evangeline glided around the corner. Despite the messy weather, she wore a white wool suit that cost more than most people spend on rent. She propped her umbrella against the counter, a puddle dripping onto the heart-of-pine floor Avery had spent most of Sunday afternoon hand-polishing.

Perfect coral lipstick accentuated the smile Evangeline bestowed upon the man. A glimpse of what looked like relief ran through his eyes.

"You're early!" she chirped. "What a doll you are for working me in." Her words bore the saccharine tone usually reserved for social occasions and never bequeathed to employees. And *doll*? Rugged, handsome, appealing perhaps. Definitely not *doll*.

Evangeline's stare went to Avery's hand, still resting on the muscular arm. A familiar look of disapproval returned.

Snatching her fingers away, Avery took a step back, then fidgeted with her heavy bracelet. His smile slight, the man looked from her to Evangeline. "I'm afraid I caught Avery off guard. We finished our last job ahead of schedule."

He knew her name? Evangeline had expected him? Avery scrolled through her memory. Was he a new handyman for the family's rental property?

"I'm sorry." Avery's gaze locked with those dark eyes, which surprisingly calmed her. "I didn't have an appointment on my calendar."

Evangeline swooped between them and placed her hand on the man's back in a movement so unlike her that Avery caught her breath. "You can wait in the workroom while I finish up with Avery. It won't take long."

"Don't rush on my account." His eyes met Avery's again, reflecting something she feared was pity. Evangeline's eyes, on the other hand, were as cold as the temperature outside.

Avery didn't blink. She had learned early on that Evangeline seized upon any sign of weakness, and Avery would show none. "You didn't mention you'd scheduled repairs," she said as the man picked up his tool bag and headed to the back. "I didn't budget for that."

Evangeline responded with a royal wave of a hand. "Our property manager suggested we take care of a few things."

"We agreed to wait until the closing." Avery's stomach churned. "The bank needs the final paperwork from your lawyer. Didn't you get my messages?"

"Avery, Avery." Evangeline made her name sound like a criticism. "There's been a change in plans."

"We don't have time for a change in plans. The closing is next week." The man had begun hammering in the back room, and the noise mirrored the pounding in her head.

Evangeline stared at the back door, her face impassive. "Creswell's attorney advised us to go in a different direction. Another buyer approached us."

"But . . . what . . ." A moment passed before Avery regained control. "I held up my end of our deal. The shop had its best year ever."

Evangeline stroked a scarf draped around a vintage dress form. "I'll admit you've got a good eye, but that is not sufficient."

"The details are set!" Avery gestured around the showroom. "I made this profitable."

"That you have." Evangeline took the scarf from the display and draped it around her neck. "You increased the value of my little shop quite a bit."

Avery closed her eyes for a second, then nodded. "I'll pay more. Amend the contract. I'll sign. Let's get this over with."

"That doesn't suit Creswell and me."

Avery shook her head so hard that a few whisps of blond hair escaped her updo and fell around her face. "Cash flow is good, and I have a little in savings. I can handle the note." It wouldn't be easy, but she would do whatever it took to make the boutique hers, to get her life back.

"Without our assistance, the bank doesn't find you the caliber of customer they want. Everyone agrees it's time for you to leave Samford." Evangeline's mouth was pinched, as though someone had taken a key and tightened her lips.

"My future depends on this!" Avery shouted over the hammering. "And I am not leaving Samford. It's my home."

"Must you make everything difficult? Creswell should have seen to this a year ago. The house, the car, the job—all of it."

Avery gripped the bracelet so tightly its ridges stung her hand. "I worked hard for all of that. Without me, this shop would have gone under five years ago."

Evangeline, moving from behind the counter, reminded Avery of a water moccasin about to strike. "Our name has been raked through the mud far too long. This is over." She brushed at her skirt as she said the word *mud*, as though a speck could have landed on her outfit. "You don't belong here." One more swipe. "You never did."

Anger and betrayal erupted within Avery, and she stepped toe-to-toe with Evangeline. "I'm not the one who tarnished the perfect family. I've done everything you asked. Everything." The hammering stopped, causing the words to reverberate through the store.

Gripping the counter, Avery met Evangeline's gaze, holding it until she looked away. A small victory, at least.

As the quiet grew, the handyman stepped from the rear of the store. He exchanged a quick look with Evangeline, who distanced herself from Avery. "Everything all right?"

"It will be," Avery said. *It has to be.* Focusing on an upholstered chair near the dressing room, she willed the tears not to gather. She had not cried before, and she would not cry now.

The carpenter shrugged. As he strode into the back, his steps and the ticking of the clock accentuated the heavy silence between Avery and Evangeline.

"I lost far more than you did," Evangeline said after a moment. For an instant, she looked less like a shrew and more like a grieving mother. Maybe somehow they could heal together. Then she spoke again. "You must go."

"Whoa." The handyman reappeared with two bottles of

water and took a step backward at the comment. He looked from one to the other, as though weighing what to say next. "Do you think you should sit down? Maybe calm down a little?"

Avery whirled, accidentally bumping his arm. The man didn't flinch when one bottle flew out of his hand, splashing onto his faded chambray shirt.

"Honestly, Avery," Evangeline snapped, "have some dignity. And I do not need to calm down. What gives you the right to come in here and give me advice?"

"My bad." He headed toward the back but, after a couple of steps, stopped and swiveled to face them. "Would you like me to give Ross a call?"

So he knew Ross too. *But then almost everyone knows Ross.*

"Absolutely not. He's out of town, and I won't have him bothered." Evangeline snatched up the designer handbag she had given Avery two Christmases ago. "Give me the keys, Avery. Now. This debacle is over."

"Just a minute." The carpenter's voice was calm. "Are you sure you want to do this?"

"This is not your concern," Evangeline hissed. "Get your own life straightened out before you interfere with ours." She marched to the front door and yanked it open.

The bells mocked Avery with their happy sound, and she looked through the rain-splashed windows. Streetlights had already come on, and the rain sputtered into sleet. "Without this shop, I have nothing," she whispered, as much to herself as to Evangeline.

The guy moved closer. "Let me drive y'all home."

"That's not necessary," Avery said.

"I told you to stay out of this."

Back straight, Avery headed toward a wrought-iron coatrack at the rear exit and threw a glance at the man. She wasn't certain what his part in this was, but he was no casual handyman. Their eyes fixed on each other for another moment before she spoke. "I apologize for drawing you into our . . . negotiations."

Evangeline made a production of locking the front door, then twirled Avery's key on her index finger. The man shook his head and followed Avery to the door, where she was putting on her jacket. "You shouldn't be driving." His gaze was full of a look she knew too well.

Pure pity.

She had recoiled from that look for months. But on this day, from this stranger, it gave her the strength she needed.

With Broussard support or not, she had to make a change.

"I'll be fine. But thanks." She walked through the door.

"This is for the best," Evangeline said before the door clicked shut.

Sleet hit Avery's face, its sting almost welcome.

The house was dark when Avery pulled into the driveway.

The pale yellow cottage, once welcoming, looked forlorn. Most of the trees and bushes were bare. The giant live oak, which Avery had dreamed would hold a swing for their children, loomed over her, tiny icicles forming on its branches.

She slipped on the steps but regained her balance, stumbling again when she saw the overstuffed envelope with its familiar scrawl peeking out of her mailbox. Thankfully her dad wasn't here to see the mess her life had become.

Sticking the package under her arm, she jiggled the brass lock, stubborn in the icy dampness. A small click sounded as the key snapped off in her hand.

Clutching the package and her purse, she slid onto the porch and stared out into the night. All those self-help books she'd read had lied. Fresh starts weren't as glamorous as promised.

Chapter 2

T. J. Aillet stood under the back awning at Evangeline's Boutique, sleet hitting his head. He should have listened to Bud and worn a cap. And Bud should have listened to him and turned down this job.

Evangeline peeled out of the parking lot, her Mercedes fishtailing on Vine Avenue, and he blew out his breath.

After a brief hesitation, he drew out his phone—and then stuck it back into his pocket. This was the kind of mess he had vowed to stay out of when he came back to Samford. He had more important things to deal with than a couple of rich women arguing about money.

But Avery, with those sad blue eyes—and, okay, that clingy knit dress that hugged her curves—had punched him in the gut.

He looked down Vine Avenue, neither woman's taillights anywhere in sight. He'd never seen anyone—male or female—do battle with Evangeline with such vigor. "Negotiations," Avery had called it. A *big mess* was more like it, but she hadn't seemed cowed.

With that long blond hair piled in a knot and those high-heeled boots, she looked every bit fancy society—but had shown a kind side. Instead of shoving him back out into the cold, she had asked for one of his business cards. Classy.

No one had mentioned how pretty she was, nor how much spunk she had.

T. J. gave his head a quick shake. He needed to stay as far away from this situation as possible.

He walked toward the parking lot, his boots crunching on the growing carpet of ice, his hands freezing as he opened the truck door. His phone buzzed before he could start the engine, and he looked at the number, tempted to let it roll to voice mail.

But he couldn't.

He jabbed at the button with a thumb that had gone numb. "I figured I might hear from you."

"Are you at the dress shop?" Ross Broussard sounded nothing like his usual upbeat self.

"Afraid so."

"How bad was it?"

"Pretty ugly." He cranked his engine. "Where are you?"

"Baton Rouge." Ross sighed. "I don't know what to do. My mother called from your parents' house, huffing and puffing about Avery attacking her. Said you witnessed it."

"Not exactly. I was there for a few repairs." Just what he needed. His mother involved. "They were fighting about the store."

Ross cleared his throat. "Today's the one-year anniversary of Cres's death."

"Man, I'm sorry." T. J. looked at the ice gathering on the street, annoyed at Ross for reasons he didn't understand. "No wonder they were on edge."

"Mother says Avery backed out of the deal and is moving back to Lafayette. Too many bad memories."

"That's not what it sounded like to me." Despite hammering as hard as he could, T. J. had overheard plenty of the conversation. He had packed up his tools to leave—but when he rounded the corner, Avery looked like someone had jabbed her in a tender spot, and he decided to intervene.

Which hadn't worked out particularly well.

"I want her to stay in Samford, put the past behind her." Ross's voice was hoarse. "She and my mother have never been close, but I hoped they'd work out some sort of peace." He exhaled. "We all could use that."

T. J. wasn't a betting man—not anymore—but he would never put money on peace between those two. "Avery thinks your mother tricked her, but I didn't catch the details." He gave a small cough. "I was doing my best not to eavesdrop."

"Is Avery still at the shop?"

"She took off before your mom. I offered to drive her home, but she wouldn't listen." He adjusted the heater. "It's a lousy night to be out, especially as upset as she was."

"I hate to ask, T. J., but could you check on her? Maybe go by her house?"

T. J. rubbed his neck. The alarm had gone off early that morning, the weather sending him and Bud out for a handful of emergency repairs. He was tired. Besides, Avery was the kind of Samford woman he wanted to avoid. "I don't think she's in the mood for company."

"I'll owe you one. If you check on her, I'll make sure Atilla the Mom got home. My father should be there by now, but Avery . . . she doesn't have anyone."

Avery alone. Uncertain. Mourning. T. J. could fix a broken intercom or piece of furniture. But working on a broken heart? *Not going to happen.* "How about I call Marsh? He's better at this sort of thing."

"He's down here, handling the legal work on my new office."

"Camille?"

"That'd be awkward. I don't think they've met. At least Avery knows who you are."

T. J. didn't mention that Avery hadn't a clue who he was. Her confusion had been written all over her face as she attempted to figure out how he fit into the Broussard picture. "Your father maybe?"

"That'd be worse than my mother."

"Where does she live?" He couldn't believe the question had come from his mouth.

"On Division Avenue, a couple of blocks from your place. So you'll check on her?"

"I'll drive by and make sure she got home." He paused. "Tell me again why you're in Baton Rouge?"

"It's your brother's fault. He cornered me one Friday night at the Sweet Olive Art Gallery and gave me quite a lecture."

"That's Marsh," T. J. muttered.

"Told me I should quit acting like nothing had happened. Kicked me in the butt and told me to move on with my life."

T. J. couldn't hold back a laugh. "Sounds like the same speech he gave me when he and Bud lassoed me in Seattle."

"You got double-teamed. You were a bigger mess."

"And this from a man asking me to do him a favor?"

Ross snorted. "I'm glad you're back. Maybe between us we can keep Marsh under control."

"Fat chance. Since Camille appeared, he's over the top. Says he wants everyone to be as happy as he is." By now a sheet of ice covered the street. "I'd better get going."

"So you'll look after Avery?"

"I'll drive by her house."

"She's great. You'll like her."

"I'm driving by, not moving in."

"I owe you one," Ross repeated and then exhaled, long and loud. "Will things ever get back to normal?"

"For all of our sakes, I hope so."

⁓

No lights were on in the house when T. J. pulled up to the curb, but Avery's late-model SUV sat in the driveway.

Should I go to the door?

His cell phone buzzed, and he grabbed it, ready for another call from Ross. But it was his parents' number. It all rushed back. He had stayed away from Samford for a reason.

"Is it true, Thomas?" his mother demanded before he had a chance to say hello. "Evangeline told me how awful that witch was to her. On today of all days." She drew a breath. "I wish you wouldn't get involved in things like this."

He squeezed his eyes shut. "I'm not involved in anything. Evangeline hired Bud and me to do a carpentry project."

His mother let out her trademark sigh, a long, slow inhale followed by a gust of breath. "Twenty-eight years old and doing manual labor. How demeaning, Thomas." Another sigh. "You could have gone into medicine like your father. Or law, like your brother."

"I like my work." He hated his defensive tone but could rarely ignore his mother's carping. "Bud's taught me more about design in the past year than I learned in four years of college. The business is growing faster than we can keep up with."

"I don't want to talk about how talented my ex-husband is." His mother's tone was brittle. "At least you won't be working with that Avery woman at the boutique anymore." Her voice lowered as though telling a secret. "She acts sweet, but she's awful. She hasn't accepted one social invitation since Cres died. Can you even imagine how difficult that is for Evangeline?"

He knew he would regret asking but . . . "Why does Evangeline care what parties Avery goes to?"

There came the sigh again. "The same reason it hurts me when you avoid obligations. Thomas, our station requires a standard of behavior that goes beyond whittling and picking up stray dogs."

"Mother, this is not a good time—"

"Working with Bud is a slap in the face to our entire family." She was working herself into a familiar frenzy. "Everyone in town is talking about it."

"Okay, so it's not ordinary, but does anyone seriously care? Dad's fine with it, and Marsh is half jealous he didn't think of it. I wouldn't have gone into business with Bud otherwise." Granted, not many sons worked with their mothers' ex-husbands. He wouldn't mention that his father had sent a dozen big customers their way.

"My feelings count for nothing?"

Maybe moving back had been a prodigal son fantasy. But he enjoyed working with Bud, loved spending time with Marsh and Camille, admired his father.

"You told me for years it was time to grow up." He'd spent years dodging her ideas for what he should do with his life. How he should dress. What kind of car he should drive. Hint: not a pickup truck. "I'm a man now."

"You're still my youngest son, Thomas."

He looked at the dark house. Apparently plenty of folks had opinions on what Avery should be doing too. At least they had that in common.

A movement in the side yard caught his eye. "Mom, I've gotta run. I'll check in later. Love you."

"I love you too, Thomas. I just wish—"

"Talk to you tomorrow." He hung up, watching the shadowy figure walk around the house. Avery, her back to him with both arms extended, was trying to keep her balance in those impractical high-heeled boots.

Jumping out of the truck, he planted his feet on the icy ground, then strode toward her. She turned as he neared, her feet moving back and forth like a novice ice-skater, and T. J. put his arm around her waist to steady her. The faint scent of flowers clung to her hair, a contrast to the smell of wood smoke drifting from a neighbor's fireplace.

"Easy. You're going to break your neck."

"That'd be on par with the kind of day I'm having." She tried to move away from him but clutched his arm when she nearly fell. "Did Evangeline send you to beat me up? Or are you here to evict me?"

He winked. "I try not to assault people during inclement weather. I live a couple of streets over, and Ross asked me to make sure you got home okay. I'm T. J., by the way."

"Well, T. J., you've done your duty." She saluted. "You can report to Ross that I'm safe and let Evangeline know I haven't run off with the family silver." She waggled her eyebrows. "Yet."

"Listen, Avery." He sensed this turf was more treacherous than the icy sidewalk. "Ross would appreciate a call."

She wrapped her arms around her stomach. "He's a sweet-heart, but he doesn't need to get dragged into this."

"He's your brother-in-law. He wants to help."

"Former brother-in-law." She sniffed. "And my cell phone's dead. This storm's knocked everything out."

"You're welcome to use mine." He prayed she wasn't about to get hysterical on him. "Let me help you into the house. You're freezing."

"I'm locked out."

He smiled with relief. "Now *that's* something I can help you with. I'll get my tools."

Chapter 3

$\mathcal{A}$very's champagne-colored Tahoe fishtailed as she turned at the corner of Trumpet and Vine, and for once she was thankful for the oversize vehicle. Tapping the brake, she held her breath as she spun through the empty intersection.

Sane people had stayed home today, but despite the winter-weather advisory, she had been frantic to get out of the house, the walls confining after the fight with Evangeline and the mysterious T. J.'s unexpected visit.

A vacant church sat on one corner, and an overgrown vacant lot occupied another. A bright spot was the Sweet Olive Folk Art Gallery, a renovated two-story house on the southwest corner. A motley group of folk artists had opened it at the end of the year, but Avery hadn't worked up the nerve to visit.

Nor had she met the woman who developed it, a newcomer named Camille Gardner whom Evangeline disapproved of on principle. From Samford scuttlebutt, Camille sounded like the kind of woman Avery would like, a person who didn't let road-blocks keep her from her dreams.

Trumpet Street took residents to the interstate and the Red River. Vine Avenue took them to downtown Samford, past the boutique, or to the artist's colony at Sweet Olive. The latter route was dotted with new oil wells, the catalyst for the birth of the gallery.

Avery looked at the bright-colored bottle tree on the gallery lawn and regretted avoiding the Christmas grand opening, one of a dozen invitations that had gone into the trash.

Even going to the grocery store had become a chore, making Magnolia Market—with its couldn't-care-less personality—a daily stop.

The year ahead was going to be different, however.

She would visit the gallery. Return to the trendy market where Cres had picked up gourmet meats for parties and ordered smoked turkeys for Evangeline's Thanksgiving feasts. Perhaps she would even venture back to church.

Clutching the steering wheel, Avery pulled into the parking lot and slid up to the curb. A small hand-lettered Open sign was crammed behind a metal bread advertisement on the old-fashioned screen door.

The metal building, with its peeling white paint, looked like a country store on a deserted road. Handwritten signs, including the menu for the grill, were taped to a smudged plate-glass window. Only a handful of promotions—for bottled water and sports drinks—looked like they'd been issued in this decade. Dim overhead lights glowed against the gray morning.

Her house's power hadn't even flickered on, and her cheeks grew warm at the recollection of T. J., who had appeared on yesterday of all days, guiding her through her dark house in search of a candle. That had been *after* he figured out her front-door lock had frozen.

Thank goodness she stopped short of accusing Evangeline of locking her out.

"Were you a Boy Scout?" she had asked as he pulled out a flashlight, a screwdriver, and a can of WD-40, unsticking the lock in minutes.

"Hardly." His dark eyes cut to where she squatted next to him on the cold porch. "Way too macho to be a do-gooder." He wrinkled his nose. "I was an idiot."

She stared at his mouth as he talked, his deep voice a soothing hum. No one else was stirring on her street, and the ice hit the ground with a crackle. The dark stillness and T. J.'s proximity created a feeling of intimacy, and Avery moved her gaze from his mouth to his eyes. He had clearly grown into a manly do-gooder—and a darned handsome one at that.

"Hmm," she murmured.

He smiled with such warmth that for a second she forgot she was sitting outside in January. "Hmm," he echoed and stared back.

There was no pity in his expression now.

Avery's eyes widened, and she stood so fast she slipped again. "Thank you so much for fixing my lock. I didn't mean to keep you."

T. J. rose more gracefully. "Do you have any candles?"

Her brain slipped out of gear as she processed the words. *This man and candlelight?*

"Candles?" he repeated. "Until the power comes back."

"Oh, right." Her face burned, and she pushed open the door. "I'm good. Thanks again."

But he walked in behind her. "Let's get you some light."

"Seriously?"

"What self-respecting man would leave you in the dark?" He tilted his head. "Which way?"

"The kitchen." Avery gestured to the left, the flashlight beam showing the path. She dug a haphazard collection of candles out of a cabinet and watched T. J. light them, then line them up on the bar that separated the house's front rooms. His hands were steady as the flames flickered, and the room went from desolate to romantic.

His dark eyes, shadowed in the low light, fixed on her. "That's a start. Now for the heat."

"Heat?" Avery was still appreciating the way he looked standing in the cozy kitchen.

"It's freezing in here."

"The power will probably be back on in no time. You've been great."

"You sure I can't take you somewhere?"

She wanted to push him out the door and beg him not to leave at the same moment. "I'm used to staying alone, and I've got plenty of covers."

His eyes narrowed, but he extended the flashlight. "Keep this."

"You'll need it." She fidgeted with her bracelet, cold against her wrist.

"I have another one." His fingers brushed hers as he placed it in her hand. "It's a gift."

"Well, it does happen to be my birthday." She forced a smile at this confession.

A frown raced across his face. "Today?"

She curtsied, the beam of the flashlight making a weak light show, and waited for the reappearance of that horrid look of pity.

But it didn't come.

Instead he leaned in and gave her a quick hug. "It seems a little late to say 'have a good one.'" Then he grinned.

The teasing was the best gift she had had in months, and the house did not seem as bleak when he drove off.

And this morning, gray and icy or not, looked brighter.

Once she had her coffee, she would go to the boutique. No matter how upset Evangeline had been yesterday, she wouldn't sell to someone else. Even she wasn't that vindictive.

Avery climbed out of the SUV and headed for the market, watching a white sedan pull into the place next to her. It slid uncomfortably close.

"Sorry. I'm not used to the weather," the driver said, spiky red hair glowing as she eased down the passenger window. The conservative car clashed with her hair, which had been brown the last dozen times Avery had seen the woman here.

"No problem." Pushing open the store door, Avery stomped the icy sludge off her turquoise-plaid rubber boots and smiled at the elderly man and woman behind the counter. As she did nearly every morning, she walked to the far wall and poured a cup of dark-roast coffee, dumped a pack of sweetener into it, and snapped on a plastic lid.

The market was small, slightly larger than a high school classroom, but the space was jammed with shelves. Passing the dusty display of peanut patties, she pulled a container of orange juice from a wheezing cooler and slid the stubborn door shut.

The cooler was only about half full. Inside, a bottle of Yoo-hoo lay on its side, its yellow label a bright spot. On long-ago church visits with her father in South Louisiana, she'd been rewarded with one of the chocolate drinks at a store owned by a deacon. The drink tasted cold and sweet as her father chatted under fluorescent lights, an antiseptic smell of cleaning supplies in the room.

She liked those memories.

Walking to the counter, she laid a five-dollar bill on the linoleum tacked to the wood. "I'm living dangerously today," she said with a grin. "I'll have a biscuit too."

Bill, the hunched-over owner, raised his eyebrows. "If you were gonna start eating biscuits today, you shoulda got here earlier. Electric company got 'em all this morning. They worked all night to get our power back on."

Avery looked over at the biscuit case and frowned. Sitting in the front corner was one biscuit wrapped in white butcher paper. She tapped on the case. "What about that one?"

"I'm holding that for someone."

"You can *reserve* a biscuit?" She didn't pull off the joking tone she was going for.

"I can do anything I please." Bill's words reminded her of Evangeline's, causing her face to grow hot. He punched the keys on the gigantic gilt-edged cash register. "Will there be anything else?"

"Is there a problem, dear?" A wavering voice came from behind the case, and Avery strained to see Martha, Bill's wife, crocheting in an old office chair.

The man met Avery's eyes. "Just a cranky customer."

"I'm not the one who's cranky."

"This weather has everyone out of sorts." Martha rose gingerly from the chair. She looked like she might fall to the floor as her skein of thread had done. "Is your power out, honey?"

"Yes, ma'am." Avery forced a chuckle. "I really need that biscuit."

"I should have made more." Martha steadied herself by gripping the wooden frame of the counter. "I flat ran out of steam."

Bill looked over her shoulder and withdrew the biscuit from

the case. As Avery reached for it, he snatched it back and pointed a gnarly finger at a word written in blue ballpoint ink. *Hers.* "You might come in here every day, but you don't own the place. This is sold."

"I could make you a piece of toast," Martha said. "Or would you like a package of doughnuts?"

"No one's coming in to claim that biscuit on a day like today." Avery kept her voice soft, not wanting to upset Martha, but she glared at Bill.

"Nothing would keep me from my daily biscuit," a voice said behind her.

"This gal's trying to steal it from you." Bill's tone lightened.

Avery turned. The red-haired woman laughed as she approached, a small carton of milk in her hand. Underneath an all-weather coat, she wore a pair of black slacks with a sweater. A large, middle-aged woman, she wasn't fat—more like oversize. With the new hair color and spiky cut, she looked like a punk rocker-turned-secretary.

"Sorry," Avery muttered and patted the money she had laid on the counter. "I'll just have coffee."

"If you don't want the orange juice, put it back in the cooler," Bill said.

Avery sucked in a breath.

"Give her my biscuit, Bill. My treat. And I'll put that juice back for her."

Bill stared at the biscuit for a moment and laid it on the counter.

"That's okay." Avery picked up the cardboard coffee cup. "I don't need it."

The redhead picked up the small white package and thrust it, causing Avery to step back. The woman moved with her. "I want you to have it. Today's my birthday, and my boss will probably bring a cake anyway." She stepped nearer. "Take it."

With the biscuit almost against her coat, Avery grabbed it, murmured her thanks, and bolted for the door.

"You left your change," Bill yelled.

"Give it to her." Avery pushed the door hard and flung the screen door back, cold air hitting her hot face.

Juggling the coffee and biscuit, she jerked open the heavy SUV door and slid onto the leather seat. The door eased shut, not catching, but she didn't take time to adjust it nor to put on her seat belt.

She tossed the biscuit on the seat, plopped the coffee into the cup holder, then turned the key. The woman was just trying to be nice. It wasn't her fault Bill was a grouch.

The SUV sputtered and died. *Does everything have to be a hassle?*

Avery turned the key again, mashed the accelerator until the engine steadied, and jammed the vehicle into gear. The SUV hesitated again, so she stomped it, putting all her recent frustration into the effort.

But her vehicle didn't zoom backward as intended.

It lurched forward before skidding sideways with a sound like a lawn mower running over a steel pipe. The white car next to hers moved a foot or so, right up against Avery's SUV, and then jumped forward, Avery's vehicle dragging it.

The movement flung her toward the dashboard, the coffee and biscuit flying into the air just before Avery bumped the steering wheel. The rearview mirror fell onto the seat as the SUV cleared the curb. Her purse flew off the seat and spilled onto the floor.

She had been on a roller coaster in middle school that felt like this before it stopped, jerking her right and left. Her teeth jarred, and her mind scrambled for instructions on what to do.

Right before the vehicle hit the metal-and-glass wall, Ms. Carrottop burst from the store, jumping to the side as the SUV approached. "My car!"

Chapter 4

*T*he *wham* of the impact coincided with the air bag catapulting Avery back against the seat.

She closed her eyes and laid her head forward against the bag, then jerked back from the chemical smell. People said it had a sickening thud. No one mentioned how an air bag smelled.

What had Cres smelled with his last breath?

"Are you all right?" A female voice, the redhead probably, asked while someone knocked on the passenger window.

"Did you see that?" Bill's voice rang out. "She crashed into our store."

"I called 911." Martha picked up speed as she hobbled near. "The police are at a wreck on I-20. They want to know if she's conscious."

The redhead loomed next to Martha. Their path was blocked by Avery's vehicle across the sidewalk.

Dazed, Avery turned her neck and looked down at her body. No visible blood, but her skin was ice-cold. Her pulse pounded in her ears, and she fought to draw a breath. *I've got to get out of here!*

She leaned to push open the door but instead nearly fell off the seat and into the side of the white car. Her door was gone!

No, not gone. It was crushed against the back fender like a wadded-up piece of aluminum foil.

"We need to drive her to the hospital, Bill." Martha's voice wafted through the open door. "Or get an ambulance." The trio peered through the windshield as though looking at a museum exhibit.

"I don't need an ambulance." Avery scooted across the front seat, her bottom smashing the biscuit. Sausage and mustard smeared the seat, and she groaned.

"Where does it hurt?" The redhead opened the passenger door.

"Nowhere." Avery put a hand to her neck. "Everywhere. I'm sorry about your car. I have insurance."

"You'd better." The woman's laugh was shrill.

Avery's legs wobbled when she crawled out. "I'm Avery. Avery Broussard." She grabbed at the woman to keep from falling, which seemed to be something of a habit lately.

"Whoa, steady there. We need to ice that bump on your head and get your insurance papers. I'm Kathleen Manning."

Avery touched her forehead and winced.

Kathleen's gaze followed the movement, landing on her left hand. "We need to call your husband!" The corner spun when Avery shook her head.

"Is there someone else? Family? Coworkers? A friend?"

Family? No way would she worry her dad over this, and Evangeline wouldn't welcome a call. Maybe Ross, but T. J. had said he was out of town. *Coworkers?* She wasn't sure she had a job anymore. *Friends?* For a year she'd all but been a hermit.

No answer was needed, though, the question overshadowed

by the commotion of people stopping to gawk. They'd better not be here for a biscuit, or they were in for a big disappointment.

"Avery?" A man's voice joined the ruckus, and she squinted to see T. J. sprinting toward her. "Are you hurt?"

"Oh, dear Lord." She put her face in her hands. "Just a little headache."

"You're going to have a big headache," Bill said. "I expect you to pay for all the damages. And if this messes up our deal, you're responsible."

"Now, Bill." Martha patted his arm.

The parking lot tilted.

"She needs to sit down." T. J. put his arm around Avery's waist, and she relaxed as he eased her onto the curb.

"She a friend of yours?" Bill asked.

"She is." T. J. knelt beside her, so close she caught a glimpse of herself reflected in his eyes. Despite mud on the knees of his jeans, he smelled crisp and clean, a mix of cold outdoors and soap. Not the expensive cologne Cres had favored, but ordinary soap. An enticing scent, lacking pretension.

"Who are her people?" Martha wobbled closer.

"My family doesn't live here." Avery tried to stand.

"Careful." T. J. put a hand on her arm. "Relax."

The blare of sirens joined the cacophony in Avery's head. A police car roared through the intersection, sounding a loud horn as it pulled into the run-down parking lot, blue lights flashing.

"They made it after all." Martha sounded proud. A couple of bystanders stepped closer, embellishing what had happened to anyone who would listen. Bill shook his head and a metal cane simultaneously.

An African American woman in a tan police uniform approached with her forehead wrinkled. "Anyone hurt?"

"Just my store."

"Sir," she said to Bill in the voice of a middle-school principal, "I'm trying to establish if we need an ambulance." Her gaze landed on T. J. and widened. "T. J.? What's going on here?"

"Hey, Jazz. I don't think there are any serious injuries." He peered at Avery. "Do you need to go to the hospital?"

"I need to go to work."

The officer knelt and threw T. J. a big smile, a look Avery suspected he was used to from women. He smiled back, his eyes crinkling at the corners. "Avery, this is a friend of mine, Jazz Hamilton. She'll take good care of you."

"That Broussard woman doesn't need coddling." Bill pointed at the storefront. "This mess is her fault. Arrest her."

Avery nodded. "The accident was my fault."

"It wasn't an accident," Bill protested. "You destroyed our store."

"You should have been more careful," Martha said, her voice stronger.

Officer Hamilton held up her hand, her unpolished nails clipped short. "If everyone will be quiet, we can proceed." She flipped to a blank form on a clipboard, then slipped on a pair of reading glasses, her pen poised above the paper.

"Let's start with you, Avery. Tell me what happened."

"*I* told you," Bill growled, pointing at Avery. "That woman ran into our store."

The officer tilted her head, looking at Avery over her glasses.

"The parking lot was slick," Avery started.

"The ice had melted," Bill interrupted. "She was speeding. And mad. Real mad."

"Upset," Martha corrected.

"My car was parked next to hers, and she slid into it," Kathleen said.

Avery squeezed her eyes closed, and T. J. touched her hand.

"She smashed Kathleen's car first and then the front there." Bill gestured with his cane at the broken window and the hole in the building.

"Were you upset?" Officer Hamilton asked.

Only for a few years.

Bill broke in again. "She was mad because I wouldn't sell her a biscuit."

That small furrow appeared between T. J.'s eyebrows. "Bill, why don't you let Avery give her side of the story?"

"Good idea." The officer nodded.

"I wasn't speeding, and I didn't care about the biscuit. My car stalled, and I tried to back up, but I went forward instead." Avery put her hand to her head, wishing she could escape the crowd closing in around her.

"Are you sure you don't need to go to the hospital?"

"I need to get this over with."

The officer looked at Avery over her glasses. "Your license, please."

"It's, it's on the floorboard. And my insurance card's in the glove box."

"I'll get them." T. J. fished around in the car until he came up with the items.

Ms. Hamilton squinted at the license, and her gaze moved to

the small slip of white paper in her hands. "Do you have a current proof of insurance? This one's expired."

Avery's head ached as she tried to think where the new card was. "I'm insured."

"You'd better be," Kathleen muttered.

The officer walked to the back of the Tahoe and narrowed her eyes. "Your tags are expired too."

"That can't be right. One of the maintenance guys took care of that last week. He was supposed to put the updated insurance card in there too." The words made her sound like the spoiled rich woman she had fought so hard not to become. "I should have taken care of that myself. I'll pay for the damages."

"T. J., will you stay with her while I run her license?"

Avery frowned.

The officer arched one eyebrow. "Would you rather sit in the back of the patrol car?"

Avery gave her head a quick shake, and Ms. Hamilton spoke into a radio in the car and occasionally jotted something. Bill, still grumbling, ushered Martha back into the store. Kathleen placed a call, her voice urgent as she whispered into the receiver.

"You sure you don't want to call someone?" T. J.'s brown eyes were filled with concern. "Ross would—"

"Do you always rescue nutcases, or is it just me?"

He looked as though he was considering a smile. "I've needed rescuing a few times myself . . . At least you haven't thrown up on me."

"T. J. helps everyone." Officer Hamilton returned, clipboard in hand. "You couldn't ask for a better champion."

"Okay, Jazz. Don't go overboard." He nudged a rock with the

toe of his boot. "I just stopped for a glass of tea. It was a slow morning anyway."

"Yeah, right." The officer pointed at his muddy knees. "I heard about the busted pipe at the mission."

"Bud did most of the hard work on that one."

The radio on her police belt crackled with a message, and she sighed. "Enough chitchat." She handed Avery her license, insurance card, and a ticket. "Get that insurance straightened out immediately or you'll lose your license."

"Will do. I'm a very responsible person."

The officer's expression was impassive. "You might want to keep ice on that head and take a couple of ibuprofen."

Nearby, Kathleen's phone played a twangy country-and-western song, and she answered and spoke for a few moments before holding it away from her ear. "I'm having my car taken to the garage, Mrs. Broussard. Do you want them to tow yours?"

"It's Avery."

"Do you want them to tow yours, *Avery*? Yes or no?"

"Is the place reputable?"

Kathleen laughed, a big, bold sound. "She wants to know if you're reputable," she said into the phone.

"Oh, just tell them to tow it." This probably wasn't the time to call the Broussard mechanic.

"Do you have someone to drive you home?"

Avery turned to T. J. "I'd appreciate a lift. I can pay you."

He smiled. "This one's on the house."

Kathleen's cell phone buzzed, and she glanced at the text message on the screen. A shadow ran across her eyes before she looked up. "Could you drop me off too? Thanks to all this"—she waved at her car—"I'm late for work."

"Sure."

Kathleen held out her hand. "Avery, I'll need a check to cover my deductible right now. If your insurance doesn't pay, I'll need more, of course."

"My checkbook's in the car." She flinched as she looked at the smashed SUV.

"I'll get it—and your other things." T. J. headed to her vehicle. "Go sit down."

As Avery walked toward his truck, Kathleen was mumbling. "I knew better than to dye my hair red. You don't change your life by changing your hair color, no matter what Lindsey says."

Chapter 5

Avery burrowed under the quilt, wishing whoever was hammering would stop.

She sat up.

That wasn't hammering.

Someone was knocking—make that pounding—on her door.

Shivering, she ran a hand through her tangled hair and contemplated crawling back in bed.

Wham. Wham. Wham.

Already dressed, including her coat, she slipped her feet—covered in two pairs of socks—into the fleece-lined slippers next to the bed and exhaled, her breath hanging in the air.

"Avery Broussard," a voice called out. "Open this door immediately! I need to talk to you."

Light-headed, she made her way through the living room, her eyes feeling as though they were encrusted with gravel. A small beam of daylight shone over the plantation shutters, and the angle of the sun confused her. She must have napped longer than planned.

JUDY CHRISTIE

Glancing through a slat, she saw a mop of red hair. The woman she'd crashed into! Avery's mind scrambled to recall her name—Kathleen. That was it. Kathleen Manning.

Wham. Wham. Wham.

"Give me a minute," Avery muttered. After taking off her leather gloves, a gift from Cres on their first ski trip, Avery fumbled with the key in the dead bolt and wrestled the door open.

"You have a lot of nerve." Kathleen was a blur as she stormed into the room. "To think I nearly fell for that fragile southern belle act." She paused and gave Avery a once-over. "Are you going or coming?"

Avery looked down at her coat. "Neither. The power's out."

Kathleen formed her mouth into an odd little *O*. "Not anymore. They got it back on around midnight."

"Midnight?" Avery gave her head a quick shake.

"Have you been drinking?"

Avery pushed aside a stack of magazines and sank onto the tapestry ottoman that went with the uncomfortable chair Cres had bought. "I don't drink." She looked at the tiny Waterford-crystal clock on an end table. "What day is this?"

Kathleen peered at Avery. "Wednesday. The day after Tuesday when you rammed into my car."

Avery leaped up and bolted toward the door. "I have to talk to Evangeline."

Kathleen moved too, quick for her size. "Not so fast. After your insurance problem, you agreed to pay me for the damage you did to my car."

"I did pay you . . . *that* I remember. I wrote you a check on the ride to your office." Avery still found it hard to believe she could whip out a checkbook for whatever she needed. She'd worked hard for that privilege.

36

Reaching into the pocket of her wool jacket, Kathleen pulled out a slip of paper and waved it in front of Avery's face. "It bounced."

"That's impossible."

Kathleen made a dribbling motion with her hand. "Bounced. Insufficient funds. No money. Wrong account. Math error." She looked around the room. "Not the most organized person, eh?"

Rubbing her neck, Avery wanted to flee. The living room was separated from the dining area with a wide arched door. Piles of mail covered the surface of the sleek glass dining table, looking like an avalanche about to happen. A stack of files sat on the pass-through from the dining room to the kitchen.

Kathleen's gaze landed on a black lacquer curio cabinet filled with crystal. "You'd better have cash stuck in one of those fancy pieces."

Avery lifted her chin. "Or?"

"Or I'm going to sue." Kathleen headed toward the door. "In fact, I can see this was a waste of time. I'll have my lawyer get in touch with you."

"You have a lawyer?"

"I will have." The redhead yanked open the door.

"Stop. Please." Avery drew another breath. "We'll work this out."

Kathleen looked over her shoulder and eased the door shut. She strode to the sitting area and sank onto the leather sofa. "Nice." She patted the cushion.

"I hate it." Avery's face crinkled. "It's always reminded me of an oversize baseball glove."

Kathleen leaned back. "At least it's a comfortable baseball glove. And if you didn't like it, why'd you buy it?"

"My husband—and his mother—picked out all our furniture."

"As much as I'd love to sit and discuss your pushy in-laws, I'm due at work in an hour. Now, the cash?"

"I don't have it."

Kathleen scowled.

"I don't have it here, I mean. I need to contact the bank to clear up the error."

"Then call the bank, and I'll try the check again on my way to work."

"Actually . . . my landline is dead, and I couldn't charge my cell without power."

Kathleen stood. "Go to the bank, get the cash, and bring it to me."

"My car's in the shop." Her face flushed as she looked in Kathleen's eyes. "I planned to get a rental when I woke up from my nap."

"Well, Sleeping Beauty, it seems you missed your deadline."

"There's no need to be rude."

Kathleen quirked her head, looking like one of the chickens at Avery's dad's house in Haiti. "You call that rude?" She gave a short laugh. "You must lead a sheltered life."

"If only." Avery squared her shoulders. "Give me a lift to the bank, and I'll withdraw the cash."

"How long will that take?"

"Thirty minutes max. Let me wash my face and brush my hair, and I'll be good to go."

Lowering herself back onto the sofa, Kathleen picked up a travel magazine. "Get a move on. I can't afford to be late for work again."

Avery went back into the bedroom and flipped the light switch. The room stayed dark as night. Gulping a breath of cold air, she went to the row of windows and opened the curtains. The stream of morning sun steadied her, and she soaked up the hominess of the room, the only one she had changed.

An iron bedstead, bought at an estate sale, anchored the space. Painted white, its fleur-de-lis pattern was woven with flowers. The quilt that covered it was a dogwood pattern in shades of green and pink, a wedding gift from her late grandmother. Cres had called it "girlie" and wanted to donate it to Goodwill. Avery had shoved it into the back of a closet and pulled it out after he left.

She reached down to touch it, soft and warm.

"Don't take all day," Kathleen called.

"I'm almost ready." She dashed into the bathroom, turned the faucet, and frowned. No water came out. She moved toward the fancy rain shower Cres had installed. No water there either.

On top of everything else, the pipes must have frozen.

The house sat on pier-and-beams, as did almost all of those in the River Bend neighborhood. The old southern design allowed air to flow better in summer but tended to make for drafty floors and the occasional frozen pipes in winter.

A loaner from Evangeline and Creswell Sr., the cottage was supposed to be temporary, until Avery and Cres built a bigger place.

But Avery had loved it and been reluctant to move, and as it turned out, Cres had other things on his to-do list.

She shook off the memories, and with light from a row of glass bricks dabbed on mascara and concealed the bruise from yesterday's wreck. Grabbing a ponytail holder, she twisted her hair into a knot and stepped back. Her skinny jeans were faded, a small hole in the knee, but her coat covered most of the outfit anyway.

She would come home and change before she went to the store to talk sense into Evangeline, who knew, whether she admitted it or not, that Avery kept Evangeline's Boutique running.

Adjusting the Haitian shawl that had come from her father in Monday's mail, she buttoned her coat and assembled a smile as she entered the living room. "My pipes are frozen. I've hit the trifecta—water, electricity, and phone."

"Are you sure? It warmed up quite a bit overnight."

"Not in here." Avery rubbed her hands together. "I don't have any water."

A wrinkle popped up on Kathleen's face. "No car insurance. No power. No phone. No money in your account. And now no water." She blew out a breath, causing her red bangs to flutter in the air. "I don't have a good feeling about getting the money for my car."

Avery watched as she placed the magazine next to one on jogging, one for CPAs, and one about boating. Cres had an array of interests, one of the first things to attract Avery, who had grown up in a less sophisticated world. The magazine arrivals, decreasing as months passed, were like a scolding about the failure of her marriage.

"Take all of those if you'd like," Avery said. "I don't read them."

"My nephew might want them." Kathleen shrugged. "Thanks."

"Let's go. I can pay what I owe you."

"Right," Kathleen said.

⌒

The teller referred to a computer monitor. "I'm sorry, Mrs. Broussard, but that account has been closed."

"That's a mistake. I've banked with you for nearly six years."

He swiveled the monitor a quarter inch toward her and tapped the screen, even though she couldn't see its content. His expression was part pity, part disdain. "It was closed yesterday afternoon."

"That's my account. I think I would know if I closed it."

"Is there a problem, Avery?" A man's voice at her shoulder drawled out her name, and she turned to see Scooter Broussard, her banker and her father-in-law's brother, standing behind her. He wore a purple-and-gold sweater-vest and purple tie, his gray hair slicked back. He had gained his nickname while a fullback at LSU thirty years ago and kept it, a big man gone soft around the middle.

"Thank goodness, Scooter. There's a mix-up with my account."

"Mrs. Broussard didn't realize her account had been closed," the teller said.

"Why don't we discuss this in my office?"

Avery's heart lurched with the velocity of yesterday's wreck, but she followed Scooter onto the elevator. "I see you have your power back on," she said as the door eased shut.

Scooter threw her a peculiar look and steered her into his office, touching the back of a leather chair facing his desk. "Take a seat. Could I get you anything? A cup of coffee, some water?"

"Just the money in my account." She forced a chuckle as she sank into the chair. "Someone's waiting for me in the car, and I need to get this taken care of."

Scooter frowned as he reached for a file. "Evangeline said she was going to speak to you."

"She did." Avery grimaced. "We'll have to postpone the loan closing until we work out details with her."

He rubbed his neck. "So she told you about her plans?"

Avery nodded. "She came back from the beach house in one of her moods, but we'll work it out. We made an agreement months ago."

He clicked his ink pen with the bank's logo on the side. "My sister-in-law can be hard to read at times."

"It's been a rough time for everyone. The loss of a son . . ." Avery glanced down at her hands, her voice soft. "I can't imagine how hard that was for her."

Scooter shook his head. "That boy was a handful, but she never lost her patience with him." He reached under his vest and pulled out a monogrammed handkerchief and dabbed his forehead. "We were all hopeful when Cres settled down with you."

Except, of course, Cres hadn't settled down. A platinum topic of gossip around Samford. Failure and heartbreak for Avery.

She leaned forward, her elbows on Scooter's desk. "That's in the past. Once I get this checking account problem resolved, we need to meet about the shop loan."

He wiped his brow again. "You'd better talk to Evangeline."

"I intend to. I'm ready to run the business on my own. My credit is excellent."

He put his hands behind his head and stretched out his legs. "Avery, have you considered going back to Lafayette? You could start over on your home turf."

She focused on the picture of a football game at LSU's stadium, Death Valley, hanging behind him. "Buying the boutique *is* my fresh start. If you'll get my checking account squared away, I'll be on my way."

Scooter looked over her shoulder, then down at the file, his gaze settling on his hands. He acted like a customer at the boutique about to ask for a larger size. "Do you want to open a new account?"

Wrinkling her nose, she blew out a puff of air. "I want you to figure out why your teller thinks my checking account's closed."

"Your checking account has been closed. Your savings account too."

Avery felt colder than she had in the middle of the night. "Then clear up the mistake. Because I did not close my accounts."

Scooter's Adam's apple bobbed, and another bead of sweat popped out on his forehead, but he did not wipe it away. "You'll have to take this up with Evangeline and my brother."

"You're my banker."

"Perhaps it'd be best if you found a new banking partner."

Avery inhaled. "I'm not looking for a partner. I'm looking for the money in my checking account."

Scooter swallowed hard again. "My brother came in late yesterday and reorganized their family accounts. The ones you and your late husband shared were among those." His voice softened when he said the words *late husband*, in the way people did all over Samford.

"That account was in my name!"

He picked up the file and flipped through. "You had access to it, but it was opened by your father-in-law."

"That has been my checking account since the day Cres and I got engaged."

"Creswell and Evangeline always backed Cres's financial needs." Scooter swallowed for the third time. "You've been taken off all the Broussard accounts, as of the anniversary of Cres's death."

"But those accounts have my money in them, money I earned!"

Standing, he bumped against his burgundy leather desk chair, sending it back against the wall with a thud. "I'm sorry things worked out this way."

"I'll file suit—and report you to regulatory authorities."

"With Broussard resources, we're used to frivolous suits. We'll outlast you."

Scooter was right. Her fresh start did not include another round of sordid stories, and the Broussards had lawyers for their lawyers. The couple of thousand dollars hidden at the house would last about ten minutes.

With her back as straight as a rod and her chin in the air, she moved toward the door.

"Um, Avery, there is another way around your financial problems." Scooter extended an envelope. "Evangeline and Creswell are as eager to get this taken care of as you claim to be. Here's a check for ten thousand dollars."

"That's a start." She took the envelope. "But I saved more than that from my paychecks." She had scrimped every week to accumulate a down payment for the store.

"Let me be clear. The check requires action on your part."

Her eyes narrowed. "What kind of action?"

"You have less than a month to cash it. By the end of January."

"No problem." The pressure on her chest lightened. "I can handle that on my way to the car."

Scooter cleared his throat. "By cashing it, you agree to leave town by the first week in February."

Her head felt as if she'd gotten water in her ears. "That's my money."

"Creswell and Evangeline do not see it that way."

She looked down at the short commercial carpet, back at the Death Valley poster, at the Rotary Club plaque with a gold hammer on it. Kathleen was waiting in the car.

"Ten thousand dollars?" A burst of laughter flew out of her

mouth. "They want to buy me off with ten thousand dollars of my own money?" Her pulse sped up. "What are they going to do if I don't cash it? Dump my body in the river?"

"They want you out of that house. Cutting off the utilities was just a start."

She gasped.

"Creswell made it clear a year ago that you would need to move on."

"I'll find another place to live."

"Find one away from Samford." His mouth twisted. "This can get uglier in a hurry."

She didn't doubt that. She'd been a Broussard long enough to know what ugly was.

Avery could make Creswell change his mind, but there had to be another way. She threw the envelope, aiming for the small copper trash can sitting near the door.

Scooter dove and snatched it in midair. He was breathing hard. "Use it to make a new life for yourself." He hesitated. "You deserve it."

"That's just another way for the Broussards to control my life."

He folded the envelope and slipped it into the pocket on the outside of her purse. "Just in case you change your mind."

⌒

"Let me guess," Kathleen said when Avery slid into the rental car. "It was all one big misunderstanding, and you have wads of cash under your coat."

"I can get your money."

45

JUDY CHRISTIE

"Oh, good, because for a second there, I thought you were going to tell me you *were* overdrawn."

"It's a mistake."

Kathleen held up her cell phone. "I'm sure old Bill at Magnolia Market will be glad to hear that. He's called three times since you went in the bank, wanting to know when our insurance adjustors will contact him."

Avery clutched her coat. "Our adjustors?"

"Looks like we're a team." Kathleen's voice oozed irritation. "When you threw my car into the building with yours, I became part of this disaster."

"Your car was parked."

"I left the motor running because it was so cold. Bill's insurance company has roped me into this."

"That's a technicality," Avery said. "I'll take care of it."

Kathleen rolled her eyes.

"I give you my word."

"Hmm."

"You don't believe me?"

"Let's say you haven't shown yourself to be all that helpful these past couple of days. After you hit me, you disappear and don't answer your phone. I have to come—"

"I told you—"

Kathleen held up her hand. "I know. Your phone went dead. You laid down for a long winter's nap and somehow—*uh-oh*—it's the next day. Do you ever take responsibility?"

Avery drew back. "I'm the most responsible person you'll ever meet."

"Whew. I'd hate to see your life if you let things go."

Chapter 6

$\mathcal{E}$very light was on in the boutique when Avery exited the taxi, one of three in the entire town of Samford. "Will you wait for me?" she asked. "I won't be long."

"Can't do," the driver said in a heavy Spanish accent. "Bad weather. Lots of business."

"Then please come back for me in twenty minutes." Her voice was steady, despite her nerves.

"My shift ends at five." He handed her a business card. "Call when you're ready. We'll do our best to send someone."

"Please, sir." She fished in her purse and pulled out a twenty-dollar bill, part of a supply of cash that had more uses than she could list.

He ignored the bill and shooed her from the cab as the dispatch radio squawked. "I'll come back if I can."

Avery straightened her skirt as she stepped out. She looked her best, wearing a skirt and suede blazer by Evangeline's favorite designer, with three-inch heels in the same deep shade of purple. She had forgone an overcoat.

If ever there was a time to look like old-money Samford, this was it.

As she approached the front door, her courage wobbled. The shop's lights didn't seem as cozy as they had two days ago. Two women gathered near the dressing room, visible through the bay window—one of Avery's favorite shop features.

Evangeline was nowhere to be seen, but the omnipresent T. J. was on a ladder near the rear of the showroom. He had been kind so far, so maybe this was a good sign.

Avery sucked in her breath. She had to enter if she was going to live with herself.

T. J.'s head turned as the bell on the door jingled. He threw a quick look at Avery and then his eyes darted to the pair of women. His raised eyebrows made her feel like an intruder, but then he grinned and she relaxed.

The two, in an animated conversation, hadn't paid attention when Avery entered. The older woman gestured to the front window. "We'll have to tear this out to make enough room. We can move the entrance over here for a more up-to-date look."

A sound slipped from Avery's mouth, and the pair pivoted, scrutinizing her. "What a darling outfit," the younger woman, about Avery's age, said. "Did you buy that here?"

"I chose it at market. I'm Avery Broussard, the manager here." She gave a tentative chuckle. "Or former manager."

A puzzled look settled on the face of the older woman. Maybe in her late forties, she wore a traditional black suit from a less expensive line the boutique didn't carry and a pair of flats Evangeline wouldn't be caught dead in. "Are you visiting Samford?"

Avery shook her head. "Samford's my home."

"We heard you relocated."

"Maybe we can lure her back," the younger woman said in a low voice.

"Are you the interested buyers?" It seemed a small blessing that Evangeline was not here to ambush her.

The older woman chuckled. "We're more than interested. We have a contract. We're with The Fashion Group out of Dallas. We have stores in twelve states and plan to add twenty sites by the end of this year."

"But it's been so fast," Avery blurted out.

"I wish. We've been finalizing this deal for weeks." Her voice dropped. "The owner's not the easiest person to deal with, and she spends a lot of time at her beach house."

Crazy, the younger woman mouthed, glancing to the back of the store. She wore a more expensive outfit, a short wool dress with knee-length boots. She looked great, and her attention kept straying to T. J. "*Would* you be interested in working here again?"

Avery took in the racks of clothing she had ordered, displays she had arranged, the candle whose scent reminded her of her mother. She avoided looking at T. J. She *had* come here to beg for her job, hadn't she?

But the word *yes* couldn't seem to get past the knot in her throat. "I don't know."

The older woman reached into her pocket. "I'm Sharon Denton, senior vice president. Here's my card if you want to visit further." She smiled at Avery. "You look as though you understand the market, and we'll need immediate help with renovations." She glanced at T. J., her voice lower. "We'll bring in our own crew, of course."

Avery felt as though she had stumbled into an alternate universe. "Are you really thinking of closing up that front window?"

"Definitely. It restricts the look of the front."

Avery frowned. "That's one of our most popular marketing devices. The displays draw customers like—well, like women to a dress sale."

Sharon smiled. "It is quaint, but we prefer a more standard look for our stores. That way people know what to expect from one location to another."

"But what about the personal atmosphere?"

"Our customers like a high-end sophisticated approach," the younger woman said.

"I agree with the sophisticated part," Avery said, "but our shop's unique personality drives sales."

"Pardon the interruption. That call took longer than expected." Evangeline's voice tinkled from the back before she rounded the corner. When she saw Avery, she couldn't have moved across the room quicker if she had been on a zip line.

She planted herself between Avery and the visitors. "Avery, as you can see I have guests."

A crash sounded from the back of the showroom, and everyone turned. "Sorry." T. J. climbed down the ladder. "Tape measure got away from me." His eyes focused on Avery. "My apologies."

She took advantage of the distraction to step around Evangeline toward the duo. "It was nice meeting you. I'd love to talk with you again."

"Avery!" Evangeline's voice snapped. "If you would join me in the workroom." Her fake smile did not reach her eyes. "This will only take a moment."

"We're all set and headed to the airport in Shreveport anyway." Sharon clapped her hands. "This will make an outstanding location for our brand. We'll be in touch to finalize inspections."

"Excellent." Evangeline escorted them to the door after throwing Avery another frown. "I expect a quick closing. As you know, I have another interested buyer and am eager to conclude the sale."

Avery swallowed. Did she still have a chance?

After they had gotten into their car, Evangeline whirled around. "What do you think you're doing?"

"Owning the store has been my dream. You know that. Am I not allowed to make a counterbid?"

"The Fashion Group has outstanding credentials. They will run the boutique as it ought to be run."

"You snatched the shop out from under me to sell to a chain?"

"They approached Ross with a generous offer."

"Ross was in on this?" Avery couldn't hide her dismay. "Did he know you were closing my accounts? Shutting off my utilities?"

Evangeline glanced at T. J. and lowered her voice. "Don't you mean the Broussard accounts?"

"My paychecks went into those accounts."

"To cover housing and automobile costs, plus a host of other expenses. We've carried you for a year."

"Carried me?" Avery gestured toward the showroom, her eyes stopping on T. J.'s back. He didn't seem the type to broadcast Broussard dirty laundry, but she pitched her voice low. "Without me, The Fashion Group—nor any other group—would have been interested."

"You couldn't possibly come up with the money to match their offer." Evangeline smoothed her already-smooth hair.

"At least they're willing to keep me on." Avery straightened a silk T sliding off a nearby hanger. "That will give me time to figure out what to do."

Evangeline frowned. "Didn't Scooter give you the check?"

"He did."

"And you've cashed it?" Evangeline's voice was climbing toward victory.

"I have no intention of taking that money from you." She fingered a cashmere sweater. "Working for a corporation instead of a family business might be interesting, right?"

"You're not staying here."

"I've put my heart and soul into this shop. I'm sure they'll appreciate my approach to retail."

"You've always underestimated me. I don't know what Cres saw in you."

The real question was what Avery had seen in Cres. From the first months of marriage, she had been tortured by her lapse in judgment. She would start anew.

Evangeline lifted her chin. "You still don't understand what it means to be part of a powerful family. I put a provision in the sales agreement that you are not to be rehired."

Avery fished the business card out of her pocket and twirled it in front of Evangeline. "I doubt a big company like that will agree to such a request."

"It was not a request. Cash our check and go back to Lafayette. You have a month or you're left with nothing."

"Why now? You strung me along for a year, leaving me to work while you were at the beach."

"I was in shock."

"You mean you didn't know how to spin it? Because if I left too soon, your friends might wonder . . . might not canonize Saint Cres."

"I will make things as unpleasant as needed to get you out of our lives." She glared at Avery's wedding band, a Mignon Faget band Cres gave her when she had balked at the Broussard family diamond. "Being difficult will hurt you more than us."

Avery took a look around the shop. Frowning, T. J. took one step down the ladder.

"One month," Evangeline said. "Cash the check and be gone."

꩜

From the middle of the ladder, T. J. watched Avery. He wasn't sure how someone could walk in shoes like that, much less sprint in them, but she took off like a wild animal was on her heels. Which it might as well have been.

The color had drained out of her face in the time she had been in the store, and she looked smaller, as though the conversation with Evangeline had shrunk her. And no wonder. The woman sounded like a mob boss about to take the kill shot.

"Avery," he called, but she was already to the door and did not turn around.

Evangeline walked to the counter. "That girl has caused my family nothing but trouble."

"We can't let her leave like that."

"I did not hire you to involve yourself in my family business." As though he weren't already.

He climbed from the ladder, then headed toward the door.

"If you follow that woman, you're fired. And I'll tell all my friends how unreliable you are."

"Do what you want, Evangeline." His mother was going to love this. He had told Bud this job was a bad idea. Letting Avery go alone would be like leaving a puppy by the side of the road. And he had told Ross he would keep an eye on her.

Flinging the door open, he heard Evangeline sputter behind him. Headed toward the street, Avery stumbled off the sidewalk, the spike heels sinking into the damp grass. She looked one way and then the other.

The rain had started again, and he wished he had grabbed his jacket. "Avery!" he shouted.

"Leave me alone." She hugged her arms around her, a near replay of two nights ago at her house.

"Are you all right?"

"I'm wonderful." Her head bobbled like a broken lawn sprinkler as she looked up and down Vine Avenue.

T. J. took a cautious step closer. She was shaking, and the rain had increased to steady misery. "What can I do to help?"

She turned. "Are you colluding with them? Is that why Ross called you the other night?"

"Ross and my brother are friends."

She sniffed. "Ross was the only Broussard I trusted, and he betrayed me."

He drew back a half step. "I don't know what's going on, but I can't see Ross being part of it. He's worried about you."

"Thanks to my dear in-laws I'm out of work, out of money, and I don't have any utilities." Water rolled down her face—rain, not tears. "For that matter, I'm out of a husband too."

"Let me take you home."

"I don't want to go there."

"To a friend's house."

"I don't have any friends." The statement was made without drama, and she walked up the street at a brisk clip. "I've been cut out of the Broussard circle."

He caught up with her. "Of course you have friends." He had been away so long he hadn't a clue. "Church? College buddies?"

She was silent, her chin set, her long legs eating up the sidewalk, the rain a biting downpour. He hadn't been this cold when he fixed a neighbor's leaking roof that morning.

He put his hand on her shoulder, and she jerked away. "I want to help you."

"Haven't you been listening to Evangeline? You'd do well to steer clear of me."

"I'll risk it." Avery was the most interesting woman he had encountered since returning to Samford, even if she was tied to that elite crowd he didn't care for. "I can drop you at a hotel, or at my mother's . . ."

"Right. Your mother is going to take a complete stranger in."

This wasn't the time to mention she was not a stranger to his mother. And his mother *would* throw a conniption fit if he showed up with Avery. "How about Ross's?"

"So the entire town of Samford can talk about how I ran into the arms of my brother-in-law when my mother-in-law threw me out?"

"Ross is in Baton Rouge. Why shouldn't you stay at his place?"

"I wouldn't do that to the poor guy." She tilted her head. "You don't have a lot of experience with gossip, do you?"

"More than you might think." T. J. had been gossiped about since the first weekend he went with his brother to stay at Bud's house. For two decades, the town had speculated about who T. J.'s real father was, and his mother had complained that he had let her down.

He strode forward and stopped in front of Avery, blocking

her path. "You're going to get sick if you keep walking in this weather." He gave a rough chuckle. "And if you don't care about yourself, at least care about me because I'm freezing."

Avery put her hand to her wet hair for a moment. "I'm sorry." She turned and her face lit up.

T. J.'s heart felt a peculiar warmth.

Until he saw that her joy was aimed at a taxi turning into the boutique parking lot.

Chapter 7

$\mathcal{T}$he mechanic wiped his hands on a blue rag and repeated himself to Avery.

"Yesterday morning. The tow-truck driver signed for it. Said the owner had decided to turn it in and lease something else."

"But that's my car!"

In his midthirties, with a stitched name tag that said Davis, he shook his head. "Not according to the dealership. The sales manager verified it when I called. Said the car is registered to a local business, a dress shop of some sort."

Avery breathed in the smell of oil, popcorn, and air freshener and sank into a chair in the office. "You were going to give me an estimate today. We spoke yesterday morning."

"They sent the tow truck right after that, and you didn't answer your phone when I called. That vehicle was banged up pretty bad, so you might be glad it's gone."

"But I need transportation."

"I'm sorry," he said. "Is there something I can do?"

She exhaled. "It's not your fault. I just need a ride to..." Where? She couldn't go to work. The house was cold. "I need a ride to the market."

He pointed to Kathleen on the phone in the rental, and the side of his mouth upturned.

"Maybe your friend will give you a lift."

"She's not my friend. That's the woman I ran into."

"No wonder she looks annoyed." He made a face, which would have been cute if Avery hadn't been miserable, waved at Kathleen, and tugged on a strand of his hair. *Nice*, he mouthed and rolled his eyes.

Kathleen swatted her hand at him.

She had appeared on Avery's doorstep again that morning, demanding her money. Avery surrendered another piece of her shrinking pride and asked for a ride to the garage. "The sooner I have transportation, the sooner I can get your money. It will only take a few minutes."

"It'll have to be early. My boss is stressed, and I can't afford to be late again." Now Kathleen talked on her cell phone, giving the rental-car horn two quick taps when Avery looked her way.

"We've got a couple of used cars, if you're in the market for a vehicle," the mechanic said. "They don't look like much, but they're cheap."

Cheap. That was new. She was wrung out and hungry. Even the stale popcorn made her mouth water. "Thanks for the offer, but I'll get my Tahoe back."

"Sure thing." His voice held doubt.

Kathleen popped out of the car before they reached it and gave the guy a hearty hug. "What's the deal?"

"Another misunderstanding," Avery said. "My car's not here. My in-laws had it hauled off."

Kathleen ran her hands through her hair, making it stick up even more. "Those people really don't like you, do they?"

"I'm getting my independence back," she mumbled.

"You could have fooled me." Kathleen looked back at the mechanic. "I have to get to work, Davis. Can you give Avery a ride home?"

He nodded. "I have to wait for one of the guys to get here, but we'll work something out."

Avery felt like a teenager in the midst of a carpool debate. "I don't need a ride after all."

"So you're going to walk home?" Kathleen asked.

"I'll think of something." Her stomach emitted a growl.

Davis looked at her. "The church has a food pantry, if that would help."

"I'm not homeless!" Avery said.

"She's touchy," Kathleen said.

He stepped closer. "I didn't mean to offend you. Everyone falls on tough times now and then."

"I haven't fallen on tough times. My mother-in-law is trying to run me out of town, but I'm not leaving."

"See what I mean, Davis?" Kathleen muttered. "Get in the car, Avery, and I'll drop you off. Make it snappy."

He fished in his shirt pocket and pulled out a card. "Here's my number, if you change your mind about a used car—or about the food pantry." He paused. "We have a clothes closet too."

Kathleen gave him another hug. "Thanks, sweetie."

"I don't think it's polite to call your mechanic 'sweetie,'" Avery grumbled as she got into the rental.

With her bold laugh, Kathleen started the car. "I don't know how I could have gotten through these past few years without him. He's my nephew."

"Did he really suggest I need clothes?"

⌒

"There's a dozen reasons not to ask you this," Kathleen said as they drove off, "but I can't seem to resist."

Avery closed her eyes.

"Why are the Broussards out to get you? I mean, my mother-in-law wasn't crazy about me, but she didn't sabotage my life."

Debating whether to reply or jump from the moving car, Avery fiddled with her bracelet. "She wants me to move back to Lafayette."

"Is that home?"

"Not anymore. My father's a missionary in Haiti. My mother died when I was in high school. Cancer." The words made her stomach roil. With her mother dead and her father gone, she had allowed herself to be sucked into Cres's world much too fast. When they got engaged, she imagined Evangeline as a surrogate mom, someone to fill the gap in her heart. Talk about wishful thinking.

"And the husband? I take it you got a divorce."

"He was killed a year ago."

"You're a widow? Oh, child." Kathleen's fingers gripped the steering wheel until her knuckles were white. "Illness?"

"Evangeline, his mother, blames me. He looked the wrong way on a one-way street and stepped off a curb."

"And you saw it happen?" Horror filled Kathleen's voice.

She shook her head. "I wasn't with him."

⌒

T. J. set up sawhorses in the market parking lot and pulled lumber from the bed of his pickup. He had promised Martha and Bill he would shore up his crude patch job and order replacement glass to repair the storefront.

He looked at the scar on the building. What had the building looked like when it was built? Avery's car had pulled the hideous metal siding loose across the front, revealing traditional wood underneath. Perhaps there were photographs somewhere.

"That Broussard gal did a number on us, didn't she?" Bill came out of the store wearing an old-fashioned butcher's apron and his regular scowl.

T. J. nodded. "That's quite a chunk. Thank goodness no one was seriously injured."

"No one except me and Martha."

"You were hurt?" He swung to look at Bill.

"Our buyer backed out when he saw the damage. I'll have that girl's hide."

"It was an accident, Bill. There were dozens of wrecks around town that day."

"She should have been more careful. We worked for months on that deal, and now it's gone." He snapped his gnarled fingers. "Just like that. That fellow said he hadn't realized the liability that came with a store like this."

"That's too bad."

"Martha has her heart set on retiring in Hot Springs. Now what are we going to do?"

"Things have a way of working out." T. J. reached for his toolbox. "Maybe there's a better buyer out there."

"No, sir. We're going to get a big settlement and shut this place down. Make those fat cats pay."

"I'm not sure Avery has access to money like that."

"Someone will bail her out. That's what rich people do."

T. J. wished Bud, easygoing with wisdom to spare, would show up. "Maybe you can work something out with her."

Bill scowled. "Your head's been turned by her pretty face. That woman is as flaky as they come."

"Aren't you being a little tough? She lost her husband in a tragic accident."

"I know, I know," Bill said. "That story was the talk of the store for a month or more. But that doesn't give her the right to plow into us."

Rubbing his eyes, T. J. kept his face expressionless. "We've all made mistakes. She seems like the type to take care of it."

"How do you know so much about her?"

"Her brother-in-law and my half brother, Marsh Cameron, are friends. Our families have known each other a long time."

"She grew up here?"

He shook his head. "I was in Seattle when she moved here. About the time she married Cres Broussard."

Bill's upper lip curled. "I never cared for him. Thought too high of himself, if you ask me."

"You knew him?" Cres didn't seem like the kind of guy to frequent a corner store.

"Came in a few times with another pretty gal. Must've been before he snagged Avery."

T. J. strapped on his tool belt. This conversation had gone further than he intended. "I'd better get to work."

"And I'd better get back to the biscuit counter."

Lord, help me. Doing the right thing was harder than he expected.

"Is that guy everywhere?" Avery said under her breath and pointed. "Looks like Bill's hired someone to fix that hole."

Kathleen pulled into a parking place a few spots away from where T. J. worked. "Not just someone. That good-looking carpenter who gave us a ride after the wreck. What a sweetie."

"I think it's creepy." But her protest was mostly an attempt to convince herself. T. J. had shown more care for her in a couple of days than Cres had their entire last three years of marriage. "That repair work's a positive sign, though, right?"

Kathleen put the car in Park and made a production of turning off the engine. "Maybe it means Bill's moved past the furious stage."

Avery reached for the door handle and stopped. "This is my problem. I'll work it out."

"Like I told you—"

"I know, I know. Bill's insurance agent says you shouldn't have left your car running. But I'm the one who hit the gas instead of the brake."

"It was icy. You slid."

Avery quirked her head. "Are you defending me?"

"Most certainly not. You screwed up big-time. You were annoyed and not paying attention."

"Thanks for the ride." Avery clenched her teeth. "I'll call as soon as I get your money."

With her lips pressed together, Kathleen nodded. "Sure."

"I'm not a loser."

"Don't drag it out too long. I get paid this week, but I don't have a lot stuck back."

"Who does?" Avery stepped out, her suede boots sinking into muddy slush.

With her head down, she walked toward the market door,

forced to step around T. J. and his sawhorse. He wore a plaid flannel shirt, a pair of jeans, and work boots. His back was to her, and he was cutting a piece of plywood with a power saw. As she passed, he took a pencil from behind his ear, scratched a mark on a board, and positioned the saw again.

Her shadow fell across the work, and he looked up. "Hey." His attention moved to her muddy boots.

She put her hand to her hair jammed under a felt hat, a few strands sticking out.

"Glad to see you're all right. You were awfully upset when you took off."

"No kidding."

He stepped toward her. "I came by your house, but there weren't any lights on."

"Are you spying on me?"

T. J. laughed, a pleasant sound. "I was about to ask you the same thing. I didn't expect to see you back here today." His eyes widened, and he lowered his voice. "Prepare yourself."

"It's about time you showed up." Bill's voice was so close that Avery jumped. "These repairs will cost an arm and a leg." Putting his hands in his pockets, he looked like a garden gnome. "And that don't include mental distress and loss of business. My nephew estimates—"

"Loss of business?" Avery swallowed.

"We've had half the traffic we normally have on a weekday."

"The weather's been awful. School's out and most of the businesses in town are closed." Avery tapped the sawhorse. "You didn't miss a day of sales."

"We missed the only sale that mattered—your mistake cost us the sale of our store."

She pulled off the hat, her head sweating, and fanned her face. Her hair tumbled to her shoulders. She was a mess.

T. J. took a step closer. "Why don't y'all go inside and discuss this over coffee? Avery probably needs a few more details, and you look like you could use a chair, Bill."

Eyeing her as though she were rabid, Bill didn't say anything.

T. J. drew in a breath and unplugged the saw. "I'll go with you." He steered Avery toward the door.

Bill stopped before they entered. "See?" He tapped on the glass. A For Sale by Owner sign was taped to the inner door. "You ruined it."

Avery gawked at T. J. "What is he talking about?"

"Their buyer backed out yesterday." He gestured at the gash in the wall. "He didn't want to deal with situations like this."

"I'll talk to him. I can reimburse him for any expenses he incurs because of this." *Somehow.*

"Too late," Bill said. "He made an offer this morning on another property over on Lake Bistineau."

"That was fast," T. J. said.

"He couldn't have wrapped up a deal yet," Avery said. "Didn't you have a contract?"

Bill tapped the *by Owner* part of the sign. "I took him at his word. I didn't know some maniac was going to crash into my store." He pushed open the door. "And you're going to pay."

Chapter 8

What a disaster. This situation had escalated faster than Cres had lost interest in their marriage. Avery pulled a bottle of water out of the cooler and put her money on the counter.

Martha shuffled over to the register and rang up the sale. "Bill doesn't mean any harm," she said, her voice apologetic. "The insurance man says these things take time, but at our age, you don't have much time. Bill's getting older, and he doesn't want to admit it."

"Oh, now..." Avery didn't know what to say, grateful that Bill had disappeared out the front door after his most recent diatribe against insurance companies, the weather, and her.

"We needed this sale to go through to move up to Hot Springs."

After taking a sip of the water, Avery replaced the cap with care. "Is that where your children are?"

Martha's face drooped. "The Lord didn't bless us with children. Our customers have been our family."

"And brothers and sisters?"

"We're not close." The regret in her voice was clear. "They didn't approve of me marrying Bill."

Imagine that.

"Over the years we went our own way." Martha wiped the counter with a dingy cloth. "How about you? Any children?"

Avery uncapped the water and took a long swig before shaking her head. "My husband and I were waiting until we had more money in the bank." She gripped the water bottle so hard it made a snapping noise. "If I had known what was going to happen . . ." She didn't finish the sentence because she wasn't sure the words were true. *Should I have tried to talk Cres into having a child?* The question was one of many that haunted her.

"You husband passed away, right? Accident somewhere, wasn't it?"

Looking at the clock, Avery nodded.

Martha made a tsking noise. "Such sadness, him dying on that golfing trip." She patted Avery's smooth, young hand with her chapped, bony fingers, veins popping up against the thin skin. "Poor thing, you not being with him at the end."

Avery nodded again.

Martha leaned into the counter. "A child would have been a comfort."

"Yes, ma'am." It was hard to respond.

"Not having a child changed my Bill. He wanted a boy from the day we married, but it wasn't meant to be. We only have Bill's brother's oldest boy. Haven't seen much of him through the years, but he's pushing us to sell."

"He probably wants to spend time with you." Avery tried not to pity the poor family members who had to deal with Bill.

"Or to spend what money we have. He and his wife have hit

a rough patch, and we've been helping out. It was easier when we had a buyer." She raised and lowered her stooped shoulders.

"I, uh, need to reach Kathleen, that woman I ran into. Do you happen to know where she works?"

"Certainly. She's been coming in here for years." Martha dialed from a list tacked to the wall and stretched the cord from the old phone over the counter. Avery felt like she was attached to a rubber band that might snap at any moment.

She exhaled when Kathleen picked up. "Dixie Metals. Mr. Barnhill's office."

"Kathleen? This is Avery, the woman who ran into you."

"I know who you are, but in case you didn't notice, some of us have to work. Good-bye."

"Wait! Please. This won't take long."

"That's what you said both days you made me late for work."

"I'm at the market," Avery whispered. "Bill's threatening to sue both of us. Things are escalating."

"Insurance companies handle that. I don't have time for this."

"He's planning to ruin our credit, post our pictures in the store—you name it."

"Avery."

"Says he'll put a lien on your house if we don't clear this up. His face is redder than your hair."

"Haven't the adjustors contacted him?"

"He told them he wanted money, not more questions, and hung up." Avery's voice was pitched higher now. "Martha's weaker than usual, and Bill says the wreck killed their business. He yelled at me at the top of his lungs, with customers in the store."

"Maybe that's why his business is declining." Kathleen let out a long sigh. "I'll come by when I get off work."

"Thank you." There was a second of silence. "I didn't know who else to call."

"You owe me a biscuit," she replied gruffly.

Avery handed Martha the phone and straightened a shelf of peanut-butter crackers and various nuts. She tried not to look at the haphazard mess that remained from her wreck. Canned goods had been shoved to one side, and a pile of broken glass remained, swept into a pile, the broom abandoned. A piece of string outlined the area like a crime scene. The Keep Out sign was scrawled in blue ink, in shaky handwriting.

Dust had gathered in the store's corners, most shelves were sparsely filled, and a medley of signs was stuck on various surfaces with yellowing tape.

Martha picked up the ragged white cloth and wiped the counter. "We should have sold years ago, but this store was our life." She gripped the stainless-steel edge on the linoleum-covered counter. "Now we need the money. I don't think Bill can last much longer."

Avery buried her face in her hands for a moment. Neither of the pair looked healthy. She looked at the jumble of merchandise on the floor. "At least I can help clean that mess up."

Opening and closing a wrinkled hand, Martha peered down at it as though it belonged to someone else. Her eyes had a glazed look.

"I don't know what else to do." Avery's agitation grew. "I don't even have a car. If you'll give me the buyer's name, I'll tell him this was my fault." Avery pointed to the patched wall. "We can text him a photo of the work."

"Oh no." Martha snapped back to attention. "He was madder than Bill was when New Coke came out. He told us not to contact him again, that the accident nullified the deal." She let out a puff of air. "Between you and me, I think he was looking for a reason to back out so he could buy that bait shop."

Through the door, Avery could see Bill propped against a truck, his face still crimson. She followed the direction of his hands where T. J. and a man wearing khaki pants and a khaki shirt stood. The trio looked toward the building front, Bill frowning. "Who's that other guy?" Avery asked.

Martha turned toward the door and smiled. "Bud Cameron. One of the finest men I've ever known. And what a craftsman." She swayed as she looked more closely. "If T. J. and Bud can't calm Bill down, nothing can."

Bill scowled and shook his finger at the boarded-up hole.

This looked like a *nothing can* day to Avery.

His voice rose, and T. J. let down the tailgate of his truck, patted it for Bill to sit down, and climbed up next to him. Bud, who looked about fifty, leaned on one arm against the truck. Avery couldn't hear what they were saying, but T. J. looked as patient as her father when he dealt with an irate church member.

"I heard you lost your job at that fancy dress shop."

Tearing her gaze from T. J.'s smile, Avery nodded. "I planned to buy that business, but the owner backed out." She released an awkward chuckle. "Sort of the reverse of what happened to you."

Martha picked up her rag and wiped the counter again. "Aren't you kin to those people, the Broussards?"

"They're my husband's family."

"Doesn't that make them your family too?"

"It's complicated."

"Life always is. But his parents letting you down?" She shook her head, rubbing the counter harder.

Avery searched for words. "My father taught me that things work out if we trust God."

"With the store open six days, we haven't been churchgoers, but I listen on the radio. I agree that everything happens for a reason."

"Amen," Avery said with a small smile. "Although the reason isn't always what I hoped it might be."

"So he's a religious man, your father?"

"He's a missionary in Haiti." Her heart swelled. "He has such love for those in need."

"I could never do something like that." Martha chuckled, but it sounded more like a wheeze. "I like my air-conditioning too much—and I don't like bugs."

A large water bug ran from the edge of the counter as though she had summoned it, scooting underneath a rack of chips. Avery glanced at the clock again.

"Does he collect money like that man on the radio?"

"No. Money's tight, but he doesn't need much. I've been fortunate to be able to help." *Until now.*

"It's harder and harder to make ends meet." Martha waved at the store. "This place has been our bread and butter for nearly fifty years, and look at it. If it weren't for the biscuit business, we'd have shut our doors a long time ago."

"They seem popular." Avery shifted from foot to foot. *Not that I have ever had one.*

"That's my great-grandmother's recipe from down in Natchitoches Parish. It's been handed down for four generations."

Avery smiled politely. "I bet your nephew is happy to have that in the family."

"He doesn't care about sentimental things." Martha gave her head a shake, her hand trembling.

"I'm keeping you from your work. I should start cleaning up while I wait for Kathleen."

Martha made a clucking noise. "That's right funny, now that I think about it, you and Kathleen getting so tight. She's good people. Hard worker."

"You're close to her?" How might this affect the insurance debacle?

"You know what it's like when you're a shopkeeper. Everyone wants to tell you their troubles. I could write a book of all the stories I've heard."

Avery couldn't hold back a laugh. "Our customers are—or rather, were—more discreet. They shop to cover up their troubles."

"I reckon we hear more of people's everyday lives here." Martha's frail hand trembled again as she let go of the counter. "I'm going to miss this place."

And then she fell to the floor.

Chapter 9

$\mathcal{E}$very now and then Avery sniffed, but T. J. had not seen her shed a tear since they had arrived at the hospital waiting room.

Her hair was in a messy ponytail, her feet muddy. Her gray pants had gotten a small rip in them at some point—maybe when she jumped over the counter to perform CPR on Martha. Although the room was stifling, her coat was draped across her shoulders, her arms around her middle.

Six hours had passed since Avery had screamed T. J.'s name with so much terror that he had nearly burst through the plywood patch job.

She refused to leave the hospital, even when the doctors said it would be hours before they knew if Martha would make it. And she turned down sandwiches Bud had brought around eight o'clock.

T. J. wanted to put his arm around her but figured he'd have better luck petting one of the feral cats living under his porch. Still in his work clothes, he brushed at the knees of his jeans and whispered another silent prayer. He longed for a shower.

Kathleen, who arrived at the store minutes after the

ambulance, sat next to Avery, murmuring indistinguishable words. Avery shook her head, hair flying back and forth. Her lips were pressed into a thin line.

After leaving for a few minutes, Kathleen returned with a large plastic binder and flipped through it as though cramming for an exam. Her red hair stuck up in more directions than seemed possible, and she had shed her jacket hours ago.

Bud was praying on the far side of the room with a subdued Bill, who had been shooed out of Martha's room a few minutes earlier. The only one allowed in the Intensive Care Unit, he was permitted to visit every two hours. His face sagged more with each return, his jowls reminding T. J. of Bud's dog, who had been rescued on a dirt road near Sweet Olive.

"She's not breathing on her own," was all Bill had said when he entered the room most recently. He narrowed his eyes as he looked at Avery, who hitched her breath. "What's she doing here?"

Avery had been through some bad weeks in her life.

When Cres had told her he wanted a divorce, her broken heart joined her broken marriage vows. She pleaded with him to talk to their pastor, see a marriage counselor, even move to another town. Maybe a baby would have held them together. Or maybe a child would have been hurt by the breakup.

Then he had been killed on a getaway "to clear his head." That day the shards of Avery's heart had been crushed into a fine dust.

When the pain of those weeks subsided, Avery had made the promise—to God and herself—that she would make better decisions.

Yet here she sat. *Do I cause bad things to happen?*

The sequence of events was like watching a TV show on fast-forward, everything happening too fast to comprehend. And now she hit Pause again, seeing details in slow motion. Putting her ear to Martha's chest, pumping, breathing, praying as she had prayed when cancer was wringing her mother dry. T. J. grabbing the ancient wall phone to dial 911. Bill hurling blame at Avery as Martha was loaded into the ambulance. Kathleen slapping a Closed sign on the screen door of the store, Avery standing with her hand on the stretcher.

She had not even minded begging for a ride to the hospital, had climbed in the car though Kathleen seemed unsure.

Officers who zoomed to the corner, including Jazz Hamilton, converged on Avery in the hospital lobby while curious staff and visitors inched closer, held at bay by a stoic T. J. All but Jazz seemed suspicious, tying Martha's collapse to Avery's crash, asking questions that made a medical emergency seem like a crime.

Avery wouldn't dwell on the new wave of gossip sure to be broadcast, still shaken by the memory of Martha's limp body and clammy skin when she had jumped across the counter. Had she missed a clue that could have prevented the calamity?

Jazz's husky voice was soft as she wrapped up the interview, then placed a card with her name and phone number and the insignia of the Samford PD into Avery's hand.

Avery stared at it.

"And could you tell me how to reach you? In case anyone has additional questions?"

Gulping a breath of the warm, medicinal air, Avery slipped the card into her pocket. "Here. I'll be here."

Jazz frowned. "Do you think that's wise, considering the tension you've described with Bill?"

"Where else would I be? I owe it to them to wait."

"I'll know where to reach Avery," T. J. interjected. "If she's not here, give me a call. She lives near me."

"Is there anyone else to notify?"

"A nephew," Avery murmured. "They don't have children. Martha told me they don't go to church, but she trusts—" Her voice cracked. "She trusts that things work out."

Now, in the ICU waiting room, Avery could not turn off the endless loop in her mind, dissecting her conversation, remembering how frail Martha had looked.

And while Martha clung to life, Bill disintegrated from elderly to ancient, his head bowed while Bud prayed from the seat next to him. Avery closed her eyes and begged God to listen to the prayers and heal Martha, to somehow make everything right.

A hand on her shoulder startled her, and she looked up, disoriented.

T. J.'s dark eyes shone above her. "Hey."

"Is there news?" Avery looked across at Bill as she spoke.

"She's resting comfortably."

"Who could rest with tubes up her nose and in her arm?" She put her face in her hands, too ashamed to look at him.

"Don't you want to take off your coat? It's sweltering in here."

"The heat feels good."

T. J. squatted in front of her chair. "You're exhausted. I'll give you a ride home."

"Don't." She held up her hand. "I'm staying. This is my fault."

"You can't blame yourself for this. Martha's had heart trouble for ages."

With a quick shake of her head, Avery shifted to the other side of the chair, her arms still tight around her middle. "I upset her. All the commotion from my wreck caused her blood pressure to go through the roof."

T. J. drew back. "Did the doctor say that?"

"No, but it's true. I caused her heart attack."

"That's ridiculous. When did you move to Samford?"

She tilted her head, puzzled. "Almost six years ago."

"And you knew Martha before that?"

She glanced up. "I'd never been to Samford before that. Of course I didn't know her."

"Martha had her first heart attack eight years ago. She was in the ICU for two weeks. She had triple-bypass surgery seven years ago."

He reached for her hands. "Martha's been declining for weeks. She complained of chest pains two weeks ago and again this morning before work. Bill's beating himself up for not calling a doctor."

"I should have done something different." She rocked back in her seat. "If only I had done something different."

"It's been a long day. Let me take you home."

She searched T. J.'s eyes, the hum of the waiting room sounding like a plane about to take off. "Why are you being so nice to me?"

"Because Bud's always reminding me to love my neighbor." His mouth curved into a lopsided grin.

"Be serious."

"I've been in enough messes for two lifetimes, Avery. Someone always gave me a hand. You've had a lousy week." He shrugged. "You look like you could use a friend."

The sound of footsteps approached from behind her, and Avery whirled. Bud, in battered work boots, stood nearby. "She's stable. They just called Bill back to ICU."

"Thank goodness, thank goodness," Avery said.

He reached out to touch her arm. "We met a few years back, at a fund-raiser, I believe. I'm Bud Cameron, T. J.'s friend."

"And business partner," T. J. said. "Rescuer of hurt creatures and wild teenagers."

"I'm sorry. I don't recall . . ." She studied his face and thick salt-and-pepper hair. His bright blue eyes sparkled.

"You did a fine thing today, Avery," he said.

She drew back as though he had struck her.

"I've been trying to tell her that." T. J.'s gaze locked on Avery's face.

"If you had not been there to give Martha CPR, she likely would have died." Bud enveloped her in a bear hug. "You saved her life."

Chapter 10

$\mathcal{A}$very woke up with a crick in her neck and an unfamiliar dog licking her face.

"Howie, leave her alone." Kathleen's voice held more laughter than scold. "She doesn't want you slobbering on her first thing in the morning."

"Hey, guy." Avery sat up and rubbed the sheltie's head. "Where'd you come from?"

"I let him in from the yard after you went to sleep. He stays in the yard during the day but likes to come in at night." Kathleen let out an embarrassed laugh. "He's good company."

Avery looked around the paneled bedroom where she'd slept on a daybed. The drive to Kathleen's house the night before had been solemn, and they exchanged few remarks while they put sheets on the mattress. "Do you live alone?" Avery asked now.

Kathleen picked up a throw pillow and fluffed it. "Except for Howie."

"So you're not married?"

"I'm a widow." She sat on the edge of the bed.

Avery's eyes widened. "I had no idea."

"We don't exactly move in the same circles. At least not usually."

With a self-conscious shrug, Avery sat on the side of the bed, pulling the loaned T-shirt over her knees. "Since my husband was killed, I feel like I have a sign flashing 'Widow' on and off. I sort of thought other women did too."

"It felt like that the first year or so," Kathleen said, "but not anymore."

"How long has it been?"

"Nearly four years now. Wayne was hooking up his bass boat and dropped dead of a heart attack." She paused. "One day I was fussing about his socks on the living room floor, and the next I was picking out a coffin."

Avery could not hold back a moan at the matter-of-fact words. "Were you ... there when it happened?"

"I was." Her lips twisted. "I discovered I'm not good in a crisis. You did much better yesterday than I would have."

"Do you have children?"

"A daughter who's twenty." Kathleen pointed to a framed picture of a girl with coal-black hair, a stud in her nose, and a defiant glare at the camera. "I worked for years to have a baby, and then she grows up and decides she'd rather run off to Tulsa with her boyfriend than live with me."

Kathleen picked up the photograph, then ran her fingers over the glass. "Lindsey was only sixteen when her daddy died. She took it hard. Davis says she'll come to her senses one of these days. He hangs around here with his son, Jake, to make me feel better."

Kathleen kissed the picture before placing it back on the

dresser. "We'd better hurry. Big corporate meeting at work, so I sure can't be late." She started from the room.

"Wait! Have you heard anything from the hospital?"

"T. J. called a few minutes ago."

"And?"

"Martha will be in the ICU for a few days at least. They're not sure from there." She paused at the door. "I put clean towels in the bath there. Come on, Howie, give Avery a little privacy."

"Kathleen?" Her voice was hesitant. "Lindsey's fortunate to have you for a mother."

Kathleen squeezed her lips together, then vanished into the other room.

Avery rushed into the pink-tiled bathroom and threw cold water on her face. A small glass shelf sat above the tiny lavatory, lined with a new toothbrush, a tube of toothpaste, and hotel-size bottles of shampoo and conditioner. The air smelled of floral air freshener, and plush rose-colored towels were folded on the side of the tub.

Reaching out to stroke them, Avery drew in a deep breath and stepped in the shower, turning the hot water on high. As it streamed down her dirty hair and sweaty body, she gave in to the tears.

⌒

"What are you doing here?" The gruff voice startled Avery, and she sloshed lukewarm coffee onto her hand.

"Bill! How's Martha? Is she . . . ?"

"Is she what? Dead? Do you think I'd be talking to you if she were?"

She bit her lip. "I came to see what I can do to help. Do you need breakfast?"

"What I need is to be at my store selling biscuits."

Avery, heart racing, patted a nearby sofa. "Have a seat, and I'll get you a cup of coffee."

"T. J.'s gone to get me something. Why are you here?"

"I wanted to see if you and Martha need anything."

Bill held up three gnarled fingers. "One, a buyer. Two, reimbursement for the damages." His shoulders stooped forward. "Three, to be back at our store."

Lowering herself to the couch, Avery cleared her throat. "I've told you I'll come up with money for repairs." She would cash the Broussard check, even if it meant she had to leave Samford.

"That ain't much, but it's a start." Bill ambled toward the door. "Make it snappy. I'm not getting any younger." When he reached the hallway, he turned. "Tell T. J. I lost my appetite."

Avery paced around the room, rubbing her face.

"Hard morning?" T. J. strode into the room with two white sacks and a bottle of juice. He wore a long-sleeved T-shirt advertising an art festival and a pair of worn khakis. Scuffed Doc Martens that looked like something from Avery's high school days were on his feet. His brown hair was damp, which it seemed to be every time she saw him.

"You changed," she blurted out.

He nodded. "I ran home while Bill was in with Martha."

"You spent the night here?"

Another brief nod.

"I didn't realize you were that close to them."

"Their nephew couldn't make it down from Little Rock. It wasn't a big deal." He gave up a small smile. "After years of crashing on friends' couches, I can pretty much sleep anywhere. And it's easier on my bones than it would have been for Bud."

"So he's good friends with Martha and Bill?"

"Not exactly." He sat beside her, setting the sacks on an end table. "Bud likes to help others."

"So do you, obviously."

He gave a quick shake of his head. "I've got a long way to go."

"My dad's like that. He serves wherever he goes." She sipped the coffee. "That's a gift."

"Is he in Lafayette?"

"He used to be." Her eyes widened. "So you *were* eavesdropping that day at Evangeline's."

"It was hard not to when the shouting started." He made a face. "Sorry for bringing it up."

"Half of Samford knows my business anyway." She fidgeted with her bracelet. "It's nice to talk to someone who isn't part of the Broussard circle."

An odd look ran across T. J.'s face. "My mother is—" He stopped when Bill rounded the corner into the room, face drawn, steps slow, his cane making a thunking noise.

They jumped up. "What's wrong?" Avery asked.

Bill limped over to the couch and let himself down as though the weight of his body was too much to hold. "They say Martha may not be strong enough to go home for weeks." He looked at T. J. instead of Avery. "When she's well enough to leave, she'll be sent to some sort of cardiac-rehab unit in Shreveport."

"That's good news," T. J. said. "That means they expect her to improve."

Bill sank even lower onto the sofa, like a tire with the air seeping out. "Who's going to run the store? We'll have to close."

"Only for the short term," T. J. said.

"Our customers will leave us for that new gas station down on Trumpet." He stopped and glared at Avery. "We'll never find a buyer for a run-down building without any business."

Avery reached for his arm but let her hand drop back into her lap. "I can talk to Ross Broussard. He's an expert on commercial property."

Bill opened his mouth, an argument on his face before it reached his lips. Then he shrugged. "Whatever. I should have listened when my nephew told me to sell to the outfit that wanted the land." He made a clicking sound with his tongue. "I held out to get more. Now I've got nothing."

T. J. leaned forward, arms on his knees. "This doesn't have to be resolved today. Give it a little time."

"I don't have time."

Avery squirmed in her seat, and Bill flung his hand out as though to sweep her away. "You shouldn't even be here. Without you, we wouldn't be here either. We'd be preparing to move to our new condo."

"Bill ..." T. J. said.

But Avery held up her hand. "He's right." She swallowed. "I swear I will pay for the repairs."

"No point in fixing it up now. We might as well take the money and leave the place boarded up."

T. J. looked from one to the other. "Now's not the time to make a decision like that, Bill."

"I can't afford to keep that place closed." His eyes searched T. J.'s, looking less antagonistic. "I don't know what to do."

Avery glanced at a picture of Christ in prayer on the far wall. "I can run the store."

"What you talking about?" Bill said. T. J. shook his head at the same time.

"Until you decide what to do." Avery delivered the words in a rush, an odd bubble of excitement in her throat. "I have experience and I'm . . ." She shrugged. "I'm available."

Bill sat up straighter. "What kind of experience?"

"I managed a dress shop for five years."

A strange laugh erupted from his lips. "You wouldn't last a day. We sell coffee and biscuits to working people, not frippery to high-and-mighty types."

Avery set her mouth in a straight line. "I increased profits every quarter at the boutique, and I know how to deal with people." She glanced at T. J., pleading with her eyes. "You've seen the store. Tell him I can do it."

"I don't know. A convenience store is a different kind of place."

Her heart sank at T. J.'s words. "Why not let me try?"

"You're biting off more than you can chew," Bill said, but he hadn't folded his wrinkled body back into the couch.

"Maybe I am, but it can't be worse than the store sitting closed indefinitely."

"Do you know how to cook biscuits?" Bill asked.

"I can learn. My mother made excellent biscuits."

"Hrrmph. Our customers expect the best, not Elly May Clampett rocks."

"I used to be a decent cook, when I first married, and I know how to read a recipe."

"You think that recipe's written down? Martha learned it from her mama, who learned it from hers."

Avery's momentum slowed. "Have you ever helped with them?"

"We've had that store for fifty years, open every day except Sundays, Christmas, and Thanksgiving. Of course I've cooked 'em."

"You can write the recipe down for me."

"Like I'd trust you of all people with that recipe—and my cash drawer."

T. J. leaned forward. "I suppose it could work." He paused. "I'll vouch for Avery."

She stiffened. "I don't need someone looking over my shoulder."

"That's not what I meant."

Bill rose from the couch and crossed his arms. "Ain't like I got a lot of choice, I reckon. T. J. can keep an eye on you."

"That makes it sound like I'm on parole." Avery frowned.

"You owe me and my Martha. This is only a start to repay us."

She closed her eyes. "It would be short-term, until you get your buyer back or hire someone. And I'll report to you, not T. J."

T. J. cut his eyes at her.

Bill's shoulders sagged again. "I can't fool with this right now."

"Hold on," T. J. said. "What if you work out a deal with Avery till the end of January? She'll have a job, and you'll buy time to make a decision."

"I need to check with my nephew. He likes to stay involved in what's going on."

"Just let me know," Avery said. "I can go over to the store and prepare to open as soon as you tell me."

Bill pinched the bridge of his nose. "I suppose a few days couldn't hurt."

Bill's voice was stronger as he lectured Avery that afternoon on how to run Magnolia Market. The hospital waiting room was mostly empty.

T. J. had left for a cabinet-building job hours ago, promising to check in later. Avery wasn't sure if he was talking to her or Bill.

A motley collection of keys on a plain silver circle lay on the table in front of her. "Write this down," Bill said when her pen paused. "It's important."

"Did you get that?" he asked a moment later. "The soft-drink delivery man is due tomorrow, and don't turn off the light behind the counter when you leave. It's important to Martha that it's always on."

Avery flipped through the small notebook. "I've got five pages of instructions, Bill. I can call if I have questions."

"What's your phone number?" He fished a scrap of paper and stub of a pencil from his blue work-pants pocket. "I'm sure I'll remember other things you need to do."

She wrinkled her nose. "I don't have a phone at the moment." Then she brightened. "But you can reach me at the store."

"What kind of a person doesn't have a phone?" The familiar scowl covered his face.

"My power's out. Just because I don't have a phone doesn't mean I'm not trustworthy."

"Maybe this isn't a good idea ..."

Avery took a risk and patted his arm. "Even though it hasn't seemed like it this week, I'm dependable." She smiled. "Besides, like we said, it's better than keeping the place locked up." She snapped her fingers. "Oh! That reminds me. I need the code to the security system."

"Security system?" Bill's nose wrinkled again, an expression Avery had come to think of as his default look. "We don't have an alarm. No need."

Frowning, Avery leaned forward. "With you and Martha away, maybe you should consider one."

"What would anyone steal? A loaf of bread? A jug of milk?" He laughed. "Oh, yeah, I know. A package of vanilla-cream cookies. They're always a big hit."

"Real funny. That's not the best neighborhood."

"Phooey," Bill said. "The money's in the safe, and we've never had a lick of trouble, other than a vagrant or two hanging out in our parking lot."

"Sir?" A nurse stuck her head in the door, interrupting the conversation. "Your wife is asking for you."

Bill bolted up. "Is everything okay?"

"She's weak," the nurse said, "but improving."

"That's what you've said since she arrived," he grumbled.

"And probably what we'll say for a few days," the nurse said, her white clogs slapping against the floor as she walked away.

Bill fell into step behind her and then turned. "I'll expect to hear how tomorrow's sales are. You have my cellular number." He walked back to where Avery stood and picked up the keys. "Keep these in a safe place."

"Yes, sir." Avery resisted the urge to salute. The ring of keys was heavy in her hand as she watched him scurry to catch up with the nurse.

Maybe she had been swept up by T. J.'s words on serving others, but this was better than sitting in the dark, cold house.

Chapter 11

$\mathcal{A}$very turned the key and gave the back door a shove, a hint of satisfaction blossoming as she stepped into the dim market. A blast of warm air hit her, welcome after the frigid parking lot.

She turned to wave at the nurse who had dropped her off when Kathleen had failed to return. "Everything looks fine. Thanks again."

As promised, a small light shone over the counter, but the rest of the store was dark in the evening gloom. She waited for her eyes to adjust, reluctant to turn on lights that would make customers think she was open, and considered where to start.

She walked through a tiny entryway with a closet, a bathroom, and a storeroom with a tattered armchair, a cot, and a rusty iron table with two chairs. This must be where Martha and Bill rested when the store wasn't busy. It looked like a boardinghouse room from a classic movie, minus the allure.

Stepping behind the counter, Avery felt like a student who had ventured into the teacher's lounge. From this vantage point—and in the low light—the store had a charming shabbiness. The old-fashioned fixtures and cluttered displays didn't look quite so grim by moonlight.

The kitchen area was not as big as the galley on a windjammer cruise she and Cres had taken the second year they were married. The oven, big and black, was in the corner near the back door, jammed next to a compact griddle. A sink sat next to that. A small white refrigerator, similar to the one in her first apartment, was on the far wall.

From the counter, looking out, the store seemed almost spacious.

Strolling to the front, she bypassed the accident site and checked the entrance to make sure it was secure, glancing at the littered parking lot.

Drawing in a breath, she rolled up her sleeves and inspected the big project ahead. The stock, heaped in the corner, needed to be sorted. The floor needed to be swept. Packages of cookies were crushed and had spilled onto the floor, and the newspaper rack was flattened. A few containers of oil and windshield fluid didn't appear to be damaged.

Maybe the shelves could be salvaged and she could rearrange the merchandise. She rested her hand against the patch job, not a breath of cool air slipping in around the makeshift wall. T. J.'s carpentry was solid.

Wandering through the rest of the store, she swiped her fingers through dust. Everything needed a good cleaning. A prime display spot by the front door contained out-of-date novelty items, packages faded. She could move those and put a more sellable item—candy maybe?—out front. The chips needed to be more visible too.

Avery stopped.

Bill would join Martha in the heart-attack ward if she re-arranged his store.

But she could start on the mess she had made.

Heading to the back in search of a garbage bag, she paused. *Eww.* Something smelled sour. "What in the world?" she muttered, trying not to gag as she felt her way around the bread aisle and over to the cooler. She stepped into the pool of foul-smelling slime before she saw it—sliding into the cooler door, which stood ajar.

This she hadn't dealt with at the dress shop.

Opening the door fully, she drew in a tentative breath and was slapped in the face by the pungent odor. She held out a hand and picked up a pint of ice cream, which sloshed. Purple liquid dripped from a box of Popsicles.

A whiff of a half gallon of milk had her running to the back door. She stood in the dark, gulping fresh air. After fashioning a mask from a towel, she flipped on one light and opened the storage closet. A mop and a metal pail leaned against the corner with a push broom.

A large roach—*weren't they supposed to disappear in winter?*—scurried under her feet as she maneuvered the pail out from the wall, one wheel wobbling. Stuffing a handful of garbage bags under her arm, she put the mop handle under the other. She might not make Martha well, but she darn well could straighten up this store.

With a surge of aggravated energy, she emptied the cooler shelves into the bags, wondering how much inventory Martha and Bill had lost by someone's carelessness. Hauling the stinky, bulging bags toward the back, she hoisted each over her shoulder, then grunted as she tossed them in the Dumpster.

She tackled the sticky floor next, and went ahead and

mopped the rest of the store's old vinyl floor, her back aching. Maybe she would polish the cases and rearrange the broken shelves in the morning. She could handle the windows on Sunday when the market was closed.

Propped up against the mop, she blinked when the lights came on and dropped the handle with a loud thump.

"Who's there?" a man's voice yelled. "Stay where you are."

"Don't shoot! I work here."

"Avery?" T. J., hammer in hand, rounded the counter. "What in the world are you doing here?"

"I'm helping Martha and Bill," she sputtered. "You know that."

"In the dark?"

"I didn't want customers thinking the store is open. I'm cleaning up for tomorrow."

T. J. lowered his eyes, and Avery looked down. Her clothes were splattered with a variety of sour milk products, the hem of her gray pants, the same ones she had worn yesterday, wet. He sniffed.

"Now you know," she said after an uncomfortable second. "I break into stores and clean up melted ice cream for kicks."

"After all you've been through, a sense of humor." He gave a small smile. "Even though you're on thin ice with the owner. Or should I say thin ice cream?"

Avery gave a small snort. "This from a man armed with a hammer."

"I thought someone had broken in." A scowl replaced the smile. "Why'd you leave that door unlocked? Anyone could have come in and—"

"Attacked me?" She patted her pant leg. "I'd have given a bloodcurdling scream. Or curdling ice *scream*?"

"This is serious. You need to be careful."

It had been so long since someone had fussed over her that her stomach did a weird flip. Afraid to meet his eyes, she looked at the cooler. "It's a good thing I did come by. The cooler was open and everything's ruined."

"Maybe this isn't such a good idea." T. J. glanced around as he spoke. "This place is pretty run-down."

"I want to do this. I need to help."

He ran his fingers through his hair. "Are you sure you're up to it?"

"I started this week as the soon-to-be owner of an exclusive clothing store and was threatened with a hammer while cleaning up spoiled food." She looked around. "I can take whatever this place throws at me."

"At least you're not blaming yourself for"—his nose wrinkled—"that."

"Oh, this mess is all of my making."

"You ruined that food?"

"If I hadn't crashed into the store, Martha wouldn't have had the heart attack. If she hadn't had the heart attack, Bill would have checked the cooler before he left." She nodded, her lips pressed together. "Yep. I ruined the food."

"Nice guilt trip, but . . ." He pointed toward the cooler. "That thing hasn't worked right since the Reagan administration. The door never seals properly."

"I guess Bill forgot to mention that." Avery drew herself up. "But I volunteered, and I intend to keep my word."

"Then you'd better get home and get some sleep. The biscuit hour starts early."

Biting her bottom lip, a habit Evangeline chided her about, Avery looked up at T. J. "Could you give me a ride?"

⌒

At four forty-five the next morning, Avery turned on her porch light and looked out of the shutters. Waiting for T. J. to take her to the market, she almost felt like a kid heading off on a youth trip.

Those had been such happy days.

As car lights shone in the driveway, she picked up her purse and hurried to the door, glad to leave the cold, dark house. She needed to make a dozen decisions about her future, ranging from where to live to how to earn a living. But for now, putting one foot in front of the other would be enough. She'd fallen into her chilly bed exhausted and awakened with a sense of promise.

T. J. was halfway up the walk by the time she stepped onto the porch, her coat hanging open. His hair, damp again, looked like he had combed it with his fingers. He wore his canvas jacket over a T-shirt and a pair of wrinkled warm-up pants.

A quick image of Cres heading out to work, all suit and tie, starched and stiff, ran through her mind. He had always tried to project an image, while T. J. seemed comfortable with who he was. She liked that about him, more each time she saw him.

"Morning." T. J.'s eyes narrowed as his gaze worked its way down her body.

She smoothed the skirt of the shirtwaist dress she had chosen for her market debut. With its hemline just above her knees and sleeves that could be rolled up, it was a good mix of practical and professional. "Thanks for picking me up." She glanced self-consciously at her shoes, where his gaze lingered. "Is there a problem?"

"Are you sure you want to wear those?"

She looked at the red heels, her favorites, purchased whole-sale on a trip to market. "Why wouldn't I?"

He held up a hand. "I'm no fashion guru, but—"

"Obviously," she interrupted, focusing her eyes on his worn running shoes.

"Those things look dangerous. Wouldn't some . . ." He shrugged. "I don't know, wouldn't tennis shoes or something be better for a day on your feet?"

"I'm used to being on my feet in these." She strode past him.

"Whatever you say." He fell into step behind her.

Avery settled into the truck, adjusting her coat over her dress and fastening her seat belt. "You don't think I can do it, do you?"

"Avery, this is a different world from the one you're used to." He climbed inside and started the truck. "This isn't your responsibility."

"It feels like it is. Besides, I don't have anything better to do right now." She turned her head to look at him. "You didn't have to give me a ride. I'm sure you'd have rather slept in on a Saturday."

"Not a big deal. Bud and I are behind on our jobs, and this gets me to the gym before work."

The gym. No wonder those broad shoulders filled out his shirt the way they did. And working on a Saturday? Cres had saved Saturdays for golf, out-of-town sporting events, and socializing with clients—or people he purported to be clients. She admired T. J.'s work ethic.

"Did you say you live nearby?" She knew it was snobbish, but she hadn't figured a handyman could afford a place in the River Bend neighborhood. Maybe he rented.

He stifled a yawn. "On Morgan Street, in a duplex. My friends call it twin peaks."

Avery nodded. "I think I know that house. It has palm trees out front?"

"That's the one."

"It's charming."

He gave a startled laugh. "Why do I think you just paid me a backhanded compliment?"

"I'll need to find a new place soon, and I might consider an apartment like that."

"I know the landlord." His voice sounded teasing. "I can let you know if the other side opens up."

She nibbled on her bottom lip. "First I have to master biscuits."

"Are you really attempting those?"

"A small batch. If everything goes right, I'll increase the number Monday."

"You're mighty brave. Martha's biscuits are legendary."

"I'll be her protégée." Avery tried to smile, anxiety growing. "Don't be negative."

"Fair enough," he said. "I should tell you that Martha and Bill give me my biscuits for free."

She rolled her eyes. "That doesn't sound like Bill."

"It was Martha's idea."

"Why don't I believe you?"

He grinned. "You know as well as I do that Bill hasn't given anything away in his whole life."

"What's the deal with him anyway?"

"He's one of those guys who thinks life cheated him." T. J. shrugged. "He watched his father sign their house away in the Great Depression, he never had a son, and he missed out on a city job that his brother got. He never got what he wanted."

"That's quite a list." She squirmed in the seat. "What about you?"

"What *about* me?"

"Have you gotten what you want?"

His shoulders relaxed. "I'm working on it. I like my job, and Bud's a great partner. I've got a nice little place to live." He glanced at her. "And I meet intriguing people from time to time."

Her face still felt warm when they exited the truck and entered the dark store. T. J. inhaled and looked around, squinting in the darkness. "You've already got the place looking better. Smells better too."

"Eau de Pine-Sol. Covers a multitude of sins."

He looked at the big old clock that hung on the wall behind the register. "I'm going to run." He hesitated. "Unless you need me to stay."

"I've got it." She had to do this on her own. "I've managed a store for years."

"But you didn't have to worry about grease fires and faulty coolers there." His mouth turned up in one corner, attractive crinkles at the edge of his eyes.

After shooing him to the door, Avery impulsively laid a hand on his sleeve. "Drop by later and I'll give you that free biscuit."

"I might just do that."

Avery was smiling as she locked the door and hurried over for a quick check of the cooler, which, though almost empty, seemed to be working. Next she pulled out her list of notes from Bill and rolled up her sleeves. "I'm going in," she murmured to herself.

Preheating the big oven, she pulled out the oversize wooden biscuit bowl and a vat of flour. She grabbed a white apron from a hook on the storeroom door, found the other ingredients, and began to mix, working on the worn butcher-block surface behind the register.

When the blobs of dough looked respectable, she shoved the first batch in the oven and moved to the coffeemaker. She started two pots of regular and added a pot of decaf, supposing she'd learn who in the world drank that stuff.

From there she moved to the register. The combination to the safe was in two parts—taped inside a cabinet door in the storeroom, and underneath a shelf beside the register. Bill considered this a devious way to thwart any burglar.

Avery got on her knees to read the scrawl, figuring it would take a mighty motivated robber to go to all this trouble. When she opened the safe, the cash drawer contained small bills as promised. With a practiced system, she counted the money and prepared the cash drawer, then wrote the balance in her notebook.

She glanced at the clock. Five minutes until six.

Picking up a greasy plastic lemon from the basket by the register, she wrinkled her nose and tossed it into the garbage bin by the back door. "Three points!" She dumped the remaining lemons in the trash. "Sorry, Martha, but those things were gross."

After grabbing the cluster of keys, she turned the lock and flipped the Open sign.

Victory ran up her spine.

Magnolia Market might not have the class of Evangeline's Boutique, but it had its own personality. And she was doing something for someone else.

Chapter 12

$\mathcal{T}$he soft-drink delivery guy took the next-to-last biscuit, smiling as he bit into it. "Are you sure Miss Martha's in the hospital? This tastes just like hers."

But he wrapped the biscuit in a napkin. "I'll eat the rest later."

"They're horrible, aren't they?" Avery wrinkled her nose. "I was afraid they'd burn, so I took them out too soon."

"I like them moist in the middle."

"They're gummy."

He looked at the napkin. "Other than that, how's business?"

"Slow, thank goodness. A few Saturday regulars came in. I couldn't have handled a crowd."

"It's been light for a while. Bill's cut his orders in half the past year." He looked away from Avery as he spoke. "I know you're filling in, but my boss, well, I was supposed to remind Bill that he's overdue on his last invoice."

"He must have overlooked it." She picked up her notebook. "If you'll give me the amount, I'll tell him."

"I can leave another copy of the invoice—to go with the three I've already given him."

"That bad?"

"That bad." He lowered his voice, looking at a customer choosing a candy bar. "The other salesmen have the same problem. Some of them won't sell to Bill anymore."

Avery backed toward the counter. "He seems like a straight shooter."

"A broke shooter."

Within a few hours, she had heard the same story time and again. After the lunch rush, which included throwing together sandwiches and cooking a burger while ringing up purchases, she wiped off the biscuit case.

After a moment of consideration, she pulled the lone remaining biscuit from the case and tossed it, then rested her head on the counter.

"Rough start?"

Her head popped up so fast, she pulled a crick in her neck. T. J. stood in front of her.

"If you're here to gloat, don't bother. You were right." She gnawed on her lip. "I'm afraid I just threw away the last biscuit. But, trust me, you wouldn't have wanted it. Free or not."

He held out a plastic grocery sack. "I have something for you."

She eyed it but didn't take it.

He gave the bag a shake. "It's something I had at the house."

Avery reached in and pulled out a beat-up iPhone, case scratched and glass cracked.

"I figured any phone was better than no phone. It doesn't look like much, but it works . . . most of the time." He reached across and tapped the back. "The number's written here."

"For me?" She coughed. Was she choked up over a broken cell phone?

T. J. stuck his hands in his jeans pockets and moved from foot to foot. "It's not as fancy as you're used to, but maybe it'll help until you get to the phone store."

She wouldn't have been happier with a lavish piece of jewelry. "Are you sure?"

"I got another one when Bud and I opened our business." He shrugged. "I don't need it."

"For real? I've been trying to get in touch with Kathleen and this will help. I left the store number, but she hasn't called."

"Were you expecting her?"

"She said she'd pick me up at the hospital last night, but she never showed. It—" Avery stopped and gave a half laugh. "I was going to say it isn't like her, but I've only known her a few days."

"Maybe she got tied up at work."

"She did mention some sort of corporate visit."

T. J. looked at the display case. "So the biscuits didn't work out so well?"

"Let's say there's a learning curve."

He smiled. "Anything I can do?"

"Find a buyer for the store?" She raised her eyebrows.

"I've asked Ross to help, but he called this morning and said there's not a prospect in sight. Commercial property doesn't move quickly at this time of year."

Avery blew out a breath. Her feet were killing her. Not that she would admit it to T. J. "I can't imagine property on this corner moving well any time of year."

"The gallery across the street's doing pretty well."

Avery picked up the blue pen by the register and twirled it in her hand. "Do you think Ross could contact the guy who wants to buy the land?"

T. J. drew back. "That guy wants to bulldoze this place. Bud and the other artists from Sweet Olive are counting on this corner. Art means a lot to those people."

She looked outside at the empty street. "It'd take a lot of work to turn this around. You should see Bill's ledger." She shook her head. "Revenue's low and his credit's not great."

T. J. went to the front door, gazing through the screen. "It'd be a shame to see this old place go—it's part of Samford's history. This corner used to be lively—especially when my parents were young."

"Really?"

"Bud says this store's diner counter was where everyone came to find out what was going on in Samford. Without Facebook or Twitter, they had to go somewhere, right?"

Despite her fatigue, she couldn't hold back her smile. "An Internet café without the Internet."

"Kids came here for candy after school, and Bill swears Elvis stopped here every time he played the Hayride in Shreveport."

She rolled her eyes. "I have a hard time seeing Elvis hanging out with Bill and Martha."

T. J.'s laugh was warm, sending a tingle down her spine. "Before I-20 and I-49 were built, everyone passed by Trumpet and Vine sooner or later." He pointed across the street. "That church hosted famous revivals—traveling preachers would stop because it was on their way to some other place in the Bible Belt. Crowds flowed out the doors."

Avery stood beside him. "It's sad that it's empty now."

T. J. nodded. "Ginny Guidry, the woman who organized the artists in Sweet Olive, tells a great story about how she was saved there. Walked the aisle at one of the revivals, and her mother made her have a long meeting with the pastor before she could be baptized."

"You should write a history of this corner."

"I did." He winked. "In middle school."

"Let me guess. You interviewed Bud."

"Pretty much, although even my mother had all sorts of stories."

"What did the gallery used to be?"

"A duplex with a gift shop. Martha's sister lived upstairs. She was famous for taking in strangers—mostly young women in some sort of trouble."

"Next you're going to tell me that vacant lot was a diamond mine."

He leaned toward her. For a second she thought he was about to kiss her—but instead he tapped his finger against her lips. "Don't be a skeptic."

She took a step back. "You make this corner sound magical."

"That's too whimsical for me, but there has always been a sort of chemistry here."

At the moment Avery felt a sort of chemistry, but it wasn't for the landscape. T. J.'s manner had a warmth long missing in her life, and she drew a breath as he continued.

"That lot was a cotton field until about ten years ago. The owner prided himself on producing the first bale of cotton of the season. Now the land's tied up in probate." Staring into space, T. J. put his hands in his pockets. "Don't you think it would make a great park?"

Avery looked across at the littered lot—tall, dead grass swaying in the breeze. A rusty piece of farm equipment was covered with vines that had died in the cold, approximating a dystopian sculpture. "And you're not whimsical?"

His laugh rumbled from his chest.

She tilted her head. "So you grew up in Samford?"

"Born here. I left when I was fourteen and came back about a year ago."

"Your parents moved when you were a teenager?"

T. J. straightened, his expression less genial. "I was sent to boarding school in Connecticut." He paused. "Not one of my better experiences."

"Lots of kids get into trouble."

"Not that kind of boarding school. The kind where you wear a tie and blazer." He tugged on the hem of his T-shirt. "You can imagine how well I fit in."

"Why'd you go?"

"My mother thought it would look good on my résumé—and change my mind about my career."

"Did it?"

"I made buddies from different parts of the country. Got a good education. Didn't mind living away from my mother. Her house isn't the kind of place where a teenager feels all that comfortable."

Avery frowned. Her parents' parsonage in Lafayette had been welcoming, and her father's cinder-block apartment in Haiti was cozy. "What about your father?"

"He's a great guy, but super busy."

"Ah." It dawned on her. "That's why you don't speak with a true Louisiana accent. Your voice is deep without that—" She hesitated. "Oh, never mind. That's silly."

"No one's ever described my voice before."

Avery stepped back quicker than a crawfish headed for a ditch. "That is the kind of procrastination a woman will resort to when she has a store to clean. I've got to get to work."

Chapter 13

$\mathcal{T}$he letter in the front door that evening screamed trouble, although Avery had been expecting it. The envelope, Evangeline's signature light-blue linen paper, was visible from T. J.'s truck. Whether she liked it or not, she would be making a move.

She turned in the seat. "Thanks for carting me to and from the market today. You've been a huge help."

"Want me to pick you up Monday?"

"You've gone above and beyond." She opened the door. "I'll figure out something by then."

"I'm available if you need me." The half smile he added prompted that flutter in her stomach again. "And I still expect my free biscuit."

"It's yours," she said and hurried up the sidewalk, then paused to wave as he drove off. Could she have called him back, asked for his opinion on her plan, trusted him with her secrets?

She dreaded the prospect of dating again, but T. J. seemed like a man who could be fun to go out with. He exuded kindness and was easygoing, unlike Cres and his cadre of friends. Not absorbed with himself but interested in others. Interested in her.

And despite all that happened, she refused to give up on her dream of a home, a family, a faithful husband.

Rubbing her eyes, she pulled the envelope from the door and turned the heavy paper over. The Broussard return address was engraved on the back flap. She stepped inside, the house temperature colder than the outdoors. She wrapped her coat around her and sat on the edge of the leather sofa.

She slid the single monogrammed sheet out and scanned the handwritten letter. The Broussards were selling the house. With Ross out of town, the listing would be done through an associate, and Avery's *things* would be put in storage until requested. If she cashed the check and left town, she would get a small bonus from the sale of the house.

"P.S. One way or another, this will all be wrapped up by early February," Evangeline had written.

Avery folded the letter, placed it back in the envelope, and looked around the room. This house once held all her desires. Now she could see only a thing or two she wanted. She headed into her bedroom and pulled out a large suitcase.

She fished the cell phone—*what a thoughtful gift*—out of her pocket and laid it on the bedside table. Wrapped in the shawl from her father, she was reaching for the quilt when the phone chirped. She grabbed for it, allowing herself to hope it would be T. J.

"Hello?"

"I'm sorry I must have the—" The voice paused. "Avery?"

She glanced down at caller ID. "Ross?"

"It's so good to hear your voice. But why are you answering T. J.'s phone?"

Her face warmed. "Mine isn't working."

"I thought you were avoiding my calls."

"It's sort of a long story." She fiddled with her hair. "But you can reach T. J. on his other number. I need to—"

"Don't hang up, Ave. I miss you. How are you?"

She hesitated. Ross was as close as a brother to her, but since the day of Cres's death, she'd shut him out. "I'm helping out at Magnolia Market. Turns out, selling biscuits isn't all that different from selling dresses."

He groaned. "I hate that I was gone when all of this blew up. My family has caused you more grief than anyone deserves. Cres—"

"Ross, I don't want to talk about it. Your mother's happy with the other buyer, and I'm putting my life back together."

"With T. J.?"

"Of course not. He loaned me a phone. I'm working and making a plan for the future."

"Avery, you earned that boutique. Give me time, and I'll fix what my parents did." His voice lowered. "We have a few weeks, but it's hard to work this out long-distance."

"I think we're past that point." She put one hand under the quilt for warmth. "I was surprised to hear about your new office. How's it going?"

"Baton Rouge has a lot of potential, and I needed to get out of Samford for a while." He cleared his throat. "There's great retail space here if you decide to open a new shop."

She pulled the quilt around her. Maybe she should tell Ross everything, let him help sort it out. But he didn't deserve to be pulled between Avery and his parents.

Ross, too, needed to put the past behind him and find happiness.

c

Avery slammed the cab door. The driver, the same one who had dropped her at home four nights ago, unloaded her suitcase, a stuffed black trash sack, and leather tote bag with a concerned expression on his face. "You sure you're all right?" he asked with his heavy Spanish accent.

"I am now," she said, freedom creeping into her bones.

Plopping her things in the dark alley, he looked around with a crease between his eyes. His two-way radio squawked through a crack in the driver's window. He waved a hand when she fumbled for her wallet. "No charge this time."

"I can pay."

He threw her a doubtful look and closed the door. "All the best, señora."

Bill's big ring of keys jingled as Avery rolled the suitcase toward the back door. Nervously she looked over her shoulder and inserted the key in the old lock, then shoved the door open with her hip.

As she pushed the door closed, the driver gave a wave and pulled off, brake lights glowing. The small light over the register reminded her of her night-light as a child. While it didn't throw much of a beam, it made the creepy interior bearable. She allowed her eyes to adjust, thankful Bill didn't have a security system.

He would be sleeping in a chair in Martha's hospital room, with no way of knowing what Avery was doing.

She walked to the closet of a room, stepped inside, and closed the door before turning on the overhead light, a fluorescent bulb that buzzed like an angry bee. She felt the tension in her shoulders ease.

While it was a far cry from the New Orleans Ritz where Cres had taken her on their honeymoon, it was a warm place to sleep until she figured out her future. She opened the door a crack and slipped through it, collecting the garbage bag first. From it, she pulled her pillow, a sheet, and her grandmother's quilt and arranged them on the cot.

She corraled the luggage into the tiny space, lifted it onto a kitchen chair in the corner, and pulled out a T-shirt and pair of sweatpants, her toothbrush, and the shawl from her father.

The bathroom was smaller than the pantry at Evangeline's house, the lavatory about the size of a goldfish bowl. She stashed her toiletries on the back of the commode and prepared for bed.

Sliding into the lumpy cot, she lay back on her pillow and smiled at the ceiling.

For the first time in five years, she was not beholden to the Broussards for the roof over her head.

Chapter 14

The buzzing of the phone roused Avery on Sunday morning, and she felt for it in the dark, trying to regain her wits.

"Darling, are you okay?" her father asked. "I've been worried."

She looked at the calendar on the wall and concentrated on figuring out where she was.

"I got your text with your new number. An ice storm? In Louisiana?"

"I'm sorry I scared you, Daddy. I wanted you to know why I hadn't been in touch. It's been wild around here."

"How's my birthday girl?"

"Aging." She forced a laugh. "How's the birthday girl's father?"

"Wondering how I wound up with a twenty-nine-year-old." His warm chuckle was almost as good as one of his hugs. "I miss you. I wish we could talk more."

"You don't need to waste money calling."

"Money's not that tight. I need our weekly chats. Did Cres's parents do something special for you on your special day?"

Tell him now.

The words she needed to say wouldn't leave her throat. "Since the ice storm hit, things have been out of kilter," she said instead.

"You sound a little blue. Want me to come home?"

"Daddy, you don't need to offer to come home every time we talk."

He cleared his throat. "I'm hoping you can visit this summer."

"Maybe. Things are up in the air right now." She fingered the fringe on the black-and-brown shawl. "Your gift arrived right on time. Thanks so much."

"That's one of the handmade items I was telling you about. What do you think?"

"It's lovely. I'm wearing it right now." She considered her next words. "But I don't think it's what Evangeline wants in the store."

"Then I'll keep looking for something else to sell."

"Uh, Dad, most boutique customers go for name brands. But I want to buy some for gifts." These goods would be worthy of her tight cash. "How are the children? I miss them."

"Wonderful. And challenging. New residents show up every week." He paused. "Angel said to tell you hello."

"She's still there?" Joy and sorrow collided within Avery.

"I doubt she's going anywhere. No one has come forward since her grandmother died." He sighed. "She's twelve now, all arms and legs and still talking about your last visit. She wants to grow up to be like you."

Avery flinched. She was not worthy to be a role model. "Give her a hug for me."

"Are you sure you don't want me to make a trip home? I haven't been there since, well, since Cres's service."

"You're the best, Daddy. I love you, and I wouldn't want you anywhere else. You're doing something special."

"I wish we could have been together for your birthday. This year especially." His voice softened.

"Your work's more important than a birthday dinner."

"I feel like I let you down."

"Daddy, aren't I supposed to leave you and grow up?"

He chuckled. "Are you telling me to get a life?"

"Don't fret. Something interesting's happening with me. I'm not sure how it's going to work out, but I like it."

"Uh-oh."

"What do you mean 'uh-oh'? That's a good thing."

"When your mother said something like that, I knew I'd better watch out."

"I'm finally doing something I feel good about." She reflected on the idea, unable to voice the hope she felt.

"You know I'm here anytime. I pray for you every day."

"Thank you," she said softly. "I wouldn't have made it otherwise."

When she hung up, she pulled out her battered Bible, a gift from her parents when she turned thirteen, and hugged it to her chest, inhaling the familiar smell.

She flipped it open, and it fell to the oft-read passage in Jeremiah. "'For I know the plans I have for you,' declares the Lord, 'plans to prosper you and not to harm you, plans to give you hope and a future.'"

Hope and a future.

Since the early days of her marriage to Cres, she had turned to those words—and since his death, they had been her rock.

A collage of memories moved across her mind, but T. J.'s smile and her father's encouragement overrode the familiar pain. Maybe the path was getting easier. She wanted to believe it was.

She looked back at the verse and bowed her head. "Help me, God."

Then she brushed her hand across the Bible and stood, too much to do to surrender to emotion.

She had to make a practice batch of biscuits.

⟶

The phone, a black wall model that had to be forty years old, was ringing when Avery finished sweeping the front sidewalk, and she composed herself before answering.

"Magnolia Market, Avery speaking. May I help you?"

"Are you working for me or the chamber of commerce?"

"Oh, Bill, good morning." She dusted the counter as she talked, stretching the cord.

"You were supposed to call me last night."

She wrapped plasticware in napkins. "It was late," she said after a moment. "I had to take care of a few things at home."

He made a harrumphing noise. "Seems like you could have spared a minute or two. Did we make any money yesterday?"

"Not much, but tomorrow will be better. I made a big Open sign to hang out front ... you know, in case people think you're closed because ... because of Martha's—"

"Not a bad idea," he jumped in. "Did you explain to the regulars?"

"I did. They said to tell Martha they're praying for her."

"What do they say about the biscuits?"

"That I need to take lessons from Martha." She laughed but didn't tell him she had scrapped three practice batches today, each worse than the one before.

"Did you sell all of them?"

"All but one. They buy them even if they're not as good." She puttered around behind the counter. "Is Martha still improving?"

"She's got a long way to go." Bill's voice was gruff. "Her heart was in worse shape than anyone realized, and she may have had a little stroke. I'm not real sure what kind of timetable we're looking at."

"You take care of her and don't worry about the store." Now wasn't the time to think about how fast February was approaching.

"Magnolia Market's not the same as some gal's dress shop."

"That's for sure." She bit back a laugh. "But I can hold things together for a while." She looked at the diminishing shelves of bread and hoped she wasn't making another bad decision.

"Don't forget to call and let me know how things go tomorrow." Bill hung up.

"You're welcome," she said as she put the receiver on the hook. But truth was, she hoped he would let her stay a few days more.

⌒

The faint knock startled Avery, who was rearranging a shelf of outdated seasonings, and her heart sped up. Maybe T. J. had stopped by to see how things were going.

Adjusting her ponytail and brushing the dust off her jeans, she hurried to the front door.

"Hi." The woman standing outside ran a hand through her short tawny hair.

"Hello." Avery turned the key and opened the door a crack. "I'm sorry, but the market's closed on Sundays."

The woman's smile transformed her face. "I'm Camille Gardner from the Sweet Olive Art Gallery across the street." She stepped in the store, her beat-up cowboy boots clomping on the floor. "Is Martha better?"

"She'll be in the hospital for a while, but she'll be glad to know you stopped by."

"So you're related to Bill and Martha?"

Avery gave a quick shake of her head. "I'm a . . . friend. I'm Avery Broussard."

"Avery . . ." Camille studied Avery's face. "I'm new to the area and still trying to remember who's who. Your name sounds familiar."

"I don't think we've met, but I hear the gallery's fantastic."

"You should let me give you a tour." Camille's voice rose with excitement. "We have the best regional art, and the artists are super nice." She raised her eyebrows. "Can you tell I like my job?"

"I was beginning to suspect you did." Avery grinned.

Camille took another step into the store, touching a display of chips in a crockery bowl. "You're a miracle worker. This place looks so much better." She slapped her hand across her mouth. "I'm sorry—I didn't mean that the way it sounded, but things look . . . well, cleaner."

Avery pointed to the dirt on her jeans. "Don't look too closely. I've got a long way to go."

Camille's smile broadened. "So you'll be running the market?"

"Temporarily. A few days or so."

"Darn. I hoped I might rope you into helping with the corner. I'm trying to get a crusade going, but Bill isn't interested." She picked up a peanut pattie. "I believe his exact words were: 'I'll be dead. Why should I care?'"

Avery hooted, a laugh so unexpected that she slapped her hand over her mouth. "That's our Bill. Ever the charmer."

"So would you be interested in helping?"

"I'm just lending a hand here."

"You're the kind of person we need. This corner's going to be turned into *light industry*—whatever that means—unless the community gets involved."

"I've never been part of something like this." Camille's enthusiasm was hard to ignore. "What exactly would I do?"

"Anything you wanted. We need everything from people picking up litter to someone to run for city council who cares what happens to the neighborhood. We need to find a buyer for that church and publicize the art gallery—and Magnolia Market."

Avery twirled her bracelet around her wrist. "A few of Bill's customers say the corner's doomed, that businesses are moving west of town."

"They're just naysayers." Camille grabbed Avery's arm. "We can't let that happen. The Sweet Olive artists worked so hard to get the gallery remodeled. Samford needs more character, not more cookie-cutter buildings." She looked down at her hand and slowly removed it. "Sorry, but I want this to work."

"So you've been involved for a while?"

"Not at all." Camille's mouth twisted. "I stumbled to the corner of Trumpet and Vine sort of like you. I was working for an oil-and-gas production company and met the artists. They're phenomenal." Her voice softened. "I haven't been in Samford a year yet."

"They convinced you to stay?"

"They're a persuasive bunch." Camille's smile was huge. "And I happened to . . . um, well, it's still hard to say out loud."

Avery leaned forward.

"I fell in love." She wiggled her nose. "Can you believe that? Next thing I know, I live in Louisiana and accost nice people like you." She chuckled. "I get wound up."

With a laugh, Avery gestured at the store. "It's easy to get drawn in. I'm attached to this place already."

"So you'll help us save the corner?"

A list of excuses ran through Avery's mind. She was in a monthlong battle with the Broussards. She didn't know how long Bill would want her to work at the market. Ross had hinted she could possibly get the boutique. She wanted to visit her father.

But why not help? It was the kind of thing her parents had taught her. She might run into T. J. more if she got involved in the neighborhood. He could even be part of this project. Volunteering might lead her to something better for her life.

"I can try." Avery shrugged. "I don't know how long I'll be here, but I'm happy to help while I'm here."

Camille dove straight in for a hug. "I knew God was going to send us someone."

Chapter 15

Avery prepared the paper for Tuesday's biscuits like a professional gift wrapper at Christmas.

In only three mornings, she had come to look forward to the quiet routine, alone with her thoughts and a mound of dough. Preheating the oven set the plan in motion, warming the dank space until the store came alive.

Today she had scurried from her secret nest in the back, where she slept soundly, turned on the oven, and got coffee going in the dark. After a quick splash bath, she dressed in one of her boutique outfits—a black maxi skirt and a black-and-white wraparound blouse—and smoothed the wrinkles with a damp kitchen towel.

When she pulled the biscuits out of the oven, a fluffy, golden brown, she felt like she had managed to get something right.

Bill had called a half-dozen times since Sunday to remind or reprimand, always a note of suspicion and fatigue in his voice. Even Monday night when she had been waxing the grimy floor. His lecture was a blend of a kick in the pants and a pat on the head. He started with a sharp accounting checkup, muttering about low sales, and morphed into a coach's pregame pep talk, reminding Avery she could do it.

For an ornery man, he delivered a stirring tirade.

But the one biscuit left from yesterday stared at Avery, weakening her confidence.

She snatched it from the case, yanked the paper off, opened the back door, and threw it like a major league outfielder. It sailed across the alley, and she slammed the door.

⌒

Kathleen's absence was unnerving. What had happened to her?

Avery dialed her cell number again, and this time it didn't even go to voice mail. It rang ten times and clicked off. After rummaging under the counter, Avery pulled out a battered phone book and scoured the residential pages. No Kathleen Manning was listed, nor K. Manning.

Her finger trailed up and down the columns as she tried to recall Kathleen's husband's name. Wayne. That was it. Sure enough there he was, even though he had been dead for four years.

The timer, a vintage blend of plastic and rusty metal, dinged, and Avery reached for an oversize pot holder and whispered a prayer for this latest batch. Her biscuits were improving at about the speed Martha walked.

After jotting Kathleen's phone number on a scrap of paper with a fat yellow pencil, Avery went back to work.

Preparing the biscuits, step-by-step, reminded her of her mother. A master of Louisiana meals, her mom believed working in the kitchen was a type of praise, a chance to offer thanks for the blessings of the day, an opportunity to focus on what was in front of you instead of worrying about something down the line.

Everyone felt welcome at their family table.

And then her mother had gotten sick.

Their life as a family became like life on a treadmill. Avery could not stop, going faster and faster toward death until one day it flung her off without a mother.

How were she and her father to get back to *normal*, whatever that was? How was she to believe, day after day, that her mother was in a better place and that it had happened for a reason? What kind of reason could be good enough to leave Avery?

Her father had agonized over a pending mission assignment in Haiti, an offer extended before her mother got sick. Avery listened to his hushed conversations with church members and saw their sad looks.

He had taken Avery's hands one night with that tender smile that always comforted her, the one that kept her from flying apart. "If it's okay with you, baby girl, let's stay in Lafayette for a few more years."

She gripped his hands so tightly it hurt. "But what about the kids in Haiti? Mama wanted us to help them."

"There'll be time for that. But for now, let's help each other." His gaze met hers. "Avery, it's all right to miss your mother."

She started crying. "What about those children who don't have anyone?"

He took off his glasses and wiped at his damp eyes. "We'll keep praying, and God will show us the way. Maybe if we wait we'll be able to help them more." His mouth twisted. "Your mother would be mad at me if I uprooted you from school right now."

And slowly they had gotten into a new routine, life after her mother, bearable, sometimes even peaceful.

Not until the summer after Avery's junior year in college had they gone to Haiti.

"What do you think?" her father asked.

"You're perfect for the job they have for you. You speak French. You are handy with a power saw." She smiled. "I want those children to know the kind of love I've known."

"Are you sure you'll be okay with this?"

"You need to do this—for all of us."

But she had been caught off guard by how much she missed him when she returned to school.

Then she met Cres.

Avery glided eagerly—if clumsily—into a new life, anxious to have a home to visit for holidays and a family that could be hers. But caterers made the food for parties, and housekeepers didn't let a dish sit in the sink for more than a minute. Cres introduced her to friends and family, bragging about how smart she was and how down-to-earth.

If he occasionally seemed patronizing, she pushed it aside, wanting to believe she had found the man for her. If the Broussard lifestyle seemed excessive, she lectured herself on not being judgmental and sent her father more money from her campus job.

The recollection made Avery shake her head, and she picked up the phone to send her father a *good morning* text. Maybe she could help right here at Magnolia Market.

It might not be Haiti, but it was a start.

C

Checking the handwritten recipe, she went to work on more biscuits, mixing the flour and cutting the dough with a water glass from underneath the register.

Bigger than the batch before, the biscuits rose and looked beautiful when she took them out of the oven. But the extra ten minutes she had left them in resulted in a hard crust on the bottom.

She picked it up and nibbled the top. Not too bad.

After frying bacon and scrambling eggs, she assembled the assigned number of combinations and wrapped them in white paper. One she set aside.

The store was empty at midmorning when Avery pulled the receiver to her ear by its stretched-out cord, perching on Bill's wooden stool. Her heart thumped harder as the phone rang.

"Hello," Kathleen said.

"Thank goodness, Kathleen," Avery said in a rush, but her words were talked over by the recording. Disappointment settled on her like a heavy blanket.

"Kathleen!" she said again when the beep sounded. "Call me, please, to let me know you're all right."

She slipped the receiver back and rested her head on the wall. Kathleen didn't seem unreliable. What had happened?

The rest of the day dragged. Business was light—"pitiful," as Bill described Tuesdays—with a steady rain. She sold all the biscuits, except the one, and a few cups of coffee, a loaf of bread, and a gallon of milk, hardly enough to keep the lights on.

Restless, Avery rearranged the bread, disapproving of out-of-date loaves that needed tossing. Even though stock was low, she dreaded an encounter with another delivery person frowning over the market's unpaid bills.

From the counter, she surveyed the room for the thousandth time. Despite her cleaning efforts, everything had a gray look. The packaged food had faded in the natural light from the windows. Water seeped from beneath the back cooler. The central heat thumped each time it kicked on, contributing to the industrial feel.

For a moment, she longed for the comfort of the dress shop.

When customers stepped into Evangeline's shop on a gray day, they smiled with relief. Magnolia Market, despite its lovely name, piled grim upon grime. If it weren't for the biscuits, she didn't think the store would have any business at all.

Why hadn't Martha and Bill built on the popularity of the biscuits?

Avery strolled down each aisle, assessing the mix of products and how they were placed. Then she reversed her steps and did it again. And again.

There had to be a way to make this place look better—and to make more money.

The electronic bell on the door buzzed, itself an irritation, and Avery turned with a smile. "May I—?" She blinked. "Kathleen?"

"I figured I might as well stop by since you obviously aren't going to quit calling." Kathleen's words were hoarse, and she gave a weak smile, her eyes bloodshot, lips pale. She scarcely looked like the same woman who had given Avery a ride to the hospital five short days ago.

Not only did she wear no makeup, but her hair was the light-brown color it had been when Avery first noticed her in the store. The bright-red spikes were tamed into what resembled a dull bob—choppy, but a bob nonetheless.

"What happened to your hair?"

Kathleen put her hand up to her head. "That red was silly. It was supposed to signal the new me, but . . ." She gave a huff of laughter. "What a joke."

"I liked it."

"You've left me two-dozen messages and you want to talk about my hair?"

"Did you have . . . the flu or did someone . . . is everything all right? What happened? I've been worried."

"I didn't figure you'd miss me since I was hounding you for money."

Avery gathered up the old bread and wedged it between her forearms and her torso. "I was getting used to having you around."

Kathleen looked from Avery's face to the bread and then over the counter, her expression as startled as if a ghost stood nearby.

"Is something wrong?"

"You're smashing Bill's bread. It makes him mad when customers do that."

"Oh." Avery relaxed her hold. "This stuff's stale. It needs to go."

Kathleen stared toward the register again. "I wouldn't do that if I were you. He lets it stay at least a day or two past its expiration date."

Avery looked down at the bread. "Isn't that against the law?"

"That's his business, not ours."

"Maybe I could put it on clearance." Avery walked behind the counter as she spoke, then dumped the loaves onto the wooden worktable.

When she turned around, Kathleen's mouth had dropped open. "Have you lost your mind?"

Avery cocked her head. "I was sort of wondering the same thing about you."

"Bill will kill you if he sees you behind the counter." Her eyes darted behind Avery.

"You must have skipped that message. I'm working here for a few days."

"You're working *here?*"

"I'm filling in until Bill decides what to do." Avery sat on the stool and patted the old office chair where Martha usually sat. "Come sit down, but I'll warn you. The mystery evaporates when you step back here. You'll never look at the place the same."

Kathleen gave a bark of laughter and seemed almost surprised that she had done so. "Not quite as glamorous as Dresses for Rich People?"

"The rodent count at Evangeline's isn't as high as it is here."

"You *are* a snob." Kathleen let herself through the swinging gate that led to the register. She looked down at her feet. "Because you'd better not be talking about real rodents."

Avery wrinkled her nose. "The mice apparently know Bill's away."

"Gross." Kathleen's gaze drifted to the biscuit case. "Who's making the biscuits?"

"Moi."

Kathleen's eyes widened. "*You* are making the biscuits."

"Yes, *I* am making the biscuits."

"Baking takes practice."

"My father's a preacher. I had to learn to cook for all the potluck dinners."

"But your kitchen ... it looked so ..." Kathleen's voice trailed off.

"Vacant? I haven't cooked much since Cres . . ." Now it was

Avery who couldn't find the word she sought. She nodded at the case. "That's for you, by the way."

Kathleen took a step closer to the case. "You saved me a biscuit?"

"Yep."

"I gave you my biscuit that day of the wreck."

"The one labeled 'hers.'" Avery nibbled on her lip.

"You've saved me one?"

"Every day, except for Saturday when they were inedible. Help yourself. On the house."

Kathleen shook her head.

"I'll pay for it," Avery said.

"It's not that. I'm afraid if I stick my hand in that case, Bill will appear and chop it off."

Avery chuckled. "He's staying at the hospital with Martha."

"I know. I've been by a few times to check on her." After taking the biscuit out of the case, Kathleen unwrapped the white paper and stared at it for a moment, then sniffed. "Looks good," she said, but bit into it as though it might bite back. She chewed for a moment and took another bite, still not speaking.

Avery had not been this nervous on the day she hosted her first trunk show at the boutique. So she waited. While Kathleen took another bite. And another.

"I can't stand it any longer! What do you think?"

"Not bad."

"What do I need to change?"

"A little dry, but not all that different from Martha's." She chewed more and gave a nod. "It's pretty good."

"Why do you sound so surprised?"

She motioned to where Avery sat. "If you'll let me have that stool, I'll tell you."

"I left you the chair. It's more comfortable."

Kathleen waggled her eyebrows. "But the stool's the seat of power. I can look out at Bill's empire."

"You're a nut," Avery said, but scooted from the stool to the chair.

Kathleen folded the white paper into a square. "I thought you were some prissy society woman who had a maid to cook for her."

"That's what you get for judging me." Avery sounded like her fifth-grade Sunday school teacher, a woman bigger on scolding than loving. "I'm happy to see you." She hesitated. "We haven't known each other long, but I've missed you."

"I got laid off."

Avery blinked.

"That big corporate meeting I organized, the day after Martha's heart attack?" Kathleen made a clucking noise. "They didn't want my opinion. They wanted to give me the ax. Reduction in force. Cutbacks. Blah, blah, blah."

"Hadn't you worked there for years?"

"So much for loyalty. They gave me a thanks-for-your-service speech and sent me on my way."

"Sounds familiar," Avery murmured. "Will you retire?"

"I used to think I'd retire young and travel with Wayne." She groaned. "I guess you know how that turned out. I just turned fifty-five, and I'm in the market for a job. And Wayne went and died."

"So you haven't been by because you got laid off?"

Kathleen nodded. "At home crying for the weekend. Job hunting yesterday." She grimaced. "Any of your rich friends hiring?"

"The only person I know who's hiring is Bill. Want to buy the market?"

"Are you kidding? My money's tighter than those jeans you wore to the bank."

Avery made a face. "I'm sure you got some sort of severance."

"Oh, I got a 'package' all right." Kathleen scowled. "I work for them for thirty years, and they give me ten minutes' warning and three months' pay. They escorted us from the building—twenty of us—like we were criminals."

"With your qualifications, you'll find a job."

"Have you seen what's out there?"

Avery shook her head. "I've been afraid to look."

"I called every administrative and secretarial listing—online and in the paper. There was one oil-and-gas office job. They quit taking applications after fifty people showed up the first hour." Kathleen paused. "I called a dozen friends from church. Nothing. Nada. Zip."

"I'm afraid retail's going to be the same." Avery straightened her apron. "All we can do is keep trying."

"Since when did you get all spunky?"

Avery shrugged and looked away.

"Don't just stand there. Give me something to do." Kathleen gestured around the room. "I might as well help as sit at home and stare at Howie."

"What about your job hunt?"

"I have my cell if anyone follows up." Her shoulders drooped. "Although from early indications, I'll be living out of my car by the end of the year."

"If it's back from the shop by then." Avery winced.

"Davis called yesterday. It'll be ready early next week." She lifted her eyes. "I nearly forgot. He has a 'classic clunker' you might be interested in."

"Is 'classic clunker' code for old junker?"

"Beats me."

Avery squeezed her eyes shut for a second. Cres had once teased her about the station wagon they would buy when they had "a passel of kids." She had stashed money at the house, hidden from Cres, for the emergency she always felt was sure to come. At the time, she felt guilty. Now she wished she had saved more.

"Here's his number." Kathleen wrote the number from memory on a slip of cash-register tape. "Said to call him if you're interested. He can even help you find insurance."

Could she possibly afford even everyday expenses?

"Well?"

She touched the bracelet. "I do need a car."

Chapter 16

$\mathcal{T}$he guy held out his hand to Avery, who grimaced. Her stomach felt as if it had been invaded by a swarm of butterflies. Maybe this was a dumb idea, but she took his hand.

"Davis Sonnier."

"We met when I came to check on my SUV." Avery liked his firm handshake and his calloused hand.

He made a face. "I'd rather pretend that never happened. I owe you an apology, Mrs. Broussard. I was way out of line when I told you about the food pantry."

"It's Avery, and don't be silly. I was miserable that day—and it was thoughtful of you to be concerned."

A big guy, tall and muscular, the mechanic carried himself as though comfortable in his own skin, which for some reason made Avery nervous. With his light-brown hair and hazel eyes, he resembled a younger version of his aunt.

Kathleen had scooted out midafternoon for another job interview. The notion of her future desertion propelled Avery to take a cab to the garage.

Now she felt vulnerable, on turf more alien than Evangeline's coronation at the Samford Spring Cotillion. Life had crashed in on Avery in the past week and a half, and she had darned well better figure out how to right things.

"I sounded like a jerk," Davis continued, "presuming you needed help and that I might bestow it on you." His mouth quirked at one corner. "It's enough to give churches a bad name."

"I did need help, but I wasn't sure how to accept it." She clasped her hands. "It took a few days for your offer to sink in."

"My aunt Kathy told me you're lending a hand at the market in your spare time." His gaze roamed over her. "Looks like things have turned around for you."

"Right." She rolled her eyes. "That's why I'm here to buy the cheapest car you've got."

"I hope I'm not out of line again, but you look great." He offered a grin, and her anxiety faded.

She looked down at the black slacks and houndstooth blazer finished off with her favorite red heels. "I wasn't sure what to wear to buy a 'classic clunker,'" she said with a wry smile.

A familiar burst of laughter erupted. Clearly that ran in the family as did the eye color.

"I've never bought a car on my own before." She held out her hands. "I'm at your mercy."

"Just the way I like my customers," he said with a mock sneer. "You're going to love this baby—as long as you don't do a lot of driving."

"That's a ringing endorsement."

"It doesn't get great gas mileage, but I know the old guy who owned it. It's dependable—and fast too."

"What color is it?"

Davis furrowed his brow. "Don't you want to know what model it is first?"

"That too." Her face heated.

"Follow me."

On either side of the glossy royal-blue door into the waiting area, two cone-shaped junipers perched in large blue ceramic pots. Oversize white rockers sat to the side, a small wrought-iron table between them. A sisal welcome mat lay before the door, and Davis stopped to wipe off his work boots before entering.

The entrance was a disturbing contrast to the shabby entrance of the corner market. If only Bill and Martha had not let the store slide, perhaps someone might actually buy it. This place showed what a little creativity could do.

The chairs weren't the usual industrial vinyl of auto shops but a glossy orange plastic with an embossed gray chevron stripe. Magazines were arranged on an orange coffee table, and they lacked the usual battered look of waiting-room reading material.

"The car's out back." Davis led her through a small hall with restrooms, a watercooler, and a coffeepot. Everything looked clean.

"This shop's so inviting," Avery said. "The owner has quite an eye for design."

Davis scrunched up his face. "Not really."

"It looks great. I kind of want to live here."

He laughed. "I'll pass along your compliment to Aunt Kathy. She helped me put it together."

"You're the owner? I thought you just worked here." As soon as the words were uttered, she clapped her hand over her mouth. "That sounded incredibly rude."

"No problem." Davis waved his hand. "You can't believe how many people tell me they'd rather talk to the owner."

She laughed. "You look young."

He patted his cheek. "Baby face. I'm thirty-five, which gives my aunt hives. Makes her feel old." He smiled. "She was twenty and had married her childhood sweetheart when I came along. She practically raised me and would rather people think she's my big sister."

"So you lived with Kathleen?"

"Most of the time. My mom got pregnant in high school, and Aunt Kathy and Uncle Wayne stepped right in, let Mama stay with them. They are the kind of people who will do anything for anyone."

"I've seen glimpses of that."

"Wayne was a mechanic here and helped get me a job cleaning the garage after school. I stayed on and bought it five years ago." A shadow ran across his face. "He died not long after. What a shocker. And then . . . life sucked for a while."

Avery laid her hand on his shoulder for an instant, the pain in his eyes familiar. "I'm sorry."

"My aunt's a rock." His hazel eyes were intense as he met Avery's. "But I guess you know how it feels to lose someone like that."

"Yes, well . . ." She looked away. Until recently she had focused on the loss—when she awoke alone and unsure, when a memory skittered forth, when she caught a whiff of someone who smelled like Cres or a glimpse of someone who looked like him. But not now. "I guess we move forward a day at a time."

Nodding, he looked around. "This place has been a refuge for me. Work therapy, I suppose."

Davis had created what she had wanted with the boutique. She clasped her hands and fought an instant of envy. "How'd you come up with all these ideas?"

"I minored in marketing."

She smiled. "I was a marketing major at LSU."

He grinned, shaking his head. "I did my first two years at the community college in Bossier and finished up at Louisiana Tech. I'll try not to hold that LSU business against you."

"Geaux, Tigers."

"Dawgs."

She laughed, relieved at the shift of mood. "I've always loved businesses that do nice things for customers."

"Getting your car fixed ranks right up there with going to the dentist, so we try to make it easier."

"I'm impressed. Since I'm helping out at Magnolia Market for a few days, maybe I could get a few pointers for the owner."

"Good luck with that. Bill's a pretty change-averse guy."

She peered at him. "You know Bill?"

"I stop by the store occasionally, but I'm a single dad, so mornings are crazy." His smile grew. "But if I'd known you were there . . ."

Avery clutched her purse. *Is he flirting?*

"I'd better check out the car and get going." Her words sounded sharper than intended, so she added a smile. "But if this clunker is a classic, the biscuits will be on me next time you come by."

He extended his arm with a flourish. "Judge for yourself."

A gargantuan wood-paneled station wagon sat before her. The back fender was scraped, but the car shone as though recently waxed and polished.

"A Buick Roadmaster," Davis said as though she had won the grand prize in a contest. "And you're not going to believe this—it has a Corvette engine."

Her eyes widened. "It's huge."

His face fell. "I knew it was an acquired taste."

"I appreciate the effort, but I had something . . . I was expecting something smaller." *And more colorful.*

"Smaller cars cost more. This one you can get for a steal."

Her wallet didn't contain much to bargain with. "A Corvette engine, you say? That car's looking better all the time."

⌒

The Tahoe had been big, but Avery's new station wagon made the SUV seem like a MINI Cooper. The car drove like an 18-wheeler, with about the same turning radius.

But she was mobile again.

With a sense of freedom, and feeling certain Davis had given her a feel-sorry-for-you discount, she drove up Trumpet and back down and across Vine, like a college student checking out her old haunts. She shook her hair out of its ponytail and let the window down, despite the chilly weather.

Using the stainless-steel buttons, she found a classic rock-and-roll station and cranked it up loud enough to draw a stare from an old man walking a dog. Or was he admiring her new car? She inhaled, giddy, the car replete with the smell of old leather, pine air-freshener—and a hint of dog. This was definitely a car for a dog and a couple of . . .

The giddiness slid away. How she longed for a child. Davis had been so proud showing her a picture of his son, Jake, his face beaming.

She let off the accelerator and coasted back down Trumpet, the weight of memories exhausting. *How did I let myself be drawn into Cres's world?*

Praying for guidance, she wandered through the neighborhood that should have been a wonderful place to call home. Ancient live oaks, squat and sprawling, and tall, skinny pines boasting green leaves and needles despite the winter weather. Purple pansies and yellow snapdragons filled flower beds, and the occasional bike and wagon sat in front yards, as though left during play.

She could almost see the neighbor's preschool son dashing in from a hard morning of pedaling or the babysitting grandmother pulling the petite twins in the wagon. Although the grandmother had taken to looking the other way after the rumors swirled about Avery. Those small, unexpected slights hurt more than the big cuts.

Avery turned onto Division and drove by the house she had shared with Cres. A Contract Pending sign had been added to the realtor's sign in the front yard, and she pulled up, tires scraping against the curb. She shoved the door, heavier than a piece of furniture, then stepped into the yard—and stopped.

What good would it do to look around?

The place had little of her and Cres left within its four walls. Even before his defection, he had badgered his parents to make a down payment on a new house, disparaging the cottage as too old and shabby for their lifestyle. House plans had been delivered from the architect the week of his death, a two-story McMansion in a gated community north of town.

When they first married, the house had brought Avery a sense of peace each time she walked through the door. But as the months passed, it stood as a symbol of how different she was from her husband, how she had let loneliness and fear draw her to the wrong man.

She shook her head. There was nothing here for her. She had started over.

Avery wished she could tell the people who whispered about her perfect life that nice houses, designer clothes, and extravagant vacations didn't make anyone happy. None of those meant as much as being available to others. Dropping in for a chat. Calling to check on a friend, offering a prayer. Her father's love for those who couldn't help themselves. Kathleen's and T. J.'s help with her problems. Those mattered.

She returned to the car, turned up the radio with a determined twist of the dial, and pulled away, almost but not quite ready to sing along.

She wound past T. J.'s duplex, admiring the neat gray-green paint and the front doors flanked by two large camellia bushes loaded with pink blooms. Incongruous cabbage palms stood nearby almost like Florida tourists.

She couldn't hold back her smile at the inviting home, wondering who owned the place and who lived in the other side. She would need an apartment. The driveway was empty, and she was both thankful and disappointed, unsure of what she would say to T. J.

A flood of longing washed over her. Maybe they could become friends.

Avery pulled out onto Vine and turned toward Cres's childhood home, a brick mansion that looked like a community center. Evangeline's car, the small Mercedes, sat under the porte cochere. The new road warrior wouldn't even fit between the columns.

Driving on, she couldn't resist going to the boutique. For the past six years, she had been here almost every day, often late into the evening. During Cres's increased absences from home and after his death, she migrated more and more to the shop, distancing herself from those who wanted to help, friends and family who bemoaned the passing of her husband.

She shook her head. The wound from the lost boutique was not as bad as she had expected. And despite another call from Ross, she had lost interest in fighting The Fashion Group.

Another plus for a fresh start.

Manuevering the station wagon behind the shop, she gazed at the row of unfamiliar cars where she and Evangeline once parked. Had the sale already gone through? Evangeline relished the cotillion and debutante seasons, when her friends flocked to the store for long visits and expensive purchases. But maybe The Fashion Group deal had been too good to wait on.

The shop looked classy, the front window intact and freshened with the bold colors Samford women adored for winter. Yet another contrast to the market, whose color of the day was gray. The moldy market had the personality of grumpy Bill. Surely she could do better. Prepare it for a buyer perhaps. Couldn't she?

As Avery left the discount craft store, her arms were loaded and excitement danced through her blood for the first time in months. With a trio of cardboard display boards, glue sticks, a stack of magazines, and a rainbow of markers, she opened the hatch of her car and bit back a grin.

Maybe she would add a page to her new notebook listing the positives of owning a plus-size vehicle. The tanker might not steer easily, but she could move a household. In fact, if her bedroom at the store went away, she could live back here. It was almost bigger than the room she inhabited.

Debating where to park the beast at the market, she inched toward the far side of the front, riding the brake. If this baby went through the wall, the entire building might fall. She bit back a giggle.

Her mishap had set so many things in motion, but the memory of the wreck, just as the boutique drive-by had been, was not as painful as expected. Before pulling her materials from the car, she walked out to the street and surveyed the building.

The Magnolia Market sign was peeling, its post rusted. Its redeeming quality was the faded magnolia on the logo, a nice piece of advertising art.

Beyond that, things went downhill. A neglected planter underneath had been knocked loose, bricks sitting where flowers should be. Weeds grew in cracks in the asphalt, with a pothole or two big enough to knock a hubcap off.

Litter collected at the corner, due in part to the lack of a receptacle out front. A pile of railroad ties were stacked at one end of the building, with the look of a project gone awry. She sniffed, hating the creosote smell, and as she kicked at the stack, a rat ran out and skittered to the back of the building.

No wonder Bill's business was sliding.

Grasping for the happiness she had experienced when driving off Davis's lot, she retrieved her materials from the car, a lot of stuff for a little cash, and let herself in the front door.

At least the store smelled fresher.

Kathleen had picked up a bag of lemons, and Avery put them in baskets near the register. Their citrus scent mixed with the lingering smell of coffee, which was better than the stale smell of cardboard and sour milk the store had when Avery took over.

Stashing her purchases in the back room, she grabbed a bottle of water from the cooler and put a dollar in the cash drawer. Taking a long swig, she focused on what to tackle next.

You must not begin to think of Magnolia Market as your own.

She glared at the shelves and went back to work.

Chapter 17

$\mathcal{K}$athleen drove into the parking lot before daylight Thursday, humming at the idea of surprising Avery with her early arrival. Something about having a copy of Bill's store key made her lighthearted.

But she frowned when she saw the big, old station wagon out front. Had someone abandoned his car in the lot—or worse, broken in?

She skidded to a stop, reached into her purse for her pepper spray, and jumped out of the car. She pounded on the door as she turned the key. "Avery! Avery!"

With her hand quivering, she held the spray up as she barged in. "Show yourself! I'm armed. I'll shoot. I swear I will."

Something—or was it someone?—rustled near the cooler, and she hunkered down, ready to fire. A large water bug ran across the floor in front of her, and she stifled a squeal. *So much for heroics.*

She needed to call the police.

A light flickered in the back, and a figure stepped into the kitchen area. "Kathleen?" Avery's sleepy voice said. "What time is it?"

"Oh, thank goodness." Kathleen's knees went weak, and she grabbed the candy display to steady herself. "Are you all right?"

Avery rubbed her eyes, which suddenly widened. After tugging on the hem of her T-shirt, she pulled her messy hair into a ponytail. Her gaze shifted to the clock behind the counter. "What are you doing here?"

"What are *you* doing here?" Kathleen's anxiety turned the words strident. "I was going to surprise you."

"You surprised me all right." Avery hurried over to the coffeepot. "I . . . I got here early too."

"You look like you just rolled out of bed."

"Thanks a lot," Avery said, but her voice lacked sarcasm. "I'll get things underway and then get dressed."

"You're going back home?"

"I . . . I brought some things."

Kathleen wrinkled her nose. "What's with the boat out in the parking lot?"

Avery's eyes shifted from side to side.

"That car." Kathleen pointed to the station wagon.

"That, my friend, is a classic clunker."

Kathleen laughed, the adrenaline of a few minutes ago giving way to relief. "I'd have guessed aircraft carrier."

"It's nice not to feel like a teenager who has to beg Mom and Dad for a lift. And your nephew is a super nice guy." She halted and started toward the back of the store. "Can you finish the coffee? I need to . . . I'll preheat the oven."

Kathleen stepped behind the counter. "You're working too hard."

"No! I'm good," she said in a more normal tone. "I have a routine."

"Is that why you're acting so weird? I'm not trying to take over."

Avery fingered her bracelet. "I'm happy to have your help, but I've already gotten set in my ways. I took lessons from the grouch himself."

"Come to think of it, you're acting a lot like Bill this morning."

Rushing toward the storeroom, Avery paused to preheat the oven. "I get a little anxious every morning. I'll feel better once the biscuits are made."

Kathleen grinned and called after her. "Isn't Davis a cutie?"

c—

Avery straightened from behind the shelves of canned goods when the buzzer on the front door sounded. And then she squatted back down so fast, she snagged her gray wool slacks, already mended once.

Cres's father, who ordered coffee beans from the Pacific Northwest and had the housekeeper run his errands, strode to the counter. In a suit and tie, which he wore every day except Saturday, he looked as out of place as Cres the time they visited the orphanage.

She had scarcely recovered from the shock of Kathleen's arrival that morning. *Now this?*

Kathleen, scrubbing years of grease from pots and pans, had her back to the counter, making more noise than the cymbals in a patriotic hymn.

Creswell Sr. cleared his throat, then tapped on the biscuit case.

Avery waddled backward a step or two. *Please turn around, Kathleen. Please don't turn around, Creswell.*

"Excuse me!" He clearly didn't think he was the one who needed excusing. "Ma'am!"

Avery added a bell for the counter to her mental shopping list.

Creswell turned, scowling, to scan the store.

Avery tucked her head down, studying a can of pork and beans as though it held the secrets to the universe.

"Ma'am!" Creswell barked again.

"Oh, sorry! May I help you, sir?" Kathleen's eyes widened when she noticed Avery, who gave her head a quick shake.

Tapping on the biscuit case again, Creswell held up two fingers. "With grape jelly and a side of bacon."

Avery's jaw dropped. Her father-in-law, avid jogger and health-food evangelist, was a two-biscuit person? The things you learned when you ran a corner store.

With his back to her, she scooted to the end of the aisle and eyed the distance to the door. While Evangeline could be haughty and cold, Creswell reminded Avery of a school friend's pet ferret—all friendly until he took a disliking to you and went for a vein. She rubbed the scar on her index finger from the time he smashed a wine glass on the coffee table and demanded she clean up the mess.

He liked to be in control and knew Avery could hurt him.

If she chose.

Which she didn't.

The antique cash register dinged, and Kathleen thanked him for his business. Avery remained still until she heard the buzz of the door, and she peered around the end of the counter, her knees popping as she stood. Kathleen gave her a thumbs-up, her brow cocked, and then shook her head wildly.

"Hello, again," Kathleen said, overly loud. "Will there be something else, sir?"

Avery plopped back down so fast she landed on her rear end.

"Maybe you can help me. I'm trying to get in touch with Avery Broussard." Creswell's voice had switched to pure southern charm and reminded Avery of Cres's two-faced mannerisms. "Someone mentioned that she was"—he cleared his throat—"helping out here?"

"Uh, um, A-Avery?" Kathleen stammered. "She's working some, I believe. Yes, she works here."

Creswell moved closer. "Do you know how I can reach her?"

"Avery?" Kathleen asked in that loud voice.

She rolled into a tighter ball.

"Avery Broussard. Might I leave a message with you?" He clearly didn't think much of Kathleen's reliability.

"A message?"

"A note!"

Avery peeked around the corner, Kathleen's gaze flitting to her and back to Creswell.

He pulled a business card out of his suit-coat pocket, reached for the pen chained to the counter, and scratched a word or two before letting it fall with a clatter. Out of ink. She had intended to change that and could picture the disdain on his face as he withdrew his expensive pen from his shirt pocket.

Avery knew it was expensive because she had picked it out as a birthday gift. Cres had taken credit for it when his father had fawned over it.

Creswell remained at the counter a moment longer. "Do you have an envelope?"

"An envelope?"

"Oh, never mind." He laid the card on the counter and pushed it toward her. "It's important that you get this to her."

Kathleen picked it up, her brow furrowed. "She can be a hard one to track down." She threw her eyes toward Avery and back. "Her life's been pretty tough."

Avery stifled a groan.

Creswell straightened. "So you know her?"

"She's a friend."

He leaned closer, his voice almost too low to hear. "Is she in trouble?"

Avery held her breath in the heartbeat of silence that followed. "She's doing great. I'm teaching her everything I know about business."

Almost laughing out loud, Avery willed Kathleen to quit joking and send Creswell on his way.

"Tell her I don't appreciate this game she's playing."

"I'll do that." Kathleen's gaze darted toward the door. "Have a good day." The sound of the screen door squeaking ended the conversation.

"Whew." Kathleen peered at the business card as Avery popped up. "Creswell Broussard Sr., Certified Public Accountant and Wealth Advisor." She turned the card over. "What was that all about?"

Avery rubbed her knees. "My father-in-law—or ex-father-in-law—I'm never quite sure how that works. What's the note say?"

Kathleen wrinkled her nose and began reading. "'Let's clear this up. Contact us as soon as possible. Regards, CS.'" She fingered the card. "Regards?"

"They're not an affectionate family."

Kathleen arched one eyebrow. "How'd you get mixed up with that hoity-toity crowd in the first place?"

"I married Cres." She tried to picture his good-looking face on the day she walked down the aisle and fought to recall the happy first dates and romantic gestures.

"So he caught your eye across a crowded room and swept you off to wealthy bliss?"

Avery felt the heat drain from her face. "Nothing like that. We had a marketing class together fall semester of my junior year in college. He was a senior and needed it to graduate."

She could remember with crystal clarity the first time he had asked for help with a paper. "He was about to fail."

"And you weren't?"

"I aced that class. With my help, he passed." She gave a rueful smile. "Cres was more partier than scholar."

"You don't strike me as the party type."

Avery twisted her hands. "That's one of the things Cres supposedly loved most about me, my common sense. And I loved his happy-go-lucky nature."

"That's sweet." Kathleen's voice could have been sarcastic or sincere. It was hard to tell.

"Our story felt so romantic at first, so unlikely. Like God dropped Cres right into that desk next to me." Avery gave a dry laugh. Cres's world was loud and exciting, a welcome contrast to her quiet, lonely days in the dorm. She had been seduced by his careless confidence and flattered that he chose her to take home to his parents.

What a fool she had been to jump into marriage with a man who wasn't what he seemed. After her marriage fell apart, she had made another vow: her future decisions would be wiser.

"How long were you married?" Kathleen's question poked at a spot that didn't feel as tender as it had a few weeks ago.

"Technically five years."

Kathleen stood and draped her arm around Avery's shoulder. "You hardly had time to get to know each other." She gave her a tight squeeze and then let her arm drop. "Wayne and I took five years to get used to sharing a bathroom."

Avery offered a weak smile. "I misread Cres. We weren't right for each other, after all. I prayed about it. I tried to do the right thing. But it ended so wrong."

Kathleen put her arms around Avery, holding her the way she wished someone had held her after the funeral. Close. Tight. Reassuring. Like her mother would have done. For a moment, she savored the connection and then collapsed into the chair behind the counter.

"I wanted a marriage like my parents', and I couldn't have chosen more wrong."

"You were young and probably sheltered."

"Maybe. I don't think I was ready for marriage." She cut her eyes at Kathleen. "Have you ever felt that you weren't a good enough wife?"

The air was quiet for a moment except for the hum of the refrigerator case.

Kathleen took a deep breath. "Wayne smacked his gum in movies and chewed his food too loud. He never could understand why he had to wear a tie to a wedding. For that matter, why he had to go to weddings in the first place." She paused. "I fretted over stupid stuff, and when he died, I was guilt-ridden."

She drummed her fingers on the counter. "I wish I had taken better care of him, forced him to get an annual checkup, cooked healthier meals, nagged him to exercise. But I didn't and he's gone."

"But when he died, you still knew he was the one for you."

Kathleen nodded. "It was so ordinary, our life together. I

didn't get the grand romance I dreamed of as a girl, but I learned to want what I had. I would have married him again in a heartbeat." She put her hands on her hips. "Could I have been a better wife? Oh my goodness, yes."

"When you talk about Wayne, your whole bearing changes."

Kathleen's mouth twisted. "I got married the week after I graduated from high school, so we grew up together. Every couple has their knock-down-drag-outs, though. Or the wife pouts."

Avery's brow crinkled. "Cres and I didn't fight. We didn't talk either. My folks talked about everything." She swallowed. "He was handsome and confident."

"And rich?" Kathleen punctuated her sentence by popping her knuckles. "I've never known anyone who married into money. Must be nice."

"Having money brings its own problems."

"To be so unlucky . . ."

"Seriously. You have lawyers and bankers involved in your life, and the Broussards . . . well, in my limited experience, wealthy parents tend to be overbearing."

"Pushy, you mean?"

Avery pondered how much to say. "They seemed more concerned about a return on their investment than his happiness." She met Kathleen's gaze. "In their defense, Cres could be difficult. They gave him everything. I didn't realize that before we were engaged—and I got dragged into it."

The house, the SUV, the expensive wedding the Broussards had insisted on—and subsidized. She was still learning to forgive herself for allowing them to control her with purchases. "I wish we had gone off on our own. Things might have been different."

"How so?"

"Cres leaned on his parents for everything."

Kathleen gave a quick shrug. "Lots of students do that."

"Even after he started working—at his dad's firm, by the way. Everything he did was part of their plan for him—except marrying me."

"And getting hit by a car."

Avery winced. "That too. His parents are so strong-willed. I felt shut out." She removed the apron, relishing the moment when it hid her face. "Maybe I was too critical of Cres, too needy."

Kathleen cocked her head. "That's what we do in life. We need each other. We do our best."

"Did I do my best?" That question haunted Avery. "They paid my rent, leased a car, got me going at the shop." She sat in the chair behind the counter. "I made the mistake of getting too attached to the boutique, especially after Cres was killed."

"Why not use Cres's life insurance to start your own shop?"

"My name wasn't on the policy."

"You weren't a beneficiary?"

"Nope. The Broussard family is worth a fortune, dead or alive, but they never saw me as part of the family."

"And you didn't fight that?"

Avery exhaled. "A legal battle would have eaten up any benefits. And, truth is, I didn't want their money, despite what Evangeline and her friends thought."

"That confirms it. You are officially 100 percent USDA crazy."

Kathleen's outburst lightened Avery's mood. "That money could have bought lots of good stuff for the store, couldn't it?"

"Well, yeah. And one or two thousand other things you need."

"The problem, though, was how their money made me feel. Almost dirty."

"I'm not following. Cres was your husband."

"Broussard money always has strings attached. They not only managed our checking account but our lives—who we socialized with, where we vacationed." She shook her head. "My parents taught me to make it on my own." *Although I'm not doing a great job of that at the moment.* "The Broussards helped for a year."

"While you were running their fancy-schmancy dress shop. You were doing *them* a favor."

"I intended to buy the shop." She looked up. "My brother-in-law, Ross, liked the idea, but Evangeline wasn't so hot on it." She tore a paper napkin to shreds. "I think Ross left town because he couldn't stand the sorrow anymore."

"Another unhelpful guy? Just what you needed."

"Oh, Ross isn't like that! Just the opposite. Gregarious. A charmer—but with a good heart. He went on like nothing happened, trying to cheer up his mother and live up to his father."

"Sounds like hard work being part of that family."

Avery looked at her. "I never thought of it like that, but it is. It can wear you down so fast you don't see it coming."

"You need to stand up to them. Those people left you in the cold." She tilted her head. "Where are you staying anyway?"

Avery looked away.

"You're not still in that cold, dark house, are you?" Kathleen's voice rose.

"Oh no, I found a little place."

Kathleen looked suspicious. "Does it have heat and lights?"

"As a matter of fact it does." Avery forced herself to look up. "It's temporary, but I'll find a permanent place soon." The words *permanent place* sounded good after so many months in limbo.

"Are you going to call Creswell Broussard Sr.?" Kathleen

extended the card over the counter, and Avery grabbed it. She looked down at the familiar handwriting.

"We'll see." Then she stuck it in her pocket.

When she got to know Kathleen better, she would tell her the rest of the story.

Chapter 18

$\mathcal{A}$very pushed the overloaded shopping cart down the aisle of the wholesale warehouse, Kathleen following with their growing shopping list and an accelerating look of worry.

"Do you have to be so spry?" Kathleen asked. "My feet hurt. It's been a long week."

"Fresh fruit!"

"My head aches too," Kathleen added. "This isn't the way I wanted to spend Friday evening."

"Add fruit. And markers. We need to make new signs."

"I'd kill for a pizza."

"Pizza! Maybe we could add homemade—no, that's not the tone we're going for."

Kathleen cut her gaze to the basket. "Are you sure Bill will go for this new tone?"

Perching a bouquet of early tulips on the top of the other supplies, Avery shrugged. "It's not a new tone exactly. We're improving on what he and Martha started."

"Dumpy chic?"

Avery laughed. "Surely it wasn't always dumpy, and we can help restore it. Improve it even."

"I don't think we have enough money to cover this." Kathleen's wrinkled expression intensified.

Avery patted her purse, adding up the money she had left. She wouldn't cash the check unless it was required to save the market. The insurance claim was still in limbo, but T. J. and Bud insisted they were satisfied to wait. Bill had told them to go on with the repairs and asked Avery to keep things running.

"Sales are better but they aren't *this* much better." Kathleen pulled a calculator out of her pocket and brandished it like a six-shooter in a Hollywood Western.

"Not the calculator," Avery groaned. "Come on. We're re-investing Bill's profits."

"And your paycheck," Kathleen murmured.

"I don't need much to live on. Besides, I can pay myself back when our sales improve." She paused. "Would you mind getting another cart?"

"I'm not sure who's crazier: me, you, or Bill." Kathleen walked off, stuffing the calculator into her pocket and scratching items off the list.

"Thanks for keeping us organized," Avery yelled at her back. She examined the display of apples. Picking up sacks of Red Delicious and Granny Smiths, she sniffed their fruity scent before stuffing them on the bottom of the cart.

Why not offer fresh fruit to customers? Some shoppers might prefer healthier choices—although none of their current customers had requested them—but the bright colors would liven up the store. And if they didn't sell, maybe Kathleen could use them in some sort of dessert special. She was good with dishes that included sugar.

Reappearing with a mop and push broom sticking out of the extra cart, Kathleen was surrounded by enough cleaning supplies to disinfect a hospital.

Avery bit back a smile.

Looking at the apples and back at Avery, Kathleen tightened her mouth. "Don't you think we should take this a step at a time?"

"I am." Avery drew in a deep breath, loving the smell of the produce. "If I weren't, I'd buy those expensive raspberries."

Kathleen's hand flew up like a school crossing guard's. "Halt!"

Lifting the broom out of the cart, Avery smirked. "Doesn't look like I'm the only one who wants to spruce the place up."

"Like you said, the customers appreciate a clean store. And that old mop is worn out." She sighed. "While you're spending money like a drunk monkey, you might as well look at these chalkboard thingies they have up front."

"You're actually suggesting a purchase?" Avery put her hand over her heart. "I knew I was going to like this partnership."

"Spoiled rich girl." Whipping her cart around, Kathleen bumped into another cart. "Now I'm driving like you," she muttered.

"Heaven help us," a man said.

T. J. stood in front of them, his cart loaded with an array of snacks and juice boxes.

"Got the munchies?" Avery asked.

"After-school program." He raised his eyebrows at their baskets. "And you?"

"Sam Walton here thinks we need to restock the store," Kathleen said.

T. J. moved closer to Avery's buggy. "With flowers?" The

doubt in his voice was bigger than the jar of jalapeños wedged underneath the tulips.

"A cheerful store sells more," Avery said.

T. J. and Kathleen exchanged dubious looks.

"I have a degree in marketing." Avery gripped the buggy handle. "I've studied the psychology of retail."

"How about the psychology of people who want a biscuit on their way to work?" Kathleen massaged her temples. "We'd do better to stand in the parking lot with the coffeepot than to put out bouquets."

Avery's eyes narrowed, and she snapped her fingers. "What a great idea! Some sort of quick service ... maybe a box breakfast?"

"There she goes again. If we could sell a cup of coffee for every idea she had, Bill would be a millionaire."

T. J. smiled. "I'm sure all of that will help, Avery." He waved his hand at their baskets. "But Bill's going to sell the place soon or shut it down." He tapped on a set of two commercial cookie sheets. "Do you need to buy stuff like that? I can't imagine you'll get your money back."

Avery looked at the overflowing basket, her heart sinking. At some level she had hoped T. J. might understand. "Maybe you're right."

"But on the other hand," Kathleen said, "we can take a lot of this with us when we're finished. Or donate it to a good cause." She pulled a box of peanut-butter crackers from T. J.'s buggy. "I doubt you get reimbursed for all of this, do you?"

"No, but it helps students who don't have a place to go after school," he said, his cheeks red. "I don't mind spending money on that."

"Well, this helps Bill and Martha," Avery said.

A slow smiled worked its way across his face. "You might help one of our GED students while you're at it. She wants to be a chef, but she has no experience—other than cooking for her family." He drummed his fingers on a box of granola bars in his cart. "She's young but she has an idea for a Louisiana seasoning mix with a Mexican kick."

Avery's excitement grew. "What a great—"

"Wait a minute," Kathleen said. "We're lending a hand, not launching a product."

"Come on," Avery cajoled. "It couldn't hurt to try her spices."

Kathleen crossed her arms in front of her chest and looked at T. J. "Whatever. Avery's the boss."

"I'll take you over to the mission, and you can see what you think." T. J. glanced at the list in his hand. "Now I need to find little cups of applesauce."

He was grinning as he walked off.

Avery watched him. He cared about others. He was a man who knew what it meant to work for a living. He was good at what he did. *What a combination.*

A small smile on her lips, she nudged Kathleen's cart with her own. "Did you say chalkboard thingy?"

The Brown Beast could hold enough to stock a small supermarket. Literally.

Pulling out the last cardboard box of supplies, Avery wiped sweat off her brow with her sleeve.

"Let me take that." Kathleen held the back door open with her hip.

"Whew, thanks." She handed the box to Kathleen and let the door swing shut behind them. It had been a long day. "I didn't work this hard during debutante fittings."

Kathleen let out a hoot of laughter. "If those society mavens could see you now."

"Sorry, friend. I don't know one person who uses the word *maven*." Grinning, Avery pulled a large package of white napkins out of a box and considered how to tie the cutlery. Raffia, maybe? "But you're right, my former customers wouldn't believe this."

The store was dim, the way Avery kept it in the evenings and early morning hours. Not only did she not want customers to think they were open, but also she didn't want to attract attention to the fact she was living there. The boxes from the wholesale-warehouse store covered the counter and the table nearest the grill.

Overall, the place was a mess.

And she was happy.

She laid the bright-pink tulips on the butcher-block counter by the sink and pulled out a knife to trim them. Kathleen unpacked perishables, some for resale and some for cooking.

A small lump swelled in Avery's throat as she watched Kathleen work. If she had known how much she needed a friend, she would have crashed into someone's car sooner. She grinned, and Kathleen gave her a puzzled look and turned back to the cooler.

They had bought enough nonperishables to disguise the store's barrenness—and maybe make the shelves look presentable to a potential buyer. The cleaning supplies would go a long way to spruce up the place. *And* they had run into T. J. doing another of his good deeds.

"Just what do you think you're doing?" a twangy male voice demanded.

Her butcher knife clattered to the counter as Avery whirled around. A wiry man with strawberry-blond hair stood in the doorway, the skin on his face over-tanned.

"Are you ransacking the place?" He eased toward Avery, who took a step back.

Avery looked at the piles of boxes and gave a spurt of uncontrollable laughter.

"What's so funny?" Kathleen called from across the store.

"Uh, Kathleen, we've got company."

"At this time of night?" She approached, eyes wide as she looked at the man pressing too close to Avery.

The surprise on the guy's face would have been amusing if Avery hadn't been so frightened. Kathleen wasn't cowed. She stood with her hands on her hips, a threatening pose in its own way. "Avery, step over here. Who do you think you are, mister?"

Avery picked up the knife and walked around the counter.

"I'm Greg Vaughan, Bill's nephew. I manage his business affairs. And I don't appreciate coming in to find you stealing from him."

"Stealing?" Avery said. "We just spent our own money to restock the store."

His lips curled. "You the Broussard woman?"

Nodding, she put a hand to her hair, pulled into a sloppy knot on the top of her head, and brushed at the dress jeans that had a patch of flour on them.

"You any kin to that realtor?" he asked. "I need to get in touch with him."

"I was married to his brother."

"You're divorced?"

"My husband died."

"So you come from money. Even better."

"Listen, buddy," Kathleen said. "I don't care if you handle Donald Trump's business affairs. We open early. Unless you want to stock the shelves, you'd better be on your way."

"How much are you taking from my uncle's profits, Ms. Broussard?" His gaze went to the register.

"Kathleen and I work here as a favor to your aunt and uncle." Avery stepped closer to him. "We barely scrape by. Take any complaints up with Bill."

She reached for an apron and thrust it at him, pleased to see sweat glistening on his temples. "Or maybe you plan to be here before daylight to open the store you claim to be in charge of. If so, Kathleen and I will gladly leave it in your hands."

"Go, Avery," Kathleen murmured. "Nicely done."

"How'd you get in here anyway?" Avery demanded.

"I had a key made the last time my aunt was in the hospital, and I stop in from time to time to make sure Uncle Bill's not losing it."

"Bill's going to lose it when he hears you've been sneaking around his store," Kathleen said.

"This place is not going to be here much longer," he sneered. "I drove in from Little Rock to help them wrap things up. We're putting it on the market ASAP."

"ASAP? Took you long enough to get here," Avery said. "Your aunt had her heart attack over a week ago. Have you even been by to see her?"

"You mean since you put her in the hospital?" Greg waved at the patched front wall.

"That was an accident." Kathleen's voice rose.

"We won't spend a cent for your carelessness. I intend to make you pay." He pranced toward the door. "I'll expect an accounting of all expenses. You ladies have a good evening."

"Ugh," Avery said as the door swung shut. "He makes me feel sorry for cranky Bill."

c—

"You're good in the kitchen, aren't you?" Avery watched Kathleen line up ingredients for the next day. With the tulips on the counter and the new supplies in place, the space looked almost pleasant, remnants of nephew Greg's horrid visit erased.

For the moment.

"I was raised in rural Louisiana and married for more than thirty years. Lots of practice."

"Why aren't *you* making the biscuits?"

Kathleen gave a small shrug. "You're good at it. I'm better at frying things."

"What kind of things?"

"Pies. Fish. Chicken." She looked over her shoulder. "It's probably what killed Wayne."

"Did you shovel it into his mouth?"

"Of course not."

"Then you didn't kill him."

"Hmm." Kathleen held a mesh sack of avocados that looked as out of place as a silver goblet would have. "I'll have to think about that."

"What kind of fried pies do you make?"

"Apple, cherry." Her eyebrows rose up and down. "Chocolate's my specialty."

"Want to add those to the menu?"

"I suppose we could." Kathleen drew in a breath. "But that visit with Greg wore me out. Can we talk about this tomorrow? Let's call it a day. Head on home."

"Home?" Avery squatted to put the dish detergent under the sink.

"You know, that place where you live. Where you sleep at night."

She sat back on her haunches, and Kathleen extended a hand. "You're exhausted too. Let's get out of here."

Avery popped up. "I've got my second wind. You go on. I have a few more chores to do."

Kathleen frowned. "Why are you doing this? Bill doesn't work this hard, and he owns the place."

Avery moved back toward the register. "I'd like to get the place in shape for Martha and Bill to sell. Besides it's a nice break from the boutique debacle."

"You can't run from life forever."

"It hasn't even been two weeks. I hardly think that's forever."

"What about the year before that?"

She tightened her ponytail. "Until Greg sells the place, can't we enjoy each day as it comes?"

Chapter 19

$\mathcal{T}.\mathcal{J}.$ showered and changed from his work clothes into a pair of clean jeans and a T-shirt Wednesday evening. He didn't want to look like he'd gone to too much trouble.

Then he fed Willie and let him linger outside, smiling as he ran around the yard like a maniac. The dog was another of the creatures Bud had rescued, the same way he had saved T. J.

At first T. J. had protested the animal, who leaned to the goofy side. Now he couldn't imagine the house without him, even though he had grown well beyond the "terrier-mix" prediction to out-and-out large mutt, still with reddish hair "the color of Willie Nelson's in the old days," as Bud put it.

"Come on, big guy. I've got business to handle." He had been by the hospital yesterday to check on Martha and Bill and gotten a surprisingly positive report on the biscuit business and a request to move forward with the market repairs.

He scratched Willie under the chin, rewarded with the shaggy tail swishing back and forth in pure dog happiness. "I

---

confess, though," he said as the dog bounded away and dropped the slimy ball at his feet. "I've missed Avery." The dog barked. "I know. I wasn't going to get involved in some society woman's drama." He threw the ball again and waited until Willie dashed back with it. "But I can't stop thinking about her."

The notion of getting close to Avery should have felt as uncomfortable as a suit and tie. He steered clear of women like his mother who liked stuff and status. A woman who could be attracted to Cres Broussard couldn't be his type. Could she?

So he stalled. Excuses to stay away weren't hard to come up with. Between helping Bud fix busted pipes for people at the mission and making custom cabinets for a new house in the Cotton Grove subdivision, T. J. had been so busy that he hadn't made it by the market since running into Avery and Kathleen at the wholesale store on Friday.

When Ross had called Monday, T. J. had been alone in Bud's shop, working on fancy cabinet doors. Proud of his work, he rubbed the smooth cherrywood as he listened to Ross. Bud was an excellent teacher.

"What's up with Avery?" Ross asked right off the bat.

"Is something wrong?"

"You tell me. I tried to call you over the weekend, and she picked up the phone again."

Maybe T. J. was tired. Maybe he was busy. But something in Ross's tone irritated him like nothing had in weeks. "Her phone broke, and I loaned her an old one."

"I didn't know you were that close."

T. J.'s jaw clenched. "You're the one who dragged me into this."

"Dragged you into what?"

"Why don't you come back and take care of her yourself?" He

clicked off the phone, trying to remember the last time he had hung up on someone. Maybe Bill was rubbing off on him.

Before he picked up the piece of wood again, Ross called back.

"Hey, man, I'm sorry," they both said at the same time and then laughed nervously.

"I won't babysit your sister-in-law for you."

"But you'll keep an eye on her, let me know if she's in trouble?"

"She may have had some bad luck, but she's plenty independent." T. J. brushed a layer of sawdust from his shirt. Did the Broussards even know Avery? "I get the feeling she's turned some sort of corner."

"That's good news." Ross was quiet for a moment. "But it helps to know you're there. Everything good?"

"Yeah, man." *Most days.*

"The mothers fixing you up with all of Samford's single women?"

The question rattled T. J. "Every now and then. Listen, you office guys may sit around and talk on the phone all day, but I've got real work to do."

Ross laughed.

"I'll run by Magnolia Market sometime this week. I'll let you know if there's a problem."

"Like I said, I owe you one."

Avery's smiling face popped into T. J.'s mind. "No, you don't." He hung up.

Now he could hardly wait to get over there, and if he wanted to pretend like it was a work matter, that was his business. He did need to get with her about design details and had sketched a new front on an envelope after Sunday lunch at his mother's.

When he and Bud had ripped the rest of the tin off the

shoddy front, they found a fine old facade. With some tinkering, the building could match the personality of the Sweet Olive Folk Art Gallery—and maybe attract more business.

He gave Willie's chin one last scratch. "No offense, big guy, but she's a lot prettier than you are."

Waiting until the last minute to call Avery—maybe that would make it seem less like a social call—he climbed into his pickup and pulled out his phone. But before he got out of his driveway, a horn beeped twice.

Camille Gardner, his brother's girlfriend, pulled up in her vintage pickup, the twin of Bud's vehicle.

Stepping out, Camille waved, illuminated under the streetlight. "I hoped I might catch you before you went over to your parents' house."

"My parents' house?" He looked at the date on his watch. "Is that tonight?"

"It's Wednesday, isn't it?"

"I forgot all about it." He shook his head. "I can't make it."

Camille stepped closer, a smile on her face, her short hair tousled. She had on a loose artsy dress, topped off by her standard cowboy boots. "Nice try, buddy, but if I have to go, you have to go."

"*You're* going?" Camille and his mother were not all that comfortable in the same room. His mother hoped Marsh would come to his senses and marry Valerie Richmond, a Samford princess who had moved to Houston.

"If it takes a Wednesday night supper to make your mother happy . . ." Camille shrugged.

"But we already do Sunday lunch."

"*Marsh* does Sunday lunch. You skip out with your mission crowd more than you go to your parents'."

"So now Marsh's tattling on me? He must be in love."

Camille laughed.

"I can't go tonight. I need to take care of something—" T. J. stopped at the amusement on her face. "I'm not making that up. What's this dinner all about anyway? It's not anybody's birthday, is it?"

"Your mother read a magazine article about a woman who has midweek dinner parties with the neighbors. She thinks it will be a nice tradition."

"This is going to be a tradition?"

"Marsh says she'll move on to something else in a week or two." Camille gave an impish grin. "I'm meeting him there, so hop in and I'll give you a lift."

Looking down at his jeans, he grimaced. "Can you wait for me to change?"

"You're fine. I won't even hold your boyish looks against you." She smiled, her face transformed in the look that had first drawn his brother's attention. "Come on."

"Dinner at my folks' wearing jeans?"

"Horrors!" She looked at her feet. "Maybe I should change too. Your mother's not crazy about the boots. But I like the way they look with this skirt." She winked. "And Marsh likes them."

Avery probably would too.

He froze. *Where did that come from?*

Unlocking the duplex, T. J. ushered Camille in and picked up a woodworking magazine from the khaki couch. "Sorry for the mess."

"No sweat. My place is a wreck too."

"But you just moved in." He turned. "How's the art business anyway?"

Camille sat in a wooden rocker Bud had made. "Slow. Trumpet and Vine isn't exactly a trendy location. Lawrence Martinez's glass is our best seller."

"Mom liked the piece you gave her for Christmas."

"He's going to make the gallery famous—if we can hold our corner together." She ran her hands through her hair. "We're getting some walk-in business and a few orders. And a little traffic since Magnolia Market's doing better."

"Really?"

"Marsh said you're doing some work over there."

"Bud and I are patching up the front."

"I went over to visit the new manager. Isn't she adorable? She's improved that store in just a few days."

"Um . . . adorable?" He wasn't about to talk to Camille about how much he liked Avery. Next thing he knew, Marsh would be ragging him about it. "I guess I haven't paid much attention."

"Yeah, right." Camille snorted. "You're honestly trying to convince me you haven't noticed Avery?"

"About your age? Long blond hair?" He had been much better at bluffing in his poker days.

"You're on the right track." Camille smirked. "Drives a station wagon that makes my truck look like a VW Bug?"

Finally, an escape. "She doesn't drive a station wagon."

"It's there night and day."

He shrugged. "Beats me. Avery's filling in for a few days until Bill figures out what to do."

"I wish she'd stay. The store's about our only hope to make something happen on the corner." She glanced at him. "Ross says there's an investor who wants to bulldoze the market and that vacant church."

"Bill might drive the dozer himself at this point. He's ready to unload that place."

"He's probably been listening to his nephew."

T. J. frowned.

"That guy's in town again from Little Rock to 'help.' He stopped by the gallery Friday, acted like he was shopping for a painting." She wrinkled her nose. "I went on and on about my dream for the corner—until I realized who he was. He wouldn't know a piece of original art if it fell on his head."

T. J. blew out a slow breath. "Bud says he's tried to get his hands on Magnolia Market for years. Wants to sell it and manage Martha and Bill's money." He shook his head. "I'd hate to see them with nothing to count on."

"If they tear it down, it could ruin our plans for the corner. Do you think they'll ever run the store again?"

"I doubt it. Want to buy it?"

Camille's eyes grew wide. "Is there any chance Avery might?"

He stilled. "I wouldn't think so. Avery's life's complicated."

"I heard about her husband getting killed." Camille made a small noise. "I can't imagine losing Marsh like that. She must be a strong woman."

"She's something of a contradiction." He debated how much to say. "She made Evangeline's dress store a success, according to Ross. Ran the place for five years."

"I've met Evangeline. Avery *must* be strong. She's perfect to help us do what has to be done."

T. J.'s cell phone rang, and his mouth thinned as he glanced at it. "Hi, Mom. I'm on my way. Five minutes. Ten max."

"Your father said you hadn't forgotten, but I had my doubts," his mother said. "Oh, there's the doorbell. See you soon."

"We're late," Camille wailed. "I'm going to be kicked out of the family before I'm even a part of it."

"I'll be right back." T. J. dashed out of the room. Sticking his head in the laundry room, he smiled at Willie, asleep on a towel on the floor. He grabbed a pair of khakis from a hook on the door and a shirt that could have used an iron, disappointed at the delay in seeing Avery.

Willie stirred and glanced at him with his *you're-leaving-again-already?* look, and T. J. gave him another pat as he walked out.

"Think this'll do?" he asked Camille.

"Other than that frown on your face."

"I had something else to do tonight. Plus, my brother will show up in a starched white shirt and silk tie—and he'll be right on time." He rolled his eyes.

"Your mother means well."

"I keep telling myself that."

"She's so glad you're back in Samford that she gets a little overexcited."

T. J. grabbed a lightweight jacket instead of his canvas work coat and held the door as they went outside. "I'm trying to be patient. Dad's great. Marsh and I don't quite live our lives to suit Mom."

She certainly hasn't lived hers to suit us.

He extended his arm. "Your truck or mine?"

"Mine. I'm not getting enough time behind the wheel now that I'm at the gallery."

"Go ahead and admit it. You like the look on my mother's face when you drive up in that thing."

"Well, there is that." Camille smiled.

Watching her shift the old truck, he felt a pang of happiness that his half brother had found the perfect woman for him. It would be fun to take Avery on a date with Camille and Marsh.

He shook his head. *Am I losing my mind?*

"Why don't you buy the market, Camille? Build an empire at the corner of Trumpet and Vine." He poured his idea into a grin. "Maybe Avery would run it for you."

Camille shifted gears. "Between Marsh's new law firm and the gallery, we hardly see each other as it is."

"Right."

She cut him another smile. "Okay, we do spend a lot of time together . . . but it never seems like enough. You know?"

"Not really." He had wasted so much time getting into and out of scrapes, he had never fallen in love, even though he had developed a reputation as a charmer.

"Are you dating anyone?"

He tensed. "And here we go."

"What?" Her eyes were wide.

"I'm a twenty-eight-year-old single man with all of my teeth. I can recognize someone about to fix me up. Why is it that everyone wants to talk about my love life?"

"A lot of nice women stop by the gallery."

"I'm sure they do."

She snapped her fingers. "Avery! She's perfect for you."

Yep. His heart thudded. "She's a Broussard, for heaven's sake."

"You're a reverse snob. Besides, I saw her on her hands and knees cleaning the market. She's nothing like Evangeline, nor your mother."

"No matchmaking, Camille. None."

Camille let out a hoot of laughter and pointed at the street ahead. Cars lined both sides. "Your mother will kill us before I can fix you up anyway."

"A valet? She hired a valet? I should have worn a tie."

"I shouldn't have worn my boots."

Marsh strode from the house as soon as they pulled up and kissed Camille on the lips while he helped her from the truck.

"Hey, you," she said.

"Hi," he murmured, kissing her again.

"Must you two be so perfect?" T. J. ambled around the truck, considering taking the keys from the college-aged valet and driving off. "If she mentions your adorable dark brown hair, I'm leaving."

"It *is* adorable, isn't it?" Camille ran her fingers through it.

"About time you got here, T. J.," Marsh said. "Mother's already told me I need a bigger house and—"

"You need to hire a lawn man." T. J. knew the script. "And she's fretting that I'm throwing my life away as a carpenter."

Marsh slapped him on the back with a laugh. "She may have mentioned that." Clasping Camille's hand, he led the way up the walk. "Lucky for you, though, she's more wound up about Avery."

T. J. stopped, pretending to study the elaborate Mardi Gras decorations. His mother's landscape service could work a theme. After a moment, he looked back at Marsh. "Why would she be upset about Avery?"

"Evangeline's 'devastated'—and I'm quoting here—that Avery's gone off the deep end." Marsh cocked his head, a curious gleam in his eye. "From what I overheard, Evangeline didn't want Avery around."

An uneasy feeling fluttered in T. J.'s gut. "You know I wouldn't tell most people this," T. J. said quietly. "I was doing a few small repairs at the boutique. Things got heated."

"Thomas Jacques, are you going to stand out front all evening?" His mother stood in the door of the big house that had never felt like home. She had a tight smile on her face and wore a dress fit for a wedding or the country club. "The other guests are already having cocktails."

"Sorry, Mother." T. J. gave her a tight hug. "Marsh and I were catching up."

"Hello, Mrs. Aillet." Camille held out a colorful gift bag. "Thank you for inviting me."

"Certainly." She sniffed, taking the bag but not looking inside. "Maybe your nice manners will rub off on my sons. I don't know where I went wrong."

"They have good hearts." Camille gave a nervous laugh and patted Marsh on the arm. He looked down at her with a smile and squeezed her hand. Then he leaned over and gave her a quick kiss on the lips, as though he just couldn't resist.

T. J. felt a pang. He wanted that kind of relationship, a woman he could marry and have a family with. A woman who didn't care about money or jewelry, fancy parties, and definitely not valets.

He looked into the room, wishing Avery were there. And wishing she wasn't part of the society crowd.

Yep, going crazy.

A cluster of guests stood a few yards away in the living room, a waiter in black pants and a white shirt serving crab-stuffed mushrooms and miniature boudin balls.

"This is a small supper?" Camille whispered.

"Aillet style," Marsh said, before plunging into the room with her, leaving T. J. standing in the foyer.

"There's my boy!" His father's look of delight made up for his mother's stingy smile, and T. J. bypassed the outstretched hand to give him a hug.

"Sorry I'm late."

"I barely made it myself," his father said in a low voice. "Minnette wanted to try a weeknight gathering." He looked across the room with an indulgent smile. "Your mother can put on quite a soiree."

His mother and Bud had divorced when Marsh was five, and she had married Roger a year later. T. J. had been born the next year. Somehow, despite everything, they had managed to stay together. T. J. admired his father, even though they had never spent much time together.

T. J. smiled. "How was work?"

"Same as every day," his father said. "Surgery all morning, clinic in the afternoon." In his personal life, his father followed in Minnette's wake, but professionally he was one of the state's top ophthalmologists, his absentminded professor look at odds with a brilliant mind. "I examined that man you sent from the mission. He needs cataract surgery. He can't see a thing."

T. J. furrowed his brow. "I'll have to ask around to raise the money for—"

His father headed into the living room, shaking his head. "I already scheduled it. I'll cover this one."

He followed. "Thanks for seeing those folks. Why don't you go over there one day, see their work?"

"Maybe one of these days. Between my practice and your mother..."

T. J. pushed down his disappointment. Since he had moved back to Samford, he felt most comfortable in Bud's shop or helping at the mission on the other side of town. Neither place enticed his parents.

"Don't you two know you should be mingling?" His mother glided toward them, a glass of white wine in one hand, her other hand looped through Evangeline's arm. His father glanced at T. J. and gave a quick smile. Camille was right: everyone was something of a contradiction.

Evangeline Broussard's cajoling voice addressed his father. "Roger, Minnette has promised you'll get me a glass of wine." As his father turned toward the bar, she said, "Hello, Thomas." Her voice was singsongy, in sharp contrast to its strident tone with Avery those days at the shop.

"Hello, Evangeline."

"As I was telling you, Minnette, Thomas did a first-rate job on our work at the boutique."

"He is so talented," his mother began, and T. J. tensed. "I told him he should be an architect or own a contracting firm."

T. J. refused to let his mother get him bent out of shape. He'd worked hard to clean up his act and was doing what he loved. He looked around for Marsh. At least they could smile at this together.

"Thomas's work drew high praise from the new owners."

His attention steered back to the two women. "So the sale is going forward?" He hoped his interest sounded casual.

"We've run into a stumbling block." Evangeline looked as though she had gotten a whiff of rancid shrimp. "Ross got involved, plus they wanted my manager as part of the package. I have tried to explain to them that she is no longer available, but they are most insistent."

She stared at his mother as though seeking backup. "Avery is unreliable." Evangeline accepted a glass of wine from his father. "Now she's disappeared."

"Isn't she helping at Magnolia Market?" T. J.'s question came out before he could stop it.

With a melodramatic sigh, Evangeline took a sip of wine. "So we've heard, but her phone's been disconnected, and she's not living at the Division house anymore. We've tried to give her money and she's refused to cash the check."

T. J. opened his mouth and then closed it. If Avery wanted them to have her temporary number, she could give it to them.

Once more Evangeline looked at his mother. "I don't know how Cres got mixed up with her in the first place."

T. J. gritted his teeth. He had never cared for Cres, who was more style than substance. When he heard about the accident, he had been remorseful. Now that he had met Avery, T. J. couldn't imagine a husband going off and leaving a wife like her behind.

After excusing himself, he ducked into the kitchen, where Barb, his parents' housekeeper and family cook, was ladling shrimp and grits into small crystal dishes. He gave her a quick grin and put his finger to his mouth, moving toward the mudroom. She smiled and nodded.

He dug in his pocket, then punched in the number to his old cell phone. When the call went to voice mail, his own voice greeted him. *"Leave a message. I'll get back to you."*

He hung up and dialed the market on the outside chance Avery was working. No answer.

The room felt too warm, and the chitchat was wearisome. He felt out of sorts. Maybe he should let Camille fix him up with someone or even give in to another of his mother's reintroductions to a string of "perfect" childhood friends.

Definitely going crazy.

Eager for a moment of solitude, he headed for his dad's sunken den, but it had been taken over by a group of men watching a basketball game. "Come on in, Thomas," Creswell Broussard said, "but don't let the womenfolk know we're down here. Evangeline will have my hide."

Forcing himself to meet Creswell's eyes, T. J. entered and went to his father's bar in the corner and grabbed a bottle of water out of the minifridge. On nights like these he missed his wild oats.

Twisting the top, he pretended to watch the game.

"That's some fine work you did at the boutique," Creswell said. "I wish I'd been born with talent like that."

T. J. didn't smile. "Thanks, sir."

"You still working with Bud Cameron?" Creswell's questions caused a couple of the others to turn away from the game.

Ah, the counterpunch.

"I am. He's an excellent craftsman."

"Always has been," Creswell said.

T. J. looked at the game. "Any word on when Ross will be back?"

"Not for a few more weeks." He lowered his voice. "He's opening an office in Baton Rouge."

T. J. nodded. "He mentioned some big project."

Creswell's eyes narrowed, his brows almost meeting. "I'd forgotten that he called you." His voice lowered. "I appreciate you helping out with that ugliness with Avery."

He shook his head and left the room. He could think of nothing ugly about Avery.

Chapter 20

Avery drew in her breath and turned down T. J.'s street. The Corvette engine suddenly sprang to life, and she sped up. She glanced down to make sure the fried pies hadn't slid off the seat.

At the same time she zoomed up to the curb in front of the duplex, T. J. walked around the front of an old pickup truck in the driveway. Illuminated by the headlights, he was laughing and pointing at the driver who had opened her door.

A thin beam of light shone on a pretty young woman with a perky haircut and a big smile.

Avery gasped.

T. J. was the man Camille had fallen in love with? The one who had convinced her to stay in Samford?

Together they headed toward the house, T. J. carrying a white sack.

Avery fought back tears. She had allowed herself to daydream that T. J. might be the man for her.

Another misjudgment.

With her foot already on its way to the brake, Avery hesitated and then punched the accelerator. The hiccup in timing was enough to bring the big, old car to a shuddering halt in the middle of the street.

At the noise, T. J. and Camille turned her way, their expressions hidden by winter darkness. "Great," Avery muttered, turning the key. "Just great."

The car acted as though it was going to start but sputtered and died. She tried again. And again. Staring at the street ahead, she pretended she didn't see them. That she wasn't stalled in front of T. J.'s house.

"Avery?" His voice was muffled through the car window, and she cranked the engine again. "Hey, Avery!"

The engine came to life, and she had a split second to make a decision. Inhaling, she eased up to the curb and rolled down her window. "I'm a much better driver than you might think."

"I'll take your word for it." He stepped closer, his gaze moving from the gigantic hood to the cargo carrier of the car. "New car?"

"I'd better get going." She looked beyond him to Camille, who had stopped a few feet behind T. J. "Sorry for interrupting."

"Don't go," he said. Hearing those words in that warm voice jarred something deep within her.

"Avery?" The curiosity in Camille's voice was unmistakable.

"I brought fried pies to thank T. J. for bailing me out last week. I should have called." She cranked the car, which started on the first try.

He shifted the paper sack and put his hand on the door. "Wait. Can't you come in?"

Camille, wearing a cute dress and the same boots she'd had on in the market, nudged him as he spoke.

T. J. shot a pointed look at Camille. "You two have met, right? You're neighbors at Trumpet and Vine."

"How wonderful to see you again, Avery. T. J. was just talking about you earlier."

"Camille..."

"I'd love to talk more about your plans for Magnolia Market." Camille's teeth gleamed in the darkness. "I'd stay now, but I promised T. J.'s brother I'd come right home." She looked at T. J., raising her eyebrows. "I'll pick up that book later."

"Subtle, real subtle," he mumbled. "I'll stop by the gallery."

"Bring Avery with you. I'd love to show you our new exhibit."

T. J. narrowed his eyes, but the corner of his mouth turned up. Avery watched. What was she missing?

Calling out exuberant good-byes, with a brief hug for T. J. and a wave at Avery, Camille climbed in the old truck, backed into the street, and stalled her vehicle.

Rolling the window down, she laughed. "See, Avery? Happens to the best of us." And she shifted gears and rolled away.

"Ah," T. J. said. "So you've met Hurricane Camille. She blew into town and swept my brother, Marsh, right off his feet."

"Your brother?"

"He's so in love he doesn't know what hit him." T. J. reached for the door. "Now, will you—and those pies—please come in?"

⌒

Avery followed T. J. to the left side of the duplex and stepped inside, her heart pounding.

A wooden lamp with a parchment shade glowed on an end table, and a couch covered in a khaki slipcover sat by one wall, a giant television on the other. A wooden rocking chair was pushed into a corner, and a braided rug covered wooden floors.

In the back of the house, a dog yelped, and T. J. rolled his eyes. "Willie, hush," he yelled, but his voice sounded more affectionate than stern. The dog's yelps turned into barking.

Sighing, T. J. looked at her. "Are you okay with dogs?"

"I love dogs."

"Even bratty dogs?"

"Especially bratty dogs. We had a rat terrier who was the biggest brat of them all." She smiled at the memory.

T. J. grew still. "You and your husband?"

"Oh, good heavens no." Her grin faded. "Cres wasn't a fan of dogs. Fearless was our family dog, but we had to give him away when Dad moved to Haiti."

"That's too bad."

"He was a sweet terror with these crazy super-pointy ears. He always looked like he knew something I didn't." She laughed, even though the memory made her melancholy. Avery had begged to take him to college her final semester, but as her father pointed out, he was prone to chewing. Wallets. Shoes. Furniture. Not a roommate charmer.

But the couple who adopted him was crazy about him. Avery had mailed rawhide chews at Christmas. The first year they were married, Cres found the idea cute. The next year he chided her. By the third year, she didn't tell him. It was one of two secrets she had kept from him.

"I bet you still miss him." T. J.'s gaze roamed across her face.

"Terribly. It was like losing another member of my family." She stopped, self-conscious. She hadn't told anyone, even Cres— especially Cres—that much.

T. J. reached out and rubbed her hand. "I understand."

"What kind of dog do you have?"

"Prepare to see up close and personal," he said with a laugh. "I'll free poor, abandoned Willie, who has been alone for all of two hours."

"Free Willie. Funny."

Chuckling, he started toward the rear of the house and set the sack and her tray of pies on the small pecan dining table. T. J. disappeared into the back, and minutes later an oversize reddish dog—some sort of setter maybe?—bounded into the living room. He skidded to a stop in front of Avery with a startled yelp and jumped on her.

"Willie, sit." The dog obeyed him for a split second, then spied a rope toy across the room and ran after it.

"I may have wasted my money on obedience training." T. J.'s grin was about as big as the dog-smile on Willie's face.

"He'll grow out of it." She tried to hide the doubt in her voice.

"He's only a year and a half old. That's young, right?"

"About like a ten-year-old child."

He gave a huff of laughter. "So I still have to make it through his teen years?"

"Very likely. Where'd you get him?"

"Bud gave him to me allegedly as a housewarming gift when I moved back last year. Someone dumped him by the road in Sweet Olive." He looked across the room. "Truth be known, Bud thought I needed the company."

"And did you?"

He twisted his mouth. "It's been nice having him to come home to."

The market was lonesome when Kathleen left each day. Maybe Avery would rescue a dog when she got a new place.

Willie dropped the toy at T. J.'s feet and pounced on it when he reached for it, a vigorous game of tug-of-war ensuing. "He'll calm down in a second. Maybe."

"If you say so." Avery's grin grew as she watched.

"Could I get you something to drink? Or eat?" He nodded toward the table. "I have excellent leftovers from my parents' house."

She quirked her brow.

"Some sort of fancy crawfish dip and French bread too. No telling what all's in there."

Avery's stomach growled.

"Aha!" He hopped up, causing Willie to jump around the room, slinging the rope toy. "Let me get a plate."

"I really—"

"I'll feed you, and maybe you'll tell me how you came to have that monstrosity of a car. I have to ask . . ." T. J. looked at her, his eyebrows raised. "Does that thing have a Corvette engine?"

"It does." She felt oddly proud.

Sitting at the table a few minutes later, Avery licked the fork. "That bread pudding was delicious."

"I'll tell my mother. She was fussing because it didn't have raisins."

"That's what I liked about it."

He smiled. "I knew I liked you."

"You do?" The question flew out of her mouth.

"Sure." He tilted his head. "A lot."

She plunged on. "Is that why you haven't been to the market all week?" She scraped the plate with her fork, gathering the thick sauce. "I figured you'd finished with me as a project."

"You're not a project."

"Sorry." She studied her dessert plate. "I'm sensitive about you rescuing me with that frozen lock and the wreck and everything."

"You're a friend, not a project. Keeping my life in order is project enough for me."

So they *were* friends. She liked the sound of that. "So you just started a business?"

"Only a few months ago. Bud and I became partners last fall." T. J. bit into one of the fried chocolate pies. "First he made me prove I'd learned something worthwhile since college."

"Woodwork, you mean?"

"Life work. I didn't have much use for the straight and narrow for a few years, and I needed to prove myself." He took another bite of the pie. "Wow. This is great."

"That's my first solo batch. Thanks for letting me test them on you."

"Anytime I can be of service." He reached behind him and pulled a folder out of a cluttered bookcase. "I have an idea I want to test on you."

She dipped her chin, suspicious, looking at the pencil sketch on the back of an envelope.

"Bud and I think you should go ahead and pull the old sheet metal off the market." He grabbed a pen from the shelf and tapped on the drawing. "With not much more expense, you could get back to the original wood siding. It's unique to this region, and it looks great."

"That looks like some old pictures I found in the safe. Would you use the same front window?"

"With a few minor adjustments," he said. "You have photographs of the original exterior?"

"Interior too. It was a quaint place. Martha and Bill were young—and Bill was smiling."

T. J. looked up. "You'd better frame that one."

"I don't know if Bill will go for this, though. Especially if it costs extra."

"I'm not a marketing whiz like you, but I think it would pay for itself in a few months. I ran the numbers, and Bud and I can do it pretty cheap."

She hunched over the table, pulling the envelope toward her. "The difference is startling. It might help Bill sell it."

An odd look shimmied across his face. He leaned back in the chair, his legs outstretched. "Bill told Bud the market's gaining customers."

"He's being nice."

"Bill?"

She chuckled. "We're doing better, but it's only been a few days. Nothing to bank on yet."

"You're a natural at that place. You're not ready to bail, are you?"

"Depends on when you ask. Magnolia Market has its own charm."

"I doubt the word *charm* has ever been used to describe that place."

Talking to T. J. always made her want to smile. "Charming or not, I've got to figure out what I'm going to do."

"Are you planning to stay in Samford?"

She fidgeted with her nails. "My dad wants me to visit him in

Haiti. I may do that and then get a job down around Baton Rouge or New Orleans."

His face grew serious. "I guess you want a store of your own. You made something out of the boutique."

She looked at the floor. "That was my baby."

"I don't mean to pry, but . . . why didn't you fight harder to keep it?"

She opened her mouth to spit out an answer—and didn't have one.

Bending to pet Willie, who gave a quick bark and slung the rope around, she searched for words. "It didn't feel right," she said after a second.

And the time had come to break her ties with the Broussards.

"I used to think starting over was like one of those toys you draw on and erase with one quick pull." Avery was unused to talking about this, but T. J. was the kind of man who might understand. "But then I realized it went deeper than that."

"Hmm." He appeared as taken aback by the comment as she had been by saying it. "I try to think of every day as a fresh start, I guess."

"'Morning by morning new mercies I see. Because of His great love we are not consumed.'" She gave a light laugh. "Such unexpected words from a book with the downer name of Lamentations."

"You're quoting the Bible?"

"What can I say? My dad's a preacher. That verse helps me through rough times." She adjusted her ponytail, winding her hair up in a knot. "I'm sorry you heard that argument between Evangeline and me."

"No worries."

"That day I realized I had lived in limbo way too long."

The concern in his dark eyes did not look like pity.

"I didn't intend to run into a building, but . . ." She held up her hands. "Apparently it worked."

T. J. smiled. "God works in mysterious ways."

⟳

Avery tidied the tiny room, stashing her suitcase under the cot and putting her cosmetics case behind a stained throw pillow. She found shelter in the little room. The walls of the house she shared with Cres had closed in on her, but this teeny space felt safe and warm.

Walking out into the market each morning gave her a ripple of pleasure.

"Morning by morning, new mercies . . ." She whispered the verse as she twisted the oven knob to preheat for the biscuits and flipped on the coffeemaker. The stillness of the store pleased her—in the same way the breakfast bustle buoyed her.

While the boutique's rhythm had been fluid, Magnolia Market was more staccato.

She chose a few apples from a basket and polished them with a paper towel before rearranging them. Grabbing a green marker and a piece of paper, she scrawled a fresh sign and taped it to the basket. Not bad. In fact, quite good.

With eight minutes left on the oven timer, she put a vase of daisies from Samford's biggest grocery store on the other side of the register and straightened the candy counter. With two minutes left, she wiped down the front of the cooler and scurried back to grab the biscuits. Perfect. Golden brown. Fluffy.

She was still grinning when Kathleen rushed in, brown hair sticking out. "I overslept," she said and then paused. "What are you so chipper about?"

"I don't know." Avery pulled a carton of eggs out of the refrigerator and slammed the door. She cracked the eggs on the edge of a stainless-steel bowl, then pulled out a whisk and added the usual salt and pepper. She grabbed Tabasco sauce and put in one dash and then another.

"Whoa, Chief. You want to give our customers heartburn?"

"I'll do a regular batch too. But my mother's hot eggs were a big hit with the men's prayer group in Lafayette."

"Yeah, but that's Cajun country. We're a tad more bland up here."

"Let's spice things up. We're only here for a little while. What can it hurt?"

Kathleen grabbed a serrated knife and sliced through the biscuits. "Might as well have some fun, I suppose. I could make beignets one day." She took a bow as she talked. "I'm sort of famous for them."

Avery turned with a full grin to high-five Kathleen.

"I like seeing that happy look on your face."

"Wait till you see the look on our customers' faces." Avery curtsied and wrapped the biscuits, while Kathleen moved to the stove and scrambled another batch of eggs.

Picking up the marker again, Avery wrote *HOT* on the wrappers and embellished them with flames. "Ta da," she said, adding the word *Kathleen's* to one.

Kathleen smiled, scooping the eggs onto a plate and shoveling them onto biscuits. "I can't wait to try it."

Avery laid a slice of cheddar cheese on each of them and closed the tops.

By the time she unlocked the front door and turned the Open sign around, the case was filled with plain biscuits and egg and cheese.

Chapter 21

Avery wasn't sure how to dress for a Sunday-afternoon occasion such as this. She didn't want to look like a snob. But she wanted to show her respect and serious interest.

She wasn't dressing for T. J., but if he liked what she wore, all the better. *Right?*

With a limited wardrobe—black slacks, gray slacks, two pairs of jeans, two blouses, a blazer, a couple of sweaters and Ts, a basic black dress, and combinations thereof—she didn't have the choices of her past.

The simplicity reminded her of those few years when she had more clothes than she could wear and open-ended credit at stores all over town. She liked today better.

She grinned and looked down at her feet. These black boots had been a marked-down birthday gift for herself before everything had gone so crazy that day. With the heels and a pair of running shoes, she had more than enough footwear.

In black slacks and a gray sweater with her boots, she loitered by the door like a teenager waiting for a date.

As the big clock behind the counter inched past three, she rearranged the few canned goods on the shelves, read over inventory notes she had jotted down, and slipped an apron over her outfit. She might as well wipe down the dairy cases while she waited.

She stared at the clock again but refused to get the cell phone out of the back. T. J. would call on the store phone if he couldn't make it.

And just like that, Avery was back in her old life, waiting for Cres to show up, making excuses, worrying.

Her stomach churned, and she fidgeted with the bracelet, recalling the last time she had reached out to a group of Samford people in need. With Evangeline preening for days, Avery had organized a black-tie fund-raiser at the Samford Club. A blues band played, and appetizers and drinks were served while Avery waited for Cres to arrive.

When the band paused for a scheduled break, she rushed over and begged the bearded leader to keep playing. "My husband should be here any minute to make the opening remarks."

But Cres never showed up, and when the crowd began to whisper and fidget, Avery straightened her back and took the microphone. "My husband and I thank you all for coming and helping fund school supplies and books for children in our parish. Cres has been delayed, but I hope you'll enjoy this lovely music and food."

The bearded bandleader gave a perplexed smile, and his musicians launched into a lively zydeco tune. Ross, his blond hair gleaming, his tux perfect, stepped forward and led her to the dance floor. "Smile," he said, his teeth clenched. "I'm going to kill that brother of mine."

Somehow she made it through the evening, vowing never

to put herself out there with Cres again. He weakly agreed after showing up at home after midnight, full of feeble excuses.

Unreliable and unfaithful. That had been her husband.

Her optimism of a few moments ago disappeared. She grabbed a butter knife, knelt, and scraped a piece of gum off the floor near the counter. *People are pigs!*

"Avery?" T. J.'s deep voice, unusually loud, sounded at the same time the door buzzed. "Are you all right?"

She stood, waving the knife as she regained her balance.

"Why didn't you answer the phone?" He looked behind the counter and strode toward her. He ran his fingers through his hair, which already looked messy. He wore a pair of khakis, a long-sleeved shirt, and a nicer pair of work boots than those he usually had on—and a frown.

"Uh, let me think. Because it didn't ring?"

Avery's gaze followed his to the old black phone. *Hm.* She must not have put it back on the hook after her father had called.

"Where's the cell I gave you?"

"In the back." Maybe she had miscalculated.

"You scared me to death," T. J. said. "I called four times. Then I called the store and got a busy signal. I was sure you'd been robbed or that nutcase nephew had come back. And you should keep that door locked."

"Are you yelling at me? The door is unlocked because you were coming to pick me up." She stared at the clock. "Forty minutes ago."

"I'm really sorry. I tried to call to tell you I'd be late. My mother was . . ." He trailed off. "Marsh and I usually eat there after church, and she was on a tear today. But that's no excuse."

"I'm used to it. Cres was always late."

"I'm not Cres." The words flew out of his mouth so fast that Avery stared.

He was right. T. J. was unlike Cres, from the messy hair to the work boots. Cres had never worried about something bad happening to her—and only apologized when he wanted something. He didn't help others unless he could make money out of the deal.

T. J. was a good and solid man who worked for what he got.

He let out a loud sigh. "I've made a mess out of this afternoon. Do you still want to go?"

"Of course. I'm psyched about this. Let me get my coat."

As he helped her into her jacket, T. J. was quiet. His fingers lightly lifted her hair over her collar, his hand resting for a moment on her neck. When she turned to face him, his gaze was intent, running from her boots up to her hair.

"Am I overdressed?" She put her hand to her hair.

He smiled. "You look fantastic. They're going to love you."

The mission was wedged between a nail salon and a payday loan center in the middle of a decrepit strip mall. A small sign taped to the door said New Wine Ministries, and the original sign across the front had been covered with a blue tarp.

"Ross got this space donated to us for a year," T. J. said as they pulled into the parking lot. "It was a bar for years."

"New Wine Minstries." She grinned. "A biblical pun."

He shot her a look, his mouth quirked up at the corner. "You're one of the few who get that. A couple of our participants are former customers who wandered in looking for a drink."

"Is this a church project?"

"Three churches—all different denominations—partnered to get it going. The pastors wanted us to work together to show Christ's love to a group of people who struggle to earn a living." He turned to her. "Sounds easy enough, right?"

She nodded.

"But everyone had their own ideas about what we should offer and how we should do it." He scrunched up his face. "It was a disorganized mess."

"And now?"

He gave a snort of laughter. "It's still a disorganized mess but in a better way. It's embarrassing to admit, but it took us a few months to start listening. The folks here knew the things they needed help with."

T. J. turned toward Avery, his hand on her arm. "That's why I hope you like their ideas. We need more partners to show what these folks have to offer."

"You're passionate about this, aren't you?"

He froze. "Do I sound like some sort of wacko?"

"You sound like my father. His entire life he's preached that when we love others, we're supposed to meet them where they have needs."

"Come take a look. This is your father's kind of place."

c—

T. J. followed Avery across the parking lot, his nerves jumping around like Willie after a day of being cooped up in the house. The contentious lunch with his mother, who griped incessantly about the construction work at Magnolia Market, had collided with not being able to reach Avery on the phone, putting him in a rotten mood.

Studying her as she walked around a pothole, he sighed. In those black boots and that dressy outfit, she looked ready for a corporate takeover. Until recently, Avery had been a socialite. What if she didn't *get* these good-hearted people?

But she had mentioned her father. Clearly some of that carried over to her. He saw it in the way she treated everyone who came into the market.

When she reached the door, she turned and gave him a dazzling smile before stepping inside the mission. *Lord, please work this out.* With a deep breath, he followed her into the spliced-together space.

Gabriela rushed to greet Avery. *"¡Bienvenidos a New Wine!* I'm Gabriela Rodrigues." She enveloped Avery in a hug.

He should have prepared Avery better. Gabriela, only twenty-one, tended to be exuberant and had more ideas than Bud had tools.

But Avery put her arms around Gabriela as though she hugged excited young immigrants every day. "I'm happy to be here." She gave T. J. a quick wave as she followed Gabriela, who switched to English as she introduced Avery to every person.

She asked questions about the various projects underway, from a group of children working on reading skills to the men whom he and Bud helped with woodworking. Gabriela's Uncle Fernando, who drove a cab, jumped up from the table and shook Avery's hand. *"¡Bienvenidos!"*

Avery blushed. *"De nada."* Then she switched to English. "Thank you for your help when I . . . well, you know, the rides."

"My pleasure." A huge smile broke across his usually somber face.

By the time they reached the kitchen, Avery's face was flushed and she had shed her coat, pulled out her notebook and pen, and laid her purse and tote bag on a table.

Some of the volunteers T. J. had brought here before clutched their purses as though someone might snatch them. Others looked at the floor or ceiling, anywhere but in the eyes of this motley group.

Not Avery.

"Gabriela, I can't wait to hear your ideas," she said as they entered the kitchen where volunteers were preparing Sunday supper. "May I help chop vegetables while you tell me?"

"*Gracias.*" Gabriela smiled as she dug out a knife. "I hope you'll sell our spices and mixes. They're better than anything you can find in the stores here. I learned most of the recipes from my mother. She was a wonderful cook." Her smile dimmed. "She passed away last year."

"I'm so sorry." Emotion infused Avery's voice. "I lost my own mother. It's hard, isn't it?"

Gabriela's chin dropped. "I promised her I would make a better life for my brothers and sisters. I'm getting my GED, and I want to own my own business some day. Like you."

Avery blushed. "I don't own the grocery store, but I know what you mean. I hope to have a shop one day."

T. J. tinkered with a loose faucet and listened intently to their conversation. They acted as though he wasn't in the room. Other volunteers wandered in and out, looking at the two women intently, smiling and whispering.

Avery pulled one idea after another from Gabriela and commented on each as though they were the most innovative thoughts ever. Gabriela practically hopped with excitement, her dark eyes glowing.

By the time they headed to the truck, T. J. felt like he was escorting a rock star. "She's so nice," Gabriela whispered while half the crowd hugged Avery good-bye.

"I'll let you know how these sell." Avery nodded at the box of merchandise T. J. carried. "Thank you for the delicious meal."

"Wow." T. J. opened the truck door for her. "You made quite an impression."

"They're wonderful! Gabriela is the most creative person. And to be so young! She's got amazing potential, doesn't she?"

"Apparently."

When he slid into the driver's seat, Avery was thumbing through the box. "What a great idea to have the children color the labels. Customers will like that." She turned to him. "Gabriela's a born leader. She could run a business."

He nodded. "But she doesn't read English well. We added classes last month. And she has to get her high school diploma. These folks need a hand."

"How'd you get involved?"

He hesitated. "Bud was trying to keep me out of trouble."

"What kind of trouble?"

"This and that. Mostly gambling." He turned onto Trumpet Street feeling clammy. "I screwed up, like some of these people."

"Looks like you've made things right."

"I'm working on it." He glanced at her. "So your father is involved in something like this?"

She nodded. "Gabriela reminds me of some of the girls who pass through the orphanage. Just this morning Dad was telling me about a girl who is so much like her."

"Do you talk to him a lot?"

"At least once a week, and we e-mail, and he still sends me

handwritten letters. I miss him a lot. I haven't visited since Cres died, but I hope to go when things settle down with Magnolia Market." She put her hand on his arm. "Maybe you and some of the other volunteers would like to go too. He always needs carpenters."

"You were great at New Wine." He glanced at her hand as they stopped at the traffic light at Trumpet and Vine. He liked her touch, but she moved it away.

"My dad says we underestimate what people are capable of."

"I certainly did," T. J. said.

Chapter 22

T.J. pulled up to Bud's house in Sweet Olive Monday night, wishing he had passed on the supper plans.

Work was so busy he didn't have a minute to himself. And after yesterday's visit, he wanted to run by the mission and hear Gabriela's opinions about Avery's ideas. *And maybe run by the market?*

Thoughts of Avery had kept him awake last night. She had him thinking about all the things he had fought so long to escape. *And he needed to tell her about his mother.*

Grabbing the bag of food, he hurried out to Bud's shop, gave a quick knock, and walked in, taking a deep breath of wood scent. Sawdust covered the floor, and a floor lamp, a garage-sale reject, threw yellow light on the space.

A line of carvings, mostly dogs—Bud's specialty—perched on the workbench. He had probably stopped midproject when Marsh arrived, one of the traits that made him a great friend and business partner. Bud knew how to pay attention.

That was the kind of man T. J. wanted to be. He would run

their custom-carpentry business one day. Pay attention. Use the gifts he'd been given. He breathed in again, the smell of wood tickling his nostrils.

"Hey, son." Bud turned around from the small burner in the corner with a can of soup in his hand. "We'd about given up on you."

Marsh sat on his usual seat, a beat-up wooden stool that had been in the shop since the two were boys. He held a glass of tea and inhaled at the sight of T. J. "I hope you brought enough chicken for me because I'm starving."

"Look who's here." T. J. smiled. "Camille must be busy tonight."

Marsh offered the familiar Cameron-family grin. "She had to meet with an artist from over around Choudrant. Said to tell you hello . . . and to ask you how things are going with Avery."

T. J. groaned, and Marsh erupted in laughter. "She thinks y'all would make a perfect couple. Give it up, T. You're not going to win when Camille makes up her mind." Marsh had gotten into a legal battle with Camille last fall over oil-and-gas rights. T. J. was still astonished at how fast—and hard—Marsh fell. It couldn't be long before they announced their engagement.

"Did I miss something?" Bud cleared off a pecan table T. J. had made from a tree cut down during gas-well drilling. "Are you and Avery dating?"

"Marsh is lovesick and thinks the rest of us should be too."

"It's pretty sweet," Marsh said.

"I was late because I was revising sketches for Magnolia Market." T. J. arranged the blue-and-white boxes of fried chicken on the table, while Marsh produced paper plates and another glass of tea.

"So Bill decided to finish it before he got the insurance check?" Bud sank into a gold-striped platform rocker, T. J. pulling up a lawn chair that had migrated to the shop when he was in high school.

"Yep, but he called this afternoon and wants to meet with us." He picked up a drumstick and gestured as it made its way toward his mouth.

"Mom mentioned something about a mess involving Avery." Marsh put a piece of chicken on his plate. "What's going on?"

"You getting your news from The Minnette these days?"

"You're not twelve, boys," Bud said. "And don't disrespect your mother, T. J."

"She dumped you, Bud. Why do you always stick up for her?"

"Everyone deserves to be respected. Respected and forgiven."

"I don't get it." T. J. frowned at Bud.

"I forgave her, and you should too. It's the only way for you to move on with your life, to become the man you're meant to be." He leaned forward. "You never bring that up unless you're stirred up. Something on your mind?"

"Camille says T.'s got women troubles," Marsh said.

"I hope you and Camille have a good time talking about my love life. Do you do each other's nails too?"

Marsh burst out laughing. "You've got it bad, don't you?" He paused. "Camille's hoping Avery will stay on at the market. Any chance?"

"She doesn't exactly share confidences with me."

"The man who charmed women from coast to coast can't win Avery's affections?"

"I don't even know if I want to win them."

"Riiight," Marsh said.

"How well do you know her?" T. J. asked.

"I haven't seen her much since Cres died." Marsh reached for the potato salad. "Up until recently"—he threw T. J. a look—"she pretty much kept to herself."

"What was she like before?" He tried to keep his tone laidback, but he didn't miss the looks Marsh and Bud exchanged.

"A lot of fun when I first met her," Marsh said, "but less outgoing as time went by. Valerie told me once that Cres was running around on her, but I didn't pay much attention." He made a face. "Shouldn't have mentioned it now, come to think of it."

"You're among friends." Bud spoke quietly. He and Marsh had learned years ago that whatever they said at Bud's stayed at Bud's.

Marsh picked at the chicken. "Avery used to be involved in a lot of things. She started that group at First Church, the one that provides clothes to women looking for work."

"Didn't she host that fund-raiser for the children's tutoring program?" Bud asked. "A fancy party at the Samford Club? I even dressed up and went to that."

Marsh nodded. "Cres didn't show that night."

"What an idiot." T. J. stood to pace.

"Ross thinks Avery might move." Marsh paused. "His brother did a number on Avery."

"I get that their marriage might not have been that great, but the way the Broussards have treated her . . ." T. J. shook his head. "Mob bosses look gentle compared to Evangeline."

Marsh stood, his face somber. "Dad, I'm leaving this one to you. Ross is also a client, and I—"

"Don't discuss your clients," T. J. growled, wandering to the workbench. "We know, we know."

Marsh grabbed T. J. in a bear hug from behind. "Listen to my father on this one. If Avery's for you, work this out. Trust her." He squeezed tighter. "And I quote the wise carver on that." He headed toward the door. "Tell Avery I said hey. I'm going to get by the market when things slow down."

As Bud ushered Marsh out, T. J. sat back down and put his head in his hands. So many times when he had been in trouble—and at odds with his parents—he had found solace in this shop. He'd like to bring Avery out here.

Yep. In over my head.

"Sure glad you made it tonight." Bud's voice surprised him, and he jerked his head up.

"I always feel better out here." He looked down at the sawdust on the floor. "I feel sort of bad that I dislike my parents' house so much."

Bud clasped his hands, nicked from carving. "Maybe you should spend some time with your mother now that you've settled in. Take a weekend trip or something."

T. J. made a face. "She's busy. And she doesn't know me. She doesn't like my career or my hobbies. Or my church." He waited. "Truth be known, I don't know her either." He had never voiced that—not even to Marsh. And he felt squeamish saying it. "It's high time I got past all that."

"We've all made mistakes." Bud's blue eyes were trained on T. J. as he sat back in the rocker.

"If it weren't for you, Bud, I guess I'd be in jail now or gambling away my paycheck." *And I wouldn't have met Avery.* "Have I thanked you recently for dragging me home?"

"No thanks necessary." Bud looked him in the eye. "You'd have come back sooner or later."

"With a felony record or broken legs." He choked out a laugh.

"You weren't *that* far gone. You just needed a nudge."

Only a man as kind as Bud would put it like that.

T. J.'s pleasure with gambling started with poker in prep school and traveled right on to college. With his absurdly generous allowance and an interest in sporting events, his appreciation for the campus bookie far exceeded his attention to college books.

The more he bet, the more entranced he became. When he won, he put more money down, flush with victory. When he lost ... well, he bet more, certain he would win it back.

After squeaking out of college with poor grades and plentiful lectures about wasted talent, he took a low-paying, undemanding job as a helper on construction sites in the northeast. The work, supplemented with the ongoing parental allowance, left him plenty of time to study racing forms and Vegas odds.

His parents were rarely in touch. His father busy with his practice, his mother busy with being The Minnette. But Bud would not leave him alone, calling several times a month, e-mailing almost daily, and preaching—always preaching. Or that's how it seemed.

With web links about better jobs, information about churches wherever T. J. was working, the occasional Bible verse, and a steady stream of comics and jokes, Bud persisted. Some weeks his counsel came with the force of a battering ram, but most of the time it was a steady, simple message: *"You're a good man. God has plans for your life. Don't squander your talent."*

Often T. J. groaned at how corny Bud was. Sometimes he deleted e-mails without reading them. Occasionally he didn't pick up a call. He certainly never admitted how much the contact meant.

On T. J.'s twenty-fourth birthday, Bud e-mailed him a photograph of T. J. and Marsh in Sweet Olive when they were in their early teens. "It's been fun watching you grow up," the message said. "You're talented."

His mother called later that day to demand he come home or lose his monthly stipend. His father texted him, saying how much he loved him, and wired a down payment for a new car.

Something in Bud's message nagged at him, so T. J. called the father of a college friend in Seattle, determined to get as far from Samford as he could. With connections and the cash from his father, he made a fresh start. He would prove he didn't need his parents' money—nor them, for that matter.

The position was challenging, the Pacific Northwest beautiful. He found a small apartment with a lake view—if you craned your neck—and visited church a few times. Coworkers fixed him up with pretty young women who liked to hike and cycle, and he found himself enjoying life for the first time in years.

Only after a few months did he allow himself the reward of betting on an office Final Four basketball pool.

And within days he was back to gambling more and working less, unhappy and unsettled again.

Bud's and Marsh's surprise visit to Seattle on his twenty-fifth birthday had rattled T. J. Sitting at the top of the third flight of stairs to his apartment, Bud was dozing and Marsh fooling with his phone when T. J. wandered in after midnight. "Did something happen?" he asked, his heart pounding.

"Nope." Bud stood and gave T. J. a bear hug. "We wanted to wish you a happy birthday and see how you're doing."

"Haven't heard from you in a while," Marsh said.

Tensing for a lecture, T. J. unlocked the door and ushered them in, embarrassed. A pile of overdue bills overflowed from the kitchen counter, and the sink was full of dirty dishes that smelled worse than T. J. remembered. "There's a pretty nice view of the lake during the day," he mumbled, clearing a pile of laundry off the sofa.

"So you like it here?" Marsh asked.

"Some days."

"And you're doing okay?" Bud asked.

"What do you think?" T. J. gestured at the mess.

"Is there anything we can do to help?"

With Bud's question, T. J. felt tears in his eyes. From that day, he had not placed a bet. He hunkered down at work, earning a promotion and a raise; wrote his parents a letter of apology; hosted them on a visit to Seattle; and even went to Samford for Christmas. He'd prayed for forgiveness for being a spoiled brat, then felt the load of years of not fitting in lift.

But the best thing that had happened was that through his former Seattle church, he'd begun to volunteer with a group of homeless men who needed to learn basic work skills. They made him realize what Bud had said was true. God had more important things for him to do than throw time and money away gambling.

The week before his twenty-eighth birthday, nearly a year ago, he woke up on a rare morning when Mount Rainier was visible in the distance and realized it was time to go back to Louisiana. He wanted longer summers and shorter winters, less vegan pizza and more gumbo. Mostly he missed Marsh and Bud, wanted to get to know his dad, and figured he was mature enough to deal with his mother.

So he had called Bud—who was staring at him now, his head cocked. "Look how much you've changed these past few years. Maybe you should help Minnie get to know that man."

"She's one woman in public and another in private. She's got me afraid to get involved with . . ." His voice trailed off. "What kind of son finds his mother unpleasant? I'm supposed to honor her, care for her."

"Is that what's got you worked up about Avery—that she's not who you think she is?"

T. J. surrendered a quick nod. "Partially. And that I'm not who she thinks I am."

"Don't you think it's possible she's changed too?"

"The truth is, I think she has always been a special person, far too good for Cres." T. J. hesitated. "So why would they want to run her out of town?"

"All those years ago, when Minnie and I got married, Evangeline and Creswell stood up with us. In all the years I've known them, there was only one thing they couldn't control—and that was Cres."

Bud clasped his hands in his lap. "If they can get Avery out of town, they can pretend that they did, in fact, win. It's a shame, but they'll go to any lengths to make that happen."

T. J. walked to the workbench and picked up one of the little dogs, then rubbed his fingers over the stubby ears.

"And," Bud said, "they can try to forget the circumstances of Cres's death."

Chapter 23

_H_umming after the Tuesday breakfast and lunch rushes—which had not been _pitiful_ this week—Avery straightened the handmade Louisiana items she had ordered from a potter in New Iberia and smiled.

"Good afternoon." Camille's eyes shone as she charged through the front door. "Cool! Whose work is that?"

"One of my dad's former church members." She held up a magnolia bloom. "She does Louisiana shapes. This is my current favorite."

"Oh, I like the pelican. And the alligator."

Laughing, Avery picked up a red crawfish. "What about this guy?"

Camille reached for it. "I see what you mean. We need that artist in our gallery." She looked around. "I can't believe how much you've improved the store."

"It's nothing. This part was easy."

"Says the woman who practically lives at this place." Kathleen walked from around the counter. "I'm Kathleen Manning, by the way. Avery's charming assistant."

"I'm Camille Gardner." She shook Kathleen's hand. "She works hard all right. Avery's car's here day and night."

A strange look crossed Kathleen's face.

"It is not." Heat flooded Avery's face.

"Not that I'm spying or anything," Camille said. "But my apartment's over the gallery, so I have a good view." She made a dramatic sneer.

Avery didn't meet Kathleen's eyes when the two laughed. "We'd be happy to display examples of your artists' work," she said in a rush. "And to put out flyers with your hours and special exhibits."

"That'd be fantastic. We can hand out your menus."

"Just like that." Kathleen snapped her fingers. "Avery's one of those rare people who comes up with good ideas and makes them happen."

"T. J.'s like that, don't you think?" Camille cut her eyes at Avery. "I heard he took you over to the mission."

Avery smiled. "We're going to carry as many of their products as possible. We've got their spice mixes, homemade pralines, even note cards."

Camille nodded. "It's amazing what a few people have put together. They provide free medical help and meals and make those amazing crafts. T. J.'s been huge in making that happen."

Kathleen guffawed. "What a sales job. Are you matchmaking, Camille?"

"Kathleen!" Avery tugged on her new green apron.

"Bill's had bread on the shelves longer than she's known him." Kathleen put her hands on her hips, a smile dancing in her eyes.

"I've known him longer than I've known you." Avery's voice rose.

"He's a nice guy who's turned his life around, from what

Marsh says. T. J. could use more friends, though. I think he's still finding his niche in Samford." Camille ran her fingers through her short hair. "That's his story to tell, not mine. I'd better get back to the gallery."

Camille headed to the door and stopped. "I almost forgot why I came in here in the first place. T. J. was raving about those fried pies, and Marsh asked me to order some for his parents. Doc will love those."

"I'll write it up." Avery looked over her shoulder. "Their name's Cameron, right?"

Camille gave a small laugh. "I forget that not everyone in Samford knows their weird story. Marsh's last name is Cameron, but his mom and stepdad are Minnette and Roger Aillet. Roger is T. J.'s father, even though T. J. works with Bud." She widened her eyes. "And Bud's Marsh's father."

"Could you run through that again?" Kathleen asked. "That makes Avery's in-laws look ordinary." She quirked her head. "Avery?"

"Uh, did you say T. J. is an Aillet?" Had she actually gotten involved with another member of the country-club set?

"Crazy, isn't it?" Camille said. "Samford's too big to know everyone, but small enough that everyone's connected. He must have been living out in Seattle when you moved here."

Must have been. Maybe it would have been better if he'd stayed there.

Chapter 24

Kathleen stopped at the blinking light at Trumpet and Vine and looked over at the front of the market, shadowy in the midnight darkness. Everything looked as it should.

But sure enough, Avery's station wagon sat pulled up almost to the door. Just as Camille had mentioned earlier that day.

Gliding through the intersection, she turned into the alley, turned off her headlights, cut the engine, and coasted to the back of the store.

"I should have figured this out days ago," she said to Howie, whose tail was thumping back and forth as he looked out the passenger window. "Come on, boy!" The alley was spooky, and she patted her dog to reassure herself.

Kathleen slipped her key in the lock, then eased the door open, holding the dog's mouth shut. She stepped into the gloomy hall. The dim light burned over the register, and through the front window she could see the traffic light blinking.

The door to the small storage room was closed, and she took

a deep breath, suddenly uncertain. Her husband's face flashed through her memory, helping a neighbor who had fallen on hard times. "Go for it, girl!" he'd always said.

She pushed the door open, her heart pounding louder than Wayne had snored. As she peeked around the corner, grief—mixed with a large measure of anger—rolled over her.

Avery was curled into a ball on the bed, sound asleep.

The doorknob slipped from Kathleen's grasp and the door flew into the wall. Howie barked twice and ran over to the cot.

Avery's eyes flew open, and she sprang up, yelling and brandishing a small kitchen knife. Howie jumped behind Kathleen, whimpering as though his feelings were hurt.

"Don't shoot—or stab! It's me!" Kathleen flipped on the overhead light.

She and Avery stared at each other for a split second before Avery scrambled onto her feet. "The biscuits. I was resting my eyes. What time is it?" She rubbed her back with one hand and smoothed her hair with another. Her eyes were red and puffy.

"Midnight."

"Midnight?" She started to head into the store. "I lay down for a—"

Kathleen blocked the door, her gaze roaming around the small space.

"I was just—" Avery began and then put her hand to her back again. "Did you have to sic the hound on me? I think I pulled my back when Howie jumped on me."

"My apologies." Kathleen's blend of rage and concern burned hotter than the oven when they took out the biscuits. "You could have been killed staying back here."

"It's not that big a deal." A look of trepidation ran through

Avery's eyes. "I was working on our new sign, and it got late. It seemed easier to sleep here."

"Give it up, Avery."

"I like to keep an eye on things." Avery blinked, looking as though she might cry.

"How long have you been living here?" To Kathleen's dismay, her voice wobbled too. She expected this kind of betrayal from her daughter but not from Avery. "I can't believe you kept this from me. And what's wrong with your eyes, for heaven's sake?"

"Other than the fact that they were closed a minute ago, that it's the middle of the night, and"—she looked up—"someone is shining a bright light in them?"

Kathleen switched on the small lamp on the folding table and turned off the overhead light. "I'm not going to apologize."

Avery plopped down on the cot and pulled her hair into a ponytail. Her face was scrubbed clean, and her feet were bare. In a pair of sweatpants and a long-sleeve T-shirt, she could have been a sorority girl.

"I—"

Kathleen held up her hand. "Don't speak."

"But I—"

"If you're going to lie to me again, don't even open that pretty mouth of yours." Kathleen sank into the folding chair where she often ate lunch. "I thought we were friends."

"We are friends." Avery looked down at the floor.

Kathleen's hand flew up again. "I mean it. No more lies."

"You're the best friend I've ever had." A big tear rolled down Avery's face, and Howie jumped onto the cot and licked her hand. "And you're the second-best, Howie." She buried her face in his fur.

Her voice was muffled, and she reminded Kathleen of the way Lindsey had looked before she got her nose pierced and ran away from home. And heaven knew that Kathleen had cried into Howie's fur after Wayne died.

"Enough with the tears already."

Avery sat up but kept her arm draped over Howie's body. "My mother was a special woman. My dad's fantastic."

That was unexpected.

"They taught me better than this." Avery took hold of Howie's face and stared into his eyes. "I didn't know how to ask for help." She scrunched up her face. "You're so smart and sure of yourself. It's harder than you'd think."

"Oh, I see," Kathleen said, a frog in her throat. She must be coming down with a cold. "You're turning this into a pity party." She stood and planted her hands on her hips. "It's not going to work. Get your things."

Avery looked up from the dog and met Kathleen's eyes. "I don't have anywhere to go. There. I've said it. Are you happy?"

"You're going to my house, you dolt, and if you're lucky, I'll let you sleep inside."

⌒

Avery watched Kathleen pull out a saucepan and fill it with milk. "I always made hot chocolate for Lindsey when she couldn't sleep." Kathleen adjusted the burner.

"That's sweet, but I *was* sleeping, if you'll recall." She rubbed her back for good measure.

"In the back of a grocery store!" Kathleen half turned. "You have to stir this constantly or it scorches."

"I've made hot chocolate before."

"Not like this you haven't." Kathleen pulled out another square of unsweetened chocolate and stuck it in a double boiler. "Are you good with real sugar?"

Avery clasped her heart. "After knowing me for three weeks, you have to ask? I'm wounded."

"Glad to see you're feeling better."

"It takes me a while to get my wits about me, you know, when I'm awakened from a dead sleep."

Kathleen faced the stove, measuring, stirring, pulling out mugs. She looked like an orchestra conductor. After pouring the cocoa into mugs, she pulled a can of whipping cream out of the refrigerator. Howie jumped up and ran toward her.

Squirting two perfect blobs on top of the cups, Kathleen added a taste to her finger and held her hand down. Howie licked it clean and whined. "You are such a beggar." She gave him one more small squirt before handing Avery her mug.

"This is a work of art." Avery sipped with her eyes closed. "Oh, my."

"Good, huh? My mother-in-law taught me to make this right after I got married."

"We should sell it at the store."

Kathleen snorted. "As you can see, it's labor-intensive."

"But worth it. Maybe we could hire someone to help out." Avery's face fell. "Although I guess we won't have time for that sort of thing."

"Is that why you went to bed crying tonight?"

"No!" Her hand went to her eyes.

"This is about T. J. being an Aillet, isn't it?" Kathleen narrowed her eyes. "You went all stoic on me after Camille's visit."

"It doesn't matter what his last name is."

"But?"

"Butt out?"

"So now you're a clown?" Kathleen blew on the hot chocolate, then took a sip. "You could talk to me instead of hiding out and crying."

"Are you pretending to be Dr. Phil?" Avery snapped her fingers. "No, it's Oprah, isn't it?"

"This is what friends do." Kathleen shook her head. "You sure don't make it easy."

Avery warmed her hands on the mug. "Yes, it hurt that T. J. misled me. He's no better than Cres. Another lying rich guy."

"Did you *ask* his last name? Or did it not matter because he was a carpenter?"

"That's insulting."

Kathleen arched an eyebrow.

"All right." Avery shrugged. "I've only known him a couple of weeks, and things have been chaotic. I'll admit I kind of liked the first-name thing."

"It was kind of cute, huh, until you found out his last name."

Heat crept up her face. "I didn't want him to focus on my being a Broussard, so I . . . just didn't go there."

"My point precisely. What does it matter who his parents are?"

"They're part of the Samford Bubble. His mother has been Evangeline's best friend since Ole Miss. They spent half of the last year together at the beach—talking about how I wrecked Cres's life, no doubt."

"I must be too blue-collar to figure out what you're talking about."

Avery leaned forward. "T. J.'s part of Cres's world. All I could think tonight was that they knew each other. T. J. never said a word." She hit her forehead with the palm of her hand. "Why didn't I realize?"

"Welcome to my world. At least his best friend hasn't been sleeping in a storage closet. Imagine what that feels like."

"T. J. dropped all those clues—friendship with Ross, prep school, fancy leftovers from his mother's. I knew that bread pudding tasted familiar."

Kathleen smiled.

"I won't get involved in that world again." Avery squeezed her eyes shut. "T. J. seemed different."

"Different from what?"

"Not what. Whom. T. J., the good old handyman, mission volunteer. Cheap watch. About as different from Cres as they come."

Kathleen winced. "Why don't you hear T. J.'s side of it?"

She put her head in her hands, her voice muffled. "I'll think about it."

Avery burned the biscuits the next morning, scorched the eggs, and broke a carafe full of coffee.

"It'll get better," Kathleen said.

"Thanks for last night." Avery swept up the rest of the glass. "And for letting Howie come to work today."

"You are such a sucker for a sad face."

"He looked lonely out in the yard."

Kathleen blew out a breath. "As long as Bill—and the Health Department—don't find out."

"He's in the storeroom, for goodness' sake." Avery smiled. "He makes me happy."

"He can come with us every day if you'll take me up on my offer. Move in, share the rent. I have plenty of space."

"Aren't you afraid you'll get tired of me?" Avery balanced against the broom, shifting the dustpan in her other hand.

"I'm like Howie. I like your company. Have I mentioned how mad I am that you stayed in the store when you could have been living with me?"

"Only about a dozen times . . . since daybreak."

"I'll even give you Lindsey's old room."

"She's coming home one of these days."

"I hope you're right." Kathleen's face softened. "But there's plenty of room for both of you."

"You're going to get a real job, and I'm . . . well, I don't know what I'm going to do."

"What's your father say?"

Avery looked at her hands. "He doesn't know all the details. I don't want to use our phone visits to unload my troubles."

"He's your father. Parents expect to be troubled."

"I'd rather trouble you."

Kathleen let loose her bold laugh. "You're doing a good job. Now, say you'll stay with me. It'll be like summer camp. You can leave when you're ready."

"Thanks. You can even give me some job-hunting pointers."

"Great. I can tell you about all the jobs you want if you'll bus tables or deliver pizza." Kathleen made a face. "Who knew that highly experienced middle-aged women were a dime a dozen? Looks like I learned Excel for nothing."

"Your spreadsheets helped our inventory control." Avery

straightened, balancing the dustpan full of glass shards. "We might be in the black by the end of the month." Although if the Broussards had their way, she might not be there to see it. The days were moving much too quickly.

"You like this stuff, don't you? You like business."

Avery pursed her lips. "Only the creative parts. Did you see what I did with the chalkboard today? Those markers work great."

"You're good at all of it." Kathleen turned the Open sign over. "Not just the creative part."

Avery smiled slyly. "And starting tomorrow we're serving custom-made hot chocolate."

"I noticed."

c—

The door buzzed, and Avery pulled out the notebook. *New bell*, she wrote while looking up with a smile. "May I help—? Oh, it's you."

Nephew Greg crossed the threshold, a scowl on his face. "What's that smell?"

"Um . . ." Avery pretended to consider. "Our new specialty— blackened biscuits. Want to try one? They're a big hit with the pigeons out back."

"Aren't you a comedian?" He walked to the cooler and pulled out a soft drink. "Like I told Uncle Bill, if he doesn't sell soon, you'll have this place run into the ground."

She walked to the cash register and opened the drawer with a flourish. "Cash or charge?"

He frowned.

"Nobody gets free food or drink. Inventory is money. Don't you have an accountant?"

"My CPA and I talk about bigger fish than a Coke. That's why I'm here."

"Oh?" She pretended disinterest, adding apples to the dwindling basket.

"I've got a bidding war between a downtown businessman and a U-Store-It guy who wants to put a big unit on this lot." He poked at the counter as he spoke.

Avery drew a breath.

"A storage warehouse? Here?" Kathleen came in from the back.

"Oh, good," Greg said. "I hate repeating myself."

"I can't believe Bill would ever agree to that," Kathleen said, hands flying to her hips. "This store has been here since I was a kid. It has history."

Greg glanced away. "Tell that to the dozer driver."

"I wish the first deal had gone through," Avery said.

"Not me," Kathleen said. "I'd have never gotten to know you."

Both Avery's and Greg's gazes flew to her, and she shrugged.

"Girlfriend bonding aside, this is a far better deal than the first offer. That guy's credit was no good. Turns out, Mrs. Broussard, you helped Aunt Martha and Uncle Bill dodge a bullet."

"I'll be darned." Kathleen shook her head.

Chapter 25

*A*very watched a growing number of people arrive at the Sweet Olive Folk Art Gallery, her nerves worsening. Why wouldn't the traffic light change?

Kathleen had gotten a call from her former boss about a job interview, which appeared to be running long. The combination of losing her friend and venturing to a social gathering made Avery want to throw up.

Camille had popped in that afternoon to pick up the Aillets' fried pies and practically begged Avery to attend the gallery pot-luck. "We're showing off the new exhibit and talking about the corner of Trumpet and Vine. You've got a stake in this too."

"I'd love to." The words came out before Avery had time to ponder them. She wanted to see this corner preserved. Elvis. Revivals. A cotton patch. It wouldn't be right to bulldoze all of that history.

The time had come for her to step out from behind the counter.

And it wasn't like she had anything else to do on a Thursday night.

As she stepped into the crosswalk, she looked down at the tray covered in aluminum foil and scurried while the occupants of an old minivan waited for her to cross. The driver, a woman with a mass of curly brown hair, waved at her and pulled into the small parking area at the gallery.

"Howdy." The woman climbed from the van in a tie-dyed floor-length skirt and a bright purple blouse. This wasn't the Evangeline's Boutique crowd.

"Hi," Avery said.

"I'm Ginny Guidry." The woman stuck out her hand. "Are you a new artist?"

Balancing her tray, Avery shook her hand. "I'm Avery Broussard. I help run the store across the street."

"Magnolia Market?" Ginny's lips, outlined in bright-red lipstick, curved in a big smile. "I hear you've turned that place around." She gave Avery a slap on the back. "Are those your famous fried pies? Camille says they're delicious."

Avery pulled back the corner of the aluminum foil and held it up. "Biscuits and country ham."

"Oh, my goodness. Welcome to the neighborhood."

As they started up the steps, Avery paused to admire the renovated frame house. Painted periwinkle blue with yellow shutters, it had a wide porch, a small balcony on the second floor, and what looked like a widow's walk perched on the top. An American flag blew in the winter breeze from the porch.

"Isn't it a great building?" Ginny asked. "Having this space has made all the difference for us artists."

"It's terrific." Avery pointed to the bottle tree. "Everywhere you look there's an unexpected detail."

"That's Camille for you."

Camille, standing at the top of the steps, laughed. "At the moment, Camille's flustered." She ran her hands through her hair. Wearing a pair of jeans, a "Do Your Part for Art" T-shirt, and a pair of cowboy boots, she looked like a teenager. "Would it be okay if people park at the market, Avery? The crowd's bigger than expected."

"Sure." A mini traffic jam was building at the intersection. "Why don't I direct them?"

"You're sure? Bill doesn't generally like us parking over there."

"It's good for business. Reminds people we're there. In fact, maybe your group might come over for coffee after the meeting."

"Bill could take a few lessons from Avery, if you ask me." Ginny's beaded earrings swayed as she reached for the tray of biscuits. "I'll take those."

"In the kitchen, no cheating, Ginny." Camille threw a bright smile to Avery. "You're a lifesaver."

Walking back across the street, Avery waved her arms like a traffic cop, directing a string of cars and pickups toward the market, a motley group of people piling out and heading for the gallery.

Among the last to arrive was a blue-and-white Chevy pickup, almost identical to the one Camille drove. Bud was at the wheel, and T. J. climbed out of the passenger's seat.

Avery looked the other way, unprepared to confront him.

"We haven't missed the fireworks, have we?" Bud asked. Wearing a pair of paint-splattered khakis and a white T-shirt, he looked like he had come straight from work.

T. J. walked around the truck carrying an oversize blue-and-white sack that almost matched the truck. He wore a pair of khakis as he had the night she had visited him, his oxford-cloth shirt pressed, but his brown hair was windblown and he hadn't shaved. He looked incredibly good, even if she was mad at him.

"Soup's on." He held up the sack with a grin. "Although from the looks of this crowd, we didn't pick up enough chicken."

"When have we ever run out of food?" Bud asked.

"You're part of the artists' co-op, T. J.?" Avery asked, trying not to soften. Something about him made her knees go weak.

"Bud ropes me into these hootenannies." He threw her a wicked grin.

"Keeps him off the streets," Bud said with a wink. "Besides, with Marsh and Ross both out of town, T. J.'s standing in."

"Chief cook and bottle washer. We'd better get over there." T. J. glanced around. "Looks like the whole crew's here tonight."

When he stepped up next to her, she dropped back to walk with Bud. "How are things coming with the rebuilding, Bud?" she asked, drawing a small frown from T. J.

Camille rushed to greet them at the door. "T. J., I've got you speaking after supper. Sound good?"

"That'll work." He glanced at Avery. "Bet you thought you knew all my secrets, didn't you?"

She stiffened.

"Your mother will be proud, T. J.," Bud said.

He shot Avery another glance, patted Bud on the arm, and headed into the gallery with Camille. He paused to speak over his shoulder. "It would take more than a zoning talk to do that."

Bud gestured to usher Avery in ahead of him, but she stopped on the porch. She still felt like someone had dumped a thousand puzzle pieces in front of her with no guide.

T. J. appeared back in the doorway. "Avery, is something wrong?"

She shook her head and walked on in.

⌐

After the buffet, T. J. watched Avery lope across the street, wearing a black dress that showed her beautiful long legs to full advantage, her steps certain despite the ever-present high heels.

She threw her arms around Kathleen, who had pulled up in front of the market.

"Keeping an eye on the neighbors?" Camille asked, sliding out the gallery door.

He gave an embarrassed laugh. "Yep. And against my better judgment, might I add?"

Camille scrunched up her face. "Why would you say that?"

"Something's up with Avery." He rubbed his eyes. "It's like she can't stay far enough away from me."

Running her fingers through her hair, Camille flinched. "I may have accidentally caused a problem yesterday."

"Did you try to fix her up with me?"

"Maybe, but that isn't what it was."

"Come on, Camille. You're killing me here."

"She seemed surprised to learn you were an Aillet."

"Ah." He jammed his hands into his pockets. "She's figured out her mother-in-law and my mother are best friends."

"Why hadn't you told her?"

"I've known her all of two weeks, three if I stretch it."

Camille raised her eyebrows.

"When I moved back to Samford, I wanted to simplify my life." He looked across the street. "I misjudged Avery as one of those rich women who whines when she chips a nail."

And our families have a history.

"No wonder she's not very happy with you at the moment."

"Did she say that?"

"It's obvious. And, for the record, she's a lovely person."

"Hey, I'm the injured party here. She's mad at me because of my last name."

Camille moaned. "Your move, T. J."

He looked back across the street. A new spotlight fell on the repaired window, the lot full of cars. Kathleen was telling Avery something. "I probably screwed up."

Camille narrowed her eyes. "I guess we'll have to wait and see about that." She headed for the door. "Are you ready to talk about zoning?"

～

Avery and Kathleen eased into the back of the room, every folding chair taken. Camille was in the midst of welcoming the crowd of about forty, none of whom seemed to notice how hard Avery's heart was pounding.

T. J. turned around when she entered, his gaze lingering on her face for a second before he turned back.

"Thank you for staying for this important meeting," Camille said. "I know you'd rather be creating art." She paused as the audience chuckled. "But a time-sensitive matter has arisen."

The words brought a hum of chatter, the energy in the room like a firecracker about to explode. Avery forced herself to focus.

They had gathered in an art classroom that smelled of paint. The floors were refinished heart of pine and the walls a pale blue. Partially finished art pieces lined shelves around the room and were tacked to a clothesline on the side. Shutters, painted bright colors, covered the bottom half of big, single-pane windows.

Camille held up a hand, and the crowd grew silent. "The gallery has been offered a generous sum to relocate."

"Here we go again," a thin African American woman in the front row said.

"At least, Evelyn, we own this building free and clear, thanks to the"—Camille bit back a smile—"generosity of J&S Production Co."

The crowd applauded.

"When will people quit pushing us around?" a woman said.

"We're here to stay," an identical woman added.

Twins? Kathleen mouthed to Avery, who nodded.

"Some argue we could build a newer facility with lower maintenance and utility costs," Camille said.

The knot in Avery's stomach grew. "If they move, the market's done for," she murmured.

"They're not going anywhere," Kathleen whispered back.

"How do you know?"

"They're like me. They don't like change."

Camille motioned toward T. J., who got up from his seat. "We've asked T. J. Aillet to talk about possible options for Trumpet and Vine. As most of you know, he grew up in Samford and has a degree in urban renewal."

Avery's eyes widened. Maybe she didn't know T. J. at all.

"Some of his work has involved a neighborhood similar to ours in Seattle. He'll be happy to answer your questions about what we might do here."

"I said I'll be glad to *try* to answer questions," he said with a smile.

The crowd laughed and clapped.

"Old commercial corners like Trumpet and Vine aren't

faring well in lots of cities. That makes what's happening with the gallery and"—T. J. nodded toward Avery and Kathleen—"at Magnolia Market hopeful."

A few people turned to look at them and then returned their attention to T. J.

"The best thing, in my opinion, is for old buildings to be restored—to return something to the community." His face grew serious. "But in most cases, they become blight or are torn down."

"And people call that progress," one of the twins called out.

He smiled. "In some cases, they're right. In other cases, not. New construction can change the personality of an area in an instant."

The audience murmured.

"Property owners must be brought into the discussion, of course." T. J.'s gaze met Avery's. "We can hope to find solutions that work for both owner and neighborhood. This requires planning, and it's why we're here tonight."

Inspiration displaced Avery's anger. She would find a way to beat Greg Vaughan. She wanted to be part of what was happening on this corner, and she wouldn't let him or anyone else derail her again.

If Magnolia Market were torn down, something special would die.

⌒

T. J. followed a few steps behind Avery, responding politely when he was stopped for yet another question about commercial use of the corner.

Avery, smiling at everyone but him, reminded the artists

they were invited across the street and called out to Kathleen, who was making a sandwich from potluck leftovers.

After excusing himself, he plunged outside after Avery. As he stepped onto the porch, excited chatter about art projects and concern for the corner drifted around the yard. But he was focused on Avery, who was galloping across the street.

Perhaps he should give her time to cool off.

Or maybe she should grow up and quit worrying about who was related to whom.

Right.

T. J. dashed after her.

He jumped off the porch and cut across the yard, the grass muffling his footsteps as he approached the crosswalk. "Avery!" he called out, but she either didn't hear or pretended not to, marching across the parking lot and into the store.

By the time he entered, she had turned on the lights, put on a fancy new green apron, and was measuring scoops of coffee. "That was a good talk," she said without looking up.

"Thanks." He stepped closer.

"Inspiring." She pushed buttons and the aroma of fresh coffee wafted across the room. She shrugged. "I'm going to consider how to get more involved. Who knows? Maybe I'll even run for city council one of these days."

"That'd be good, I guess." Why did he feel like he was dodging a land mine? "We need people who care about Samford."

"I'll have to think about it. Decide, you know?"

"Come on, Avery. We have a couple of minutes before people get here. Do you really want to talk about politics?" He rubbed his eyes.

"Are your eyes bothering you? Maybe you should ask *your father* to look at them." She put the counter between them.

"You don't have to get nasty about it."

"So you're Thomas Aillet?"

"I prefer T. J., but that's me."

"You didn't think that maybe, just maybe, you ought to mention that?" Her voice had a reedy sound.

He held up his hands. "We didn't exactly meet under normal circumstances."

"I'll give you that, but didn't it cross your mind the other night when I dropped by your house?"

"Yes."

"No wonder you went to prep school." She smacked the counter. "So what's with the handyman act?"

T. J. frowned. "I build things. That's no act."

She looked him over again. "You must be one overqualified carpenter." She stiffened. "And you knew Cres."

He nodded, not quite meeting her eyes.

"You went to summer camp together in North Carolina, skiing every winter in Aspen, and to someone's beach house in the summer." She drew a breath. "Flirted with the same women."

He was silent, mad at himself and at her.

"Am I on track?"

"You got some of it right."

"One big clump of well-bred friends," she muttered.

"I don't think of myself like that, but it's no secret my parents are wealthy."

"No secret to everyone but me."

He exhaled. "I knew Cres when we were kids. We went in

different directions. After college, I worked for a builder in Seattle, and he—well, you know what direction he went."

"His mother never forgave me that he headed in my direction."

Once more he remained silent.

"The rumors are true. Evangeline believes I ruined Cres's life. I'm sure your mother has told you the whole ugly story."

"I don't listen to rumors."

"You must be the only one."

The bell he had installed Thursday sounded, and Avery looked up, relief painted on her face. "Welcome to Magnolia Market."

Chapter 26

$\mathcal{A}$very opened the oven door and leaned in.

"Things that bad?" a deep, amused voice asked.

She jumped back and touched her arm against the hot rack. "Ouch!" Her face flushed as she looked up into Davis's concerned face. He wore his work shirt and a tattered Louisiana Tech cap.

"If it isn't Mr. Classic Clunker himself," she said with a smile. "You working on a Saturday?"

He nodded. "You need to put ice on that. Looks painful."

She sighed and scooted around the counter. "By the time I leave this place, I'll have an impressive collection of scars."

"I never realized the biscuit business was so dangerous." Davis followed her to the ice machine and reached past her for ice.

Avery winced when the cold hit the welt but managed a smile. His now-regular morning stops for the biscuit of the day, inspired by the success of the hot-egg biscuits, entertained Kathleen and her. Occasionally he brought five-year-old Jake, a special day brightener.

"Any more news on the sale? Aunt Kathy said the moron nephew paid you another call yesterday."

"I should be asking you for an update." She wrinkled her nose. "Your grapevine is much better than mine." Nearly everyone passed through Davis's auto shop sooner or later, and he picked up information the way her father attracted hurting souls. He had heard that Martha was being released before Bill had bothered to tell Avery, and he knew when her old house sold before she had seen the Under Contract sign out front.

"I'm still hearing storage units," he said.

A pang of regret ran through Avery. "I was afraid of that." She headed back toward the glass case. "What can I get you today?"

"Hmm . . . the special, I think." He cleared his throat looking around. "And I was hoping you might let me take you out to supper tonight."

"It's pepper bacon."

He frowned.

"Monday's jalapeño sausage."

"Are you stalling, or have I slid into an alternate universe?"

"I'm stalling." She stopped, her hand in the biscuit case. "On a date?"

He pulled a face. "Let me explain: I get a sitter for Jake. We both get spiffed up. I come to your door. That sort of thing."

She smiled. "I vaguely remember what that was like."

He looked her up and down. "Not that you need spiffing up. You look great. Always."

Her apron was draped over black slacks and a short-sleeve black T. Sweaters, as she quickly learned, were too warm for working in the kitchen.

She held back a smile. "You're desperate, aren't you? But thanks for the compliment."

"I've heard you drive a hot car." He wiggled his eyebrows. "Corvette engine."

"That thing can move." She picked up a potholder. "But I don't know. I haven't been out on a date in . . . well, years." She imagined the look on Evangeline's face if—no, *when*—word got around that she was dining with a good-looking *mechanic*.

"We can drive to Shreveport if you'd prefer." He gave her an easy smile.

"You'd do that?"

"Would you rather stay in Samford? I can cook, if you'd like. Although"—he looked at the biscuit case—"I can't hold a candle to you."

The new bell on the door jingled, and Avery looked up.

T. J. stood in the entrance, his tool belt around his waist. "Handyman reporting for duty." He strolled toward the counter. He looked as uncomfortable as a dress-shop customer trying to get into a Spandex girdle.

As he approached, his gaze moved from her to Davis. "What you having today, Davis?"

"Whatever the chef suggests." He eyed T. J. the way Howie eyed the squirrels that tormented him in Kathleen's backyard.

"How about you, T. J.?" Avery asked.

The front door opened again, and Avery drew a breath. *Thank goodness.*

Camille entered with a smile. "I love this new bell. So much better than the buzzer." She surveyed the room, stopping at the counter where the trio stood. "Will you come across the street and give me some decorating ideas?"

The hot feeling in Avery's face intensified. "We haven't done that much."

"You've changed the whole look in three weeks," T. J. said.

Avery's hand went to her cheek.

"It does look great," Davis said.

"Your garage inspired me," Avery said. "Camille, have you seen how Davis has his business decorated? It's like something out of a magazine."

"Not the look I was going for." Davis cut his eyes at T. J.

"I notice your truck over here quite a bit," Camille said. "My Chevy's sputtering. You making house calls these days?"

Davis laughed and T. J. grew still. "I'm trying but I haven't convinced Avery yet." He winked at her.

T. J. was irritated. Very interesting.

"Well, who's ready for a biscuit?" Avery asked.

⌒

The lunch "rush," although an overstatement, had passed when T. J.'s electric saw grew silent. Not that Avery was paying attention.

She filled a large paper cup with ice, then sweet tea. No matter what the temperature, T. J. couldn't get enough tea. He favored her new mint flavor, made from a tiny mint garden she had planted in a pot inside the back door.

Maybe the new owner would move it outside when the weather warmed up.

Today she put a slice of orange in the tea. Then she removed it.

Maybe that was too girlie for a guy like T. J.

Then she put it back. "Oh, good grief."

"What's the problem?" Kathleen came in through the back door, Howie running into the storeroom.

"I'm thinking of adding orange tea to the drink menu." She inhaled, the citrus smell tickling her nose. "Is that too froufrou?"

"Let me taste it, and I'll tell you what I think." Kathleen reached for the glass.

"I'm taking this one out to T. J. I'll make you another one."

Kathleen smirked. "So that's how it is."

"Whatever you're implying, you're wrong."

"T. J.'s a great guy. Next to Davis, he's the best young man I know. Go for it."

"It's a glass of tea, not an engagement ring." Avery sloshed the tea onto the counter as she snapped the lid on it. "He's been working hard, and it's warmer today."

The more she talked, the bigger Kathleen's grin grew.

"Davis asked me out for supper tonight. On a date."

"My Davis? I hope you said yes."

"He's such a nice guy." Avery fiddled with the lid on the cup. "It feels sort of like leading him on."

A crease appeared on Kathleen's forehead. "You two make a good pair."

"I'm not sure." She fiddled with the hem of her apron.

"For someone who says she wants to start dating again, you're mighty standoffish."

"I don't see *you* going out on any dates—unless you count taking me and Howie to Sonic."

"Yuk, yuk. You are so funny." Kathleen straightened the receipts by the counter. "My situation's different. Wayne and I had a good marriage, and—" She broke off. "I didn't mean that like it sounded."

In the past, the words would have felt like a punch in the stomach, but not today.

"Every man isn't like Cres." Kathleen picked up a pencil, then tapped it on the counter.

"I know that." Avery couldn't bring herself to admit she wished T. J. had asked her out.

"Forgive Cres, Avery. Heck, for that matter, forgive yourself. Go out with Davis, and see what happens. And if you can get over T. J.'s lineage, maybe you'll forgive him too." She picked up the glass of tea. "Shall I take this to him?"

"I've got it," Avery said and headed outside.

Chapter 27

$\mathcal{T}$. J. cocked his head to examine the piece of custom trim. Scowling, he strode to his pickup and pulled out a crowbar.

What a day.

"Wait!" Avery cried out as he pried it loose. "That looks great."

"It's crooked."

She stepped back, tilting her head one way and the other. Her long blond hair, usually up in a ponytail, swished back and forth around her shoulders. The omnipresent apron—utilitarian on Bill and cute on Avery—had been removed, revealing a pair of black slacks and a T-shirt. The pair of red high heels—*when did I start looking forward to seeing those?*—topped off the outfit.

He scowled and turned back to the wall. "Nothing in this building is level, so we have to adjust."

"You've just described my life."

Giving up a small grin, T. J. wrenched the metal again and looked over his shoulder. "Whoever buys this place will need to pay for foundation work."

"Unless they decide to *level* it." She smiled a tentative smile. "Get it? Level it?"

"I get it."

"I'm sorry we got crossways over the whole name thing." The words tumbled out, her face flushed. "I overreacted."

He gave her his full attention. "I should be the one apologizing. I've spent ten years figuring out who I am, and I'm sensitive about it."

"Can we still be friends?"

"Oh." His ego fell harder than a hammer off a roof. "Sure. Yeah. Great."

"I brought you a peace offering." She held out a paper cup. "See what you think."

His fingers brushed her hand as he reached for the drink. They both jerked their hands back, jostling the cup, which hit the pavement. The lid flew off, and iced tea splattered onto both of them.

"Sorry." She kneeled to pick up the cup, lid, and straw. "I'm a klutz."

He picked up the crowbar. "You seem awfully cheerful today."

"We had a good sales day. Sold out of pepper-bacon biscuits, and customers loved the muffalettas."

"I had two of those. That olive mix was good."

"Gabriela's group made that." She looked into the distance, a calculating gleam in her eyes. "If we package that and—oh, never mind." Her gaze landed on the faded sign. "Are you still planning to paint that?"

"How about asking Bud to carve something with your logo? That magnolia might add some class to the joint. And maybe an awning over that front door to pull it together—and help in bad weather. Maybe in green to play off the sign?"

She twirled her bracelet. "I've been thinking about stripes, sort of a modern look to go with the retro logo." She put her hands on her hips, studying the construction. "I love that display window you came up with."

Her face was flushed and her eyes shone. Avery was not only pretty, but she glowed. Her voice had risen as she described the display.

He pointed to his sketch with a mechanical pencil, erasing the mullions that had divided the glass. "With tweaking, we can transform the front." Avery brushed against him as she looked at the drawing, her floral scent invading his brain. He could stand here all day.

But she pulled back. "This is stupid."

It certainly didn't feel stupid to him.

"I'm getting ahead of myself. There's no point in going to a lot of trouble if it's going to be torn down."

Conversation floated across the street from the Sweet Olive Folk Art Gallery, a quartet of women exiting, each holding a shopping bag. As they climbed into a BMW sedan, Camille waved from the porch, first at the shoppers and then at Avery and him.

"The gallery business is picking up," he said. "Bud says sales are ahead of projections. He's sold a couple of bowls—he turns them on a lathe. They're nice pieces." He was babbling to keep Avery nearby.

But she didn't seem to hear, her attention on the car now headed into the market parking lot.

"If the gallery does well, that should help the market," he said. "You might make a decent living here."

Avery's laughing flush had switched to the color of the paper cup she held. "I'd better get back to work." She fled into the store.

He shook his head and picked up a hammer. Smashing his thumb might feel better than trying to figure Avery out.

"Hey, good-looking," the driver called as she disembarked, beautiful long legs unwinding gracefully.

"Hi," the woman exiting the backseat said, so softly he could barely hear.

"Good afternoon, y'all." His head ached at this combination of visitors. He still didn't understand how his mother and Evangeline had stayed friends all these years.

"Isn't this a wonderful coincidence, Thomas?" His mother came around the front of the car. He moved forward.

"Girl's day out," Evangeline Broussard, on his mother's heels, said in a tight voice.

His mother pointed to her outfit and then back to his construction project. "I would hug you, but . . . Don't you have *help* to do that kind of work for you?"

"My staff's taking a coffee break." He kept his tone light. "How do you like the way the new front's shaping up?"

"It looks nice." His mother glanced at the new window for a couple of seconds and then back at him. "Wasn't it thoughtful of Maggie to drive us?"

"Indeed."

His mother's latest interference in his dating life gave a charming snort at his comment. Margaret Ann Dillingham—Maggie since middle school—was the latest beautiful, young, well-connected woman his mother and Evangeline had encouraged him to take out. Maggie was one of the few he had dated. Already a vice president at her family's insurance business, she was a heck of a tennis player and easy to talk to.

"Isn't it serendipitous that we ran into Thomas, Maggie? It was meant to be!"

He hadn't seen his mother this revved up since she had learned that Marsh was going to be appointed by the governor to a state legal board.

"It's a pleasant surprise, for me, at least." Maggie gave him a flirtatious smile and added a big wink.

Humoring his mother—and a little lonely—he had asked her to dinner and a movie two or three times and tried to stir up a spark of feeling. But it hadn't gone anywhere, and he hadn't asked her out since . . . *Has it been since I met Avery?*

"And you remember Thora, don't you?" his mother said. "She's a tax attorney now. Very successful."

"Sure. Thora looked at my other apartment. How's—?"

"T. J. rented it right out from under me," she interrupted.

Thora might have announced she summered on the moon for the looks she got from Evangeline and his mother.

"You were going to live in that duplex?" his mother said. That piece of news had just removed Thora from the matchmaking list.

Thora gave T. J. a subtle shake of her head. "Some med-school resident got there first. I wound up renting a bigger place in Shreveport."

"A doctor? His mother must be so proud."

"I'm sure she is, Mother." T. J. was happy to have a reliable tenant, part of his plan to make enough to acquire more property.

"You drive back and forth from Shreveport every day?" Evangeline asked. "Why in the world would you do that?" Her eyes had zoomed in as if she'd spotted a loose thread on Thora's shirt.

"I'd have a longer commute if I'd taken one of the big-city

jobs." A flush mottled Thora's neck. "The drive's only thirty minutes. Gives me time to clear my head."

What was going on here?

Thora had called T. J. in a panic at the first of December. "I start a new job in a couple of weeks, and Ross said you rent out the other side of your house. I need to get settled in a hurry." She hesitated and then her words came in a rush. "Do you allow children?"

The next day she had left a message that she had found something else.

T. J. had met her at a party years ago, but he didn't know her well. She had grown up in Samford and started college about the time he graduated. She looked more like a soccer mom than a high-powered lawyer.

His mother clapped her hands as though calling for attention. "Shall we go inside?"

"T. J.," Maggie said, "is the hot chocolate as good here as everybody says?"

"I'm more of an iced-tea guy. They have excellent mint tea."

"Can I get anyone anything?" Maggie included T. J. in her smile. She was attractive in a perky sort of way—and, as his mother often reminded him, very thoughtful. "Or shall we all go in?"

Evangeline pursed her lips. "That sounds lovely." But she looked as though the idea ranked up there with having a colonoscopy.

Thora slid a clunky white-gold bracelet up and down her arm, her face solemn. "I think I'll make a call. I'm not hungry."

"Oh, sure," Maggie said. "Make me the pig in front of T. J." She laughed, a fun, tinkly sound. Maybe he should try harder with her.

"Join us, darling." His mother deigned to tug on his sleeve.

"I'd better finish up."

"I heard Avery's working here." His mother's voice dropped

almost to a whisper. "Evangeline and I are curious about what's going on."

Ah. So this visit wasn't about throwing Maggie and Thora at him. Evangeline wanted to spy on Avery.

He smiled at his mother. He needed to try harder with her too. "Avery's been a big help to Martha and Bill, the owners. The place was kind of a mess."

"Everyone in town is talking about the food," his mother said, her face impassive. "Claire Richmond served chicken and biscuits from here at a brunch last week, and Maggie's mother ordered fried pies for our canasta group." She patted her narrow waist. "Thank heavens they were miniatures."

"They've tried quite a few things, and they're sending a lot of business to the mission."

"They?"

"A friend helps Avery." He glanced at the front wall, frustrated that he could still care that she didn't ask about the mission.

"I'm going to have a look." His mother talked as though she were about to investigate a homicide. Maggie had paused, holding the screen door open for Evangeline. Thora was rooted in place.

Avery facing this battalion might be a bit much, even for her. "Mom," said T. J., "there's not much room to sit down. I know you don't like to eat in the car."

An odd expression—relief maybe?—crossed Thora's face. "Perhaps we could try that tearoom on Trumpet."

"That might be best, Minnie." Evangeline—the only person other than Bud who had *ever* called his mother Minnie—threw his mother a look.

"Let's see what all the fuss is about," his mother hissed. "You said you wanted to know."

Thora glanced at her phone. "I didn't realize we were going to be out all afternoon. I need to get home."

Evangeline rubbed her temples. "We won't stay long."

"I need to check my messages," Thora said. "I'll wait in the car."

T. J. ran his hand through his hair, watching her practically run to the car. Confused, he followed the other three into the store, smiling at the jingle of bells on the main door. Removing the sterile buzzer and installing the bells had taken him all of fifteen minutes and put a silly grin on Avery's face. For a while, anyway.

⌒

Avery glanced in the mirror, patted her hair, then pulled it back into a ponytail. She was a clerk, not a hostess.

"Wish me luck," she whispered to Howie, who dozed on the cot. She hurried out, wishing Kathleen hadn't taken the afternoon off.

Moving behind the counter, she picked up a rag and dusted off an invisible crumb, not yet looking at the entourage. She took a deep breath and plastered on a smile. "May I help you?"

"Hi, Avery." Maggie Dillingham stepped forward, wearing an outfit Avery had sold her at the boutique. She had the legs to pull off that skirt. "Everyone in Samford's talking about this place. We were at the art gallery across the street, and it seemed like a good time to visit."

T. J., hovering near the door, stepped from behind the women. "Maggie wants to try Kathleen's famous hot chocolate."

A sizzle of jealousy ran through Avery at the sound of Maggie's name on his lips, and she tried to shake it off. A few years younger than her, Maggie had been nothing but gracious in visits to the boutique and a variety of the usual Samford social occasions. She had even brought a home-cooked meal after Cres was killed—Caesar salad, chicken enchiladas, chips and hot sauce, and blackberry cobbler with vanilla ice cream.

"The cocoa takes a couple of minutes." Avery pulled out the ingredients as she spoke. "Feel free to look around or"—she gestured to a bistro table with a vintage floral tablecloth on it and four metal chairs—"have a seat."

"How cute," Maggie said.

Before she could reply, Evangeline strode forward, wearing a dress Avery had never seen. "Hello, Avery," she said in her patented society drawl. "How's the biscuit business?"

Gripping the edge of the counter, Avery fought the urge to shove one down her throat. "Good afternoon, Evangeline. Welcome to Magnolia Market."

Her mother-in-law looked as though she had wandered into a strip club.

"It's darling, isn't it?" Maggie murmured, gazing around the room. "Avery, you can transform a space better than anyone I've ever met. Are you still living in that cute house on Division?"

Avery lowered her gaze to her apron. "I moved in with a friend."

Evangeline's eyes widened, and she turned away but remained close enough to eavesdrop.

"I bet your new place is perfect," Maggie said. "I'm in a plain, old town house. Nothing as spiffy as what you have."

Avery visualized the daybed in Kathleen's spare room and smiled. It was perfect.

"I'm glad you found a new place," Maggie said. "I know you must have been lonely after Cres . . ."

Here it was again. Well-meaning words drifting off. But they didn't bother her as much as the fact that the coffee was running low.

"I was lonely," Avery said, "and it's been great having someone to talk to." She looked at her mother-in-law. "Evangeline was right. I needed a fresh start."

Chapter 28

*A*very was sitting on the couch, brushing dog hair off her skirt when Kathleen ushered Davis into the living room. "Your date's here," Kathleen said, her hands on her hips. "He brought flowers."

Davis, looking like a stranger in slacks and a white shirt, smiled. "Don't get too excited. I cut them from my backyard."

"They smell so good." Avery buried her nose in the bouquet of bright-yellow jonquils in a Mason jar. "These always make me hopeful that we might make it through winter."

"One of the great things about life," Kathleen said. "Spring always comes." She patted them both on the shoulder. "Come on, Howie. Let's leave these kids to themselves."

"Are you sure you don't want to go with us?" Avery said.

Davis looked mildly taken aback. "I made reservations at the Bayou Steak House over on Lake Bistineau. I can add another."

"Nice recovery," Kathleen said, "but I've got a big night planned watching British comedies."

"My dad loves those," Avery said.

"He must be a good man." Kathleen walked off, Howie on her heels.

Davis put his hands in his pockets. "Does that restaurant sound good? We might have more privacy there. Away from all our nosy Samford neighbors." He grinned.

"You don't mind driving that far?"

"I look forward to it." He reached to pull her off the couch, but she dodged his hand and stood, the black dress swirling as they headed for the car.

Walking through the front door of the Bayou Steak House was like stepping back in time—both in the restaurant and in her own life. She had not been here since long before Cres died, even though it was one of his favorite restaurants.

Gold leather booths glowed under hurricane lanterns mounted on the walls. The carpet, unchanged through the years, and the lack of televisions gave a hushed feel, almost like the sound right before church started.

A mirror behind the bar reflected the colors of paintings of regional scenes. The art, she saw upon a closer look, was on loan from the Sweet Olive Folk Art Gallery and available for purchase.

Camille needs ideas. Right.

The waitstaff, dressed in black pants and white shirts, was mostly the same—formal serving veterans who poured water and related the specials with solemnity.

"Save room for their King Cake bread pudding," Davis said as they ordered.

"Might I recommend the strawberry shortcake made with Ponchatoula berries and homemade pound cake?" the waiter asked.

A child's squeal distracted Avery, and she didn't reply. In the mirror, her eyes met those of Thora Fairfield, seated across the room in a red T-shirt. A blond toddler giggled from a booster seat at the table, while an older couple smiled indulgently.

Davis looked at her and back at the waiter. "We'll be a moment."

"Yes, sir." The waiter stepped toward the kitchen.

Avery watched him walk away, remembering not one of her dinners here with Cres but her first visit to Cres's office, days after her graduation from college and weeks before their wedding.

She had been excited to be invited into this part of his life, and Cres greeted Avery in the lobby of the office tower, draping his arm around her while he signed her in. "Isn't she something?" he said to the security guard who answered with two thumbs up.

On the elevator, she stepped closer to Cres, feeling shy, almost like she didn't know him. That was silly. He wore one of his standard outfits—a pair of slacks, a golf shirt from a resort in Florida, and a pair of leather loafers he had bought from an exclusive men's store in Dallas.

"I can't wait to see your office. Now I'll be able to picture it when you're working all those long hours. I'm so glad we're together again." She reached for his hand, but he pulled away as the door glided open.

"Here we are. My home away from home this past year." He shepherded her through the glass door, the words Creswell Broussard & Son, CPAs painted in small letters.

"Classy." She smiled and reached for her phone.

"What are you doing?" His voice was sharp, a tone she had heard a handful of disturbing times.

"I want to get a picture of you by the sign. Daddy will love it."

"That's silly." He looked toward a young brunette who sat at a receptionist's desk. "We're not in college anymore."

Stung, Avery fumbled to put the phone back in her purse.

"We'll do it another time," he said in a low voice. "I'll get someone to snap the two of us. Now, come see my new office." Ushering her through the lobby, he nodded at the receptionist, his steps increasing as he headed for the hallway.

The young woman had beamed at Cres as he strolled by, her gaze lingering on Avery. Her wavy dark hair flowed to the middle of her back, her face heavily made-up—but still gorgeous. She wore a tight red sleeveless top, cut in at her tanned shoulders.

"Shouldn't we have stopped to say hello?" Avery asked as they stepped through the door. Cres was walking so fast, she struggled to keep up with him, but he slowed at her question.

"To whom?" he asked with a frown.

"That secretary. It felt rude rushing by like that."

Cres rubbed his earlobe, a nervous quirk Avery found endearing. "Thora's just an intern. I pass her a hundred times a day. I can't visit with everyone in the office."

"But I want to get to know your coworkers. I've got a year of catching up to do." She smiled. "After all, I am going to be the boss's wife."

He returned her smile, but it didn't quite make it to his eyes. "You'll be crazy about my secretary. She's been at the firm forever."

Brenda Bottoms was middle-aged and overweight, and she wore her hair, prematurely gray, cropped short. Her sleeves were long and her blouse navy blue. She looked from Cres to Avery and back at Cres.

"Brenda, this is my fiancée, Avery." He gave Avery a tight squeeze as he said the words, bringing a warmth to her cheeks. "Avery, this woman runs the office. She's something."

"Nice to meet you, Avery. I hope Cres knows what a fortunate man he is." The soft-spoken words were delivered with a quick look toward Cres, the kind a parent gives a child acting up in church. "She's lovely, Cres."

His quick laugh sounded peculiar, more like a croak. "Brenda thinks she's my mother. You two are going to love each other."

"I'll keep a close eye on this man of yours, Avery. You call or pop in anytime."

"You're my secretary, not my probation officer."

"Cres!" Avery exclaimed.

"Just kidding. Brenda and I joke around all the time, don't we?"

For a moment, Brenda stared into Cres's eyes and then looked back at Avery. "I look forward to your wedding."

"I'm glad you're coming." Avery hunched her shoulders and lowered her voice. "I won't know most of the people there, so it'll be great to see a friendly face."

"I've known this one since he was a boy, and it'll be nice to see him settle down."

The phone rang, and a frown crossed Brenda's face as she glanced down. "Excuse me." She punched one of a dozen lines and picked it up.

Cres tugged on Avery's hand. "Come see my new desk."

"He's busy right now," Brenda said into the phone as they walked away. "I told you not to call again."

Avery paused, taken aback by her tone, but Cres pulled her into his office and closed the door. "Don't mind Brenda. She's used to having her way."

That day Thora had watched Avery, but tonight she quickly looked away. Her attention seemed locked on the boy, whom she lifted out of his seat and held against her chest.

Davis reached out and touched Avery's arm, causing her to start. "Is something wrong?" he asked, his voice pitched low.

"I am so sorry. Would it be okay if we left?"

He jumped to his feet and pulled out her heavy chair. "Are you sick?"

"I think I'm going to be." She rushed from the restaurant.

⁓

Davis insisted on taking her to his house. "It's closer."

Clasping her clammy hands, Avery nodded. At least she wouldn't have to talk to Kathleen yet. The drive had been silent, except for Avery's occasional sniffle.

"Do you need to pick up Jake?" Avery asked with a hiccup as they pulled into the garage.

"He's spending the night with a friend from church." He paused. "That makes them both happy."

"And you?"

He gave a sheepish smile. "I miss the little squirt when he's not around."

"You have a pretty home," Avery said as they entered. A large island with a granite countertop dominated the kitchen. A bar stool was pulled up before a *Sesame Street* cereal bowl and spoon resting on a fire-truck place mat.

"I wish I had Kleenex." He looked around before he grabbed a roll of paper towels. "Will these help?"

She gave him a watery smile. "I'm so, so sor—"

"Stop." He shepherded her to a big leather couch. "You've apologized plenty. In fact, you've got a credit for future dates."

She looked up. "You'd actually go out with me again?"

"There aren't that many single women in Samford," he said with a wink. Then his face grew solemn. "But I would appreciate it if you'd tell me what's going on."

Avery closed her eyes, remembering the boy who looked like the child she had planned to have with Cres. "I'm not sure I can talk about it."

"O-kay." He drawled the word out and tossed a small blanket covered in monkeys her way. Then he moved to the fireplace and placed a couple of logs onto the andirons. Sticking a long match to kindling, he blew a time or two, and the fire crackled to life.

"You're way too nice to me. I ruined our plans." Avery sank back into the couch and absorbed the warmth of the room. The brick house sat in a subdivision lined with similar new homes and was filled with personality.

A watercolor of deer in the edge of woods hung over the fireplace. Pictures of Jake from infancy to preschool graduation were scattered about. Two guitars—one full-size and one child-size—hung on stands in the corner.

"Do you ever wish you could go back in time and start over?" She shook her head before he answered. "Of course not. You have it all together."

"I've made mistakes. What I lack in quantity, I make up for in quality." His grin didn't quite meet his eyes. "And that's a *no* to having it all together."

She gestured around the room. "You have a beautiful home, a great business, a cute son. You even get along with your aunt." The fire popped and Avery jumped.

"It's easier to judge people by what's outside. But that's like thinking TV dinners taste like the picture on the package. And I can tell you from lots of experience, they don't."

Their laughter eased the tension in the room.

"How long have you lived here?" Avery asked after a moment.

"About two years. My wife died when Jake was three, and I bought this place a few months later. I hoped it would offer him stability. Me too, I guess."

"She had cancer, right?" Avery had seen people walk to the other side of a room to avoid talking to her about death, and right now she understood what they were feeling.

He gave a slow nod. "We didn't know until right after Jake was born." He put his hands on his knees. "Losing a spouse . . ." He shrugged. "It puts you into a weird sort of club."

She looked back down at her hands. "I shouldn't be a member of that club."

"Nobody wants to be. But what choice do we have?"

She picked up a picture of Jake from the end table, rubbing her hand on the glass. "You're so lucky to have a son. I wanted to have a baby."

His gaze locked with hers. "I don't know how I would have gotten by without my boy."

She stood and walked to the fireplace, inhaling the aroma of smoke. The wood popped again as she held her hands out for warmth. "Cres didn't want a child," she said into the flames. "Not with me anyway."

She turned, and Davis leaned forward in the chair. It took a few moments for her to compose herself. "Our marriage was falling apart."

"I had heard that." His voice was quiet.

"You and your grapevine," she said with a shaky smile.

"I don't know what happened in your marriage, but I'll tell you what Kathleen always tells me. You have to move on."

"That's what I'm doing—or trying to do." She sat on the hearth.

"Sorry." He grimaced. "I hate it when people tell me what to feel and when I should feel it."

"I wish I could be more like you. I hibernated for a year—hardly left the house except to go to work. I was a coward."

He stood and walked to the fireplace, then leaned against the mantel for a second before turning to face her. "Be thankful you hibernated. I messed up so many lives." He cleared his throat. "I rushed into a second marriage and made everything worse."

"You're married?" She sprang off the hearth, her gaze flying around the room.

"Of course not! I wouldn't have asked you out if I were married." He threw her a wounded look. "We divorced after six months, and she moved back to Atlanta."

"Another strike against my grapevine."

"I was going to tell you at dinner, but things veered off course."

"Wow."

He closed his eyes for a moment, looking ten years older. "I was stupid."

"And scared and lonely?"

"That's putting it kindly."

She sat again and Davis sat beside her. "I like the way your mind works," he said.

"That's a new one." She tried to smooth her hair.

"Seriously. You've turned a run-down corner store into a popular place." He leaned forward. "And you're a lot prettier than Bill."

She saw the spark in his eyes—and wished she felt it too. But she didn't. She turned, rubbing the wood on the mantel. "Is this cypress? Wouldn't something like this make a good display at the market?"

Davis didn't say anything, just studied her.

"Did you buy it around here?" she rambled on. "It's fantastic."

The spark vanished. "T. J. Aillet made it. Maybe you should give him a call."

Chapter 29

$\mathcal{A}$very pawed through her closet at Kathleen's house. Maybe the black dress could work. It wouldn't show dirt, and she could swap out her shoes after the breakfast rush.

"I'm out of here," she said a few minutes later. "See you at the store."

Kathleen put her hands on her hips, surveying her. "Didn't you forget the pearls?"

Smoothing her hair, Avery pasted on a nonchalant smile. "I have to run errands this afternoon."

"At a funeral home?" Kathleen frowned. "It's Monday. Aren't we working on our offer to Bill today?"

"That may need to wait until this evening. We'll talk about it at work. The biscuits aren't going to make themselves."

Kathleen's eyes narrowed. "See you there."

Morning customers were always rushed, most on a tight schedule. One of Avery's unexpected pleasures was chatting about their lives while serving them, and this morning she allowed herself to savor each conversation.

"Hope the presentation goes well," she said to a young insurance agent.

"Is your daughter ready for her recital?" she asked a middle-aged pediatrician.

Davis held the door for the doctor, smiling as he entered. "Could I interest you in a job?"

Avery laughed. "I doubt your aunt would appreciate that."

He made a face. "Good point. But you have a knack for this."

"And she dresses well," Kathleen said from the grill, her eyes suspicious.

"It's part of the tone we're going for," Avery said with a teasing grin.

"Oh, brother. And to think I once planned to retire at fifty-five and travel the country in an RV."

"Really?" Avery turned to Kathleen. "My dad said the same thing the other day. Maybe we'll all go together one of these days."

"After we make our first million." Kathleen rang up Davis's breakfast. "Could you ever imagine I'd wind up trying to buy a business? At my age?"

"I've wanted you to work at the garage for years. You're a natural entrepreneur."

"This is your aunt Kathy you're talking to." She ran her hands through her hair, the misshapen bob standing up.

"Uncle Wayne always said you had the talent to do whatever you wanted."

"He should have told that to a few HR directors." But she smiled as she spoke. "Thanks for that, Davis. You're the best."

He looked toward Avery, who was getting andouille sausage out for lunch. "Or second-best, depending on whose eyes you're looking through."

Telling Davis she couldn't date him Saturday night had been a rough conversation at the end of a rough day. "You're such a nice guy," she had said.

"Oh no." He held up his hand. "Stop right there, before you get to the *but* part of the sentence."

Avery's laugh felt sad in her throat. "I really, really like you . . . and you sold me the best classic clunker in the world. Helped me get my insurance. Everything."

"That's not enough to build a relationship on?"

"I live with your aunt. Jake's like my own nephew."

"Maybe he could be your son one day. He loves you, and you'd make a great mom. We can see where this goes."

"I talked myself into marrying the wrong man once. You're a great friend, but . . ."

He looked up at the ceiling and back at her, his mouth curled in a crooked smile. "Maybe we should agree to erase tonight from our history."

Avery had leaned over and kissed him on the cheek. "It's a deal."

⌒

Pulling into the parking garage, Avery eased her way around compact cars and SUVs, unable to find a spot large enough for the station wagon.

She wound her way to the top level, nearly vacant on the gray winter day, and swerved into a row. With a quick look in the rearview mirror, she touched up her lipstick, patted her hair, and confirmed that the check was in her purse.

Leaning on the door, she pushed hard with her shoulder and stepped out. The wind whipped around her, and she buttoned her light wool coat, peering down at Samford, bustling on this Monday afternoon.

Like many southern cities, downtown looked worn. The blue of the Louisiana flag flew next to the US red-and-white stripes at the courthouse, barely visible past the office building that housed the Broussard CPA office.

Camellias bloomed outside the public library, a spot of color even in the dead of winter. In the distance the Red River sat as still as a lake, trees bare on its bank. If she strained, she could almost make out the neighborhood where she and Cres had lived, and she could see the faint peaks of T. J.'s roof.

She liked Samford, its personality different from Cajun country, where she had grown up. Its feel was gentler somehow, a fact she hadn't realized until her recent weeks in the store.

As she stepped toward the stairwell to the street, the wind blew a piece of hair across her face, evoking another memory of that first visit to Cres's office. He had chastised her for not taking one of the reserved spaces down below as he walked her to the roof. The wind had blown that day too, a hot summer wind.

"No wonder your hair's such a . . ." He seemed to catch himself. "You look great all windblown." He brushed the hair out of her eyes and kissed her. "I like that natural look."

She eased back from him and put her hand to her hair. "Did I look all right when I met your coworkers?"

"You were perfect." He opened the door of the SUV his parents had loaned her when she graduated. They were trading up and didn't need it anyway, they said. And, of course, she would get a new one when she and Cres married.

Today a sports car revved its engine nearby, jolting Avery.

She tidied her hair and straightened her sleeve, glancing at the heavy white-gold bracelet.

The sports car backed out and idled nearby. Stepping back, she motioned the driver on, but the car stayed put. "Oh, thanks." She waved again, although the driver was obscured by his sun visor. When Avery stepped in front of the car, though, the driver honked the horn, long and loud.

She jumped back so fast, she stumbled and scurried to get out of the way.

"Shouldn't you be minding our store, Mrs. Broussard?" Bill's nephew climbed out of the car, the door squeaking.

Avery tightened her grip on her purse. "What are you doing here?"

"Probably the same thing you are." He leaned back against his car, arms crossed. "Calling on your dear old daddy-in-law. That's the kind of man I like to do business with." Greg lifted his chin and eyebrows at the same time. "Was mighty happy when I tracked him down. Says you're trying to cheat me out of my inheritance."

"I'm trying to keep you from cheating Martha and Bill out of their life savings."

"Oh, the three of us will make out just fine. Turns out, your dead husband's daddy's interested in investment property. Likes that old neighborhood." His smile revealed what looked like a dip of snuff. "Guess you should have paid more attention to me."

Avery drew in a breath. Whatever happened would be for the best, and she was trying to help Martha and Bill. It might not be Haiti, but it was a start.

And she wasn't afraid.

"I'd watch out for Creswell, if I were you," she called over her shoulder as she walked away. "He doesn't like to lose." Greg's tires squealed as he zoomed out of the garage, and he threw her an obscene gesture.

Head held high, she entered the office building for the first time in four years. "It interrupts my work when you stop by," Cres had said early in their marriage.

Right.

The same security guard sat at the counter, but he didn't seem to recognize Avery and asked her to sign in while he called for an escort. Avery read the list of the building's occupants while she waited—Slattery Richmond, a sneaky lawyer; J&S Production Co.; and Creswell Broussard CPA.

"Hey, Avery." She jumped even though the voice was soft spoken. Brenda Bottoms, looking the same except for slightly longer gray hair, stood behind her. "It's good to see you."

"Did you tell him I called?"

"You asked me not to." She looked uneasy. "I could lose my job over this."

"I hope the element of surprise might work in my favor." Avery placed her hand on Brenda's arm for a moment. "Thank you. You've always been nice to me."

"I should have said something before the wedding," Brenda said as they stepped onto the elevator.

"I should have opened my eyes." Avery kept her voice even.

The elevator jolted to a stop and the doors slid open. Brenda exited first, holding the door. Avery didn't move. "The first time's bound to be hard," Brenda said. "You might as well get it over with."

Nothing seemed familiar when Avery stepped off the elevator. The carpet was new, a checked pattern, and the walls were painted gray instead of ivory. Even the entrance was changed, the glass door replaced with wood.

And then she saw the small painted sign: Broussard & Associates.

"No more *Son*," she whispered.

"No." Tears popped into Brenda's eyes, and she opened the door.

Walking down the hall, Avery's steps were steady as she neared Cres's old office.

"Avery? What a . . . surprise." Creswell Sr.'s voice rang through the hall as he stepped out of his office. The heads of a pack of assistants and accountants popped up and then ducked back down, like a game at the fair.

"Good luck," Brenda murmured and scooted to her desk outside Creswell's office, where she had sat since the week Avery and Cres married.

Avery held herself rigid when her father-in-law moved in for an unexpected hug. "You had us worried sick," he said loud enough for the entire floor to hear. "Why did you move out of the house on Division?" His voice dropped several decibels. "Your time is running out."

Curious eyes peered at her from every direction.

"Perhaps we could speak in your office?" she said.

"Of course. Brenda, how about getting Avery coffee or water. What would you like, dear?"

She gritted her teeth. "I need a few minutes of your time." She moved first and glided to a chair in front of his desk. "You were my CPA, and you stole money from my account."

He smirked as he sat in his leather desk chair. "I gave you ten thousand dollars, and you have"—he turned the calendar on his desk around to face her—"a week to cash it. A week to leave town.

Best offer you'll get." Pulling the calendar toward him, he put a finger to his chin. "Ross has been suggesting I invest in that corner for months." His laugh was ugly. "That Greg Vaughan makes it sound quite attractive. Even if your involvement drove up the price."

"You're not going to win. I will find a way, with or without Broussard money, to save that store. To save that corner."

"That's so cute, you running that little grocery store. I don't recall you being much of a cook." He leaned forward. "Cres would have appreciated that. He wanted nothing more than home and family."

The image of the little boy came into her mind. Was it possible Creswell didn't know he had a grandson?

Creswell continued. "He was earning a living, building a future for you two."

"In New Orleans? Or in the Turks and Caicos before that? Oh!" Avery snapped her fingers. "There was all of that work in Palm Springs that second winter we were married."

His gaze darted toward the door. "You weren't right for him." His voice was low and angry.

She stood. "I want my money, and I don't want any connection, ever again, with you or Evangeline."

"I bet you haven't even told your dear do-gooder father what happened. Cash that check or be left without anything. The end of January, Avery. Bye."

"I haven't told *anyone* what happened."

"Are you blackmailing me?"

"I want the money I earned. Nothing more." She leaned forward. "Now that you mention how fast this month is going, I'll expect it . . ." She tapped on his calendar. "By the first week of February."

He stiffened but the smirk remained on his face for a second before his attention went to the door.

"Creswell, do you know if Brenda…?" Thora's voice trailed off as she entered his office, the color fading from her face. "Excuse me, I didn't realize you were busy." She put her hand on the door frame, as though to steady herself. She wore black pants and a red blazer today and had a pencil stuck behind one ear, which would have looked contrived on anyone else.

"Hello, Thora."

"Avery, excuse me."

Creswell's mouth quirked. "Thora provides legal counsel for our clients."

"I didn't know you'd gone to law school."

"Three years ago," Thora said. "I graduated in December."

"We hounded her to get her back. She left us so abruptly." He looked from one to the other, like a football fan deciding which team to root for. "But when she finished law school, all footloose and fancy-free, we lured her back."

Thora's eyes looked as they had in the mirror at the restaurant. She pushed her auburn hair behind her ear, dislodging the pencil. As she bent to pick it up, her white-gold bracelet slid down her arm.

Identical to the one Avery wore, the one Cres had given Avery for her twenty-sixth birthday.

Chapter 30

"I paid Creswell Broussard Sr. a visit today."

Kathleen plunked the mug down on the kitchen table. "So that's what the fancy outfit was all about."

"Nephew Greg made the connection. Thus Creswell's sudden urge to develop that corner."

"You should have taken me with you."

"Would you have beaten him up?"

"You didn't have to face him alone." Kathleen sank onto a bar stool.

"I also saw Cres's girlfriend. She works there now."

"Oh, dear God." Kathleen popped up like a toy on a spring and moved in to hug Avery. "I'm going to kill you for not taking me with you."

"I needed to do this on my own. No matter how this all plays out, I'm not cowering in my room anymore. Ever." She pushed back her hair. "Cres went on that golfing trip because he needed, as he put it, 'space.'" She held up her wrist. "The week before my twenty-sixth birthday, he gave me this bracelet. Then he told me he wasn't the kind of husband I needed."

Kathleen narrowed her eyes but didn't speak.

"He was tired of being married." She took the bracelet off and twirled it on her finger. "Like I was a chore he had had enough of. He didn't want to be married anymore. When I reminded him we had taken sacred vows, he laughed and said I was so 'old-fashioned' it was almost cute. He sounded like a frat boy who had wrecked his parents' car."

"I wish you had let me go with you today."

"The strangest thing, Kathleen. During these past few weeks, I've forgiven myself. I think I've almost forgiven him." A feeling of lightness rose up within Avery. "His girlfriend was with him when he died. She was wearing this same bracelet at his funeral, and she was wearing it today."

The confession hung in the air. "I rushed out of the service, everyone convinced it was because I was distraught over his death."

"Avery, you were heartbroken."

"I'll never know if I could have forgiven him, if we could have lived up to our vows." She paused. "Til death do us part."

"Is that why you shut yourself off for a year?"

Avery's head bobbed. "People pity me because I lost my husband, but they don't know I lost him long before that accident." She clasped her fingers. "I've never even told my father. I was too ashamed."

"Honey, it's a miracle you haven't exploded."

"I knew who Cres was the day I walked down the aisle, the moment I saw Thora sitting in the church, her eyes red from crying. If I had been braver, I would have kept on walking."

"That would have been mighty hard for anyone." Kathleen leaned forward.

"But easier than all that followed."

"Was today the first time you've seen her?"

"I followed Cres once and saw them having dinner, but I never told him." She shook her head. "He reduced me to one of those weak wives paralyzed by uncertainty."

"You're not weak, Avery."

"I saw her the night Davis and I went out too. She was with a child who looks like Cres."

Kathleen drew in her breath. "No wonder your date crashed and burned."

"I'm pretty sure the Broussards don't know about their grandson." Avery looked up. "I've prayed about this. I don't know what to do." She plunged ahead. "There's something I have to tell you, but it can never leave this room."

"You know you can trust me."

"Creswell Sr. was in New Orleans at the time of the accident, with . . . a family friend. I'm not sure if Evangeline ever heard that. Nor Ross." Avery stared at the bracelet. "I found out when I got the call about the wreck. I know it's why Creswell wants me away from Samford. Maybe why Evangeline does. They tried to pay me to leave town, but I haven't cashed the check. He's getting nervous."

Kathleen reached over and stroked Howie. "It's possible you've rendered me speechless."

"I don't know what to do with all these secrets. I need to tell my dad about Cres and me. He'll be hurt."

"Cres's affair doesn't make you a bad person."

"Daddy wishes he had been here for me. He's always felt bad about moving. Maybe I'll go see him after the store business is settled. But the other . . . whew."

"Perhaps you should let that stay between the people involved."

She looked Kathleen in the eyes and shared the one secret that could ruin everything.

Chapter 31

$\mathcal{A}$ car coasted to the curb Tuesday after lunch as Avery wrestled the chalkboard from the sidewalk toward the store. Preparing the colorful listings was entertaining, but this thing was heavy. Two car doors slammed.

"Let me get that door for you," a woman said.

"May I help you?" Avery couldn't see around the sign.

"Let's hope so," the woman said.

"Are you closed?" a second voice said.

"Never." Avery gave a small laugh. "I'm working on the sign."

The two followed her into the store and stood inside the door. They looked around as though they had never seen a corner market before. Each wore pieces from designer lines that had been big sellers at the boutique.

"Oh," Avery said. "You're from The Fashion Group. I met you at Evangeline's shop."

The older woman nodded. "I'm Sharon Denton, and this is Jen Montgomery. You're Avery Broussard, right?"

"Good memory."

"Hard to forget," Jen said. "The customers keep asking when we're bringing you back."

"Jen's managing the store," Sharon said.

"Temporarily."

"Until we find a full-time replacement. These acquisitions are crucial." The two women eyed each other like bantam roosters about to fly into each other.

Avery gave a small cough. "It's nice to know I'm missed."

"According to the regulars, no one has an eye for color like you." Sharon glanced at Jen over her glasses.

"You must have spoiled them," Jen said.

"They do appreciate the personal touch." Avery tugged on her apron. "Although they wouldn't be as interested in my opinion if they saw me now."

"Very girl-next-doorish," Jen said. "That's in."

Avery choked back a laugh. *Wait until Kathleen hears that I am "in."*

Jen eyed Avery as though she were a mannequin in a window. "It's the look I'm putting together for our next catalog."

Avery kept her face blank. "Would you like something to eat? Or drink?"

"You serve food?" Jen's mouth dropped open.

"Good Louisiana food. Breakfast and lunch six days a week."

Sharon looked at the menu posted on the wall behind the register. "Do you honestly have homemade fried pies?"

"The best around."

Sharon closed her eyes for a moment. "I haven't had one of those since I was a kid."

"We have one chocolate left today." So much for her dessert tonight. Business was business.

Sharon patted her flat stomach. "I'm going to be naughty."

Jen gave a tinkling laugh. "Just water for me."

While Avery grabbed the pie and two bottles of water, Sharon and Jen walked around the store, stopping at the small collection of artwork from the Sweet Olive gallery. After Camille's first visit, Avery had began to display samples. In return, the gallery handed out menus with Magnolia Market's specials.

The partnership gave Avery energy, something lacking in her job at the boutique. Kathleen and Camille made her realize what she was missing.

"Are these original paintings?" Jen asked.

"By local artists," Avery said. "The gallery across the street has a terrific collection of regional folk art."

Sharon took a step back. "This reminds me of that area near downtown Dallas."

Jen nodded, looking at Avery. "They added shops and galleries, and people have snapped up the houses around there."

They are comparing Trumpet and Vine to a trendy neighborhood in Dallas?

"We've made a small start," Avery said, "but we're hopeful."

It hit her. *"Yet this I call to mind,"* the passage in Lamentations said, *"and therefore I have hope: Because of the Lord's great love we are not consumed, for his compassions never fail."*

She *was* hopeful.

"I suppose that answers that." Jen arched her carefully shaped eyebrows at Sharon. "We came by to check you out."

There was an uncomfortable pause. "I don't understand," Avery said.

"Forgive us." Sharon sat at another bistro table Kathleen had found at a flea market and patted the chair beside her. "Evangeline implied you—"

"Were a prima donna." Jen finished the sentence, her gaze falling on Avery's apron.

"She said you had issues after the loss of your husband, but that you'd be great for a store in a town like Santa Fe. Anywhere, really, but here."

Avery opened her mouth but couldn't summon criticism of her mother-in-law. She was beginning to think she owed Evangeline a huge thank-you. "That was a hard time for all of us. My work at the boutique was my refuge, as pathetic as that sounds."

"It's obvious you're doing a great job here," Jen said.

"This is temporary, but the break has been good for me."

Sharon nibbled at the fried pie like a fish eating a piece of bread in a pond. "Do you have any interest in going back into the clothing business?"

"Possibly." She drew a breath. The afternoon smells of coffee and lunch, and the basket of apples pleased her. January sunshine, a treat, glimmered off a shelf of canned goods in a kaleidoscope of color.

T. J.'s pickup pulled up front, and he hopped out and leaned over to pull out his tools.

The two women turned.

"Ooh la la," Jen said. "What have we here?"

"He's repairing the damage to the store." Avery's voice had grown frosty. "You were saying . . . ?"

"We're opening that Santa Fe store," Sharon said, "if you'd consider relocating."

Jen continued to stare at T. J. Maybe he would get right to work and not stop to say hello as he did most days.

Okay, every day.

"We also have plans for stores in Nashville and Little Rock," Sharon continued.

The bell tinkled as T. J. stepped in with a piece of canvas in his hand. "Believe it or not, I found those stripes you like," he called out, his eyes scanning the store. Avery loved the way he looked for her like that.

Then his gaze picked up the women, and he grimaced. "I didn't know you were in a meeting. I'll show you later."

"You can show me anytime," Jen said under her breath.

Avery wanted to punch her, but before she could shoo T. J. away from the pair, Sharon spoke. "Come join us." She almost cooed the words.

"These women are from The Fashion Group," Avery said, making introductions.

"We're trying to drag Avery back to the clothing business," Jen said, "but I see why she might want to stay in Samford."

T. J. looked stunned. "You're thinking of leaving?"

"No. Not yet. I'm n-not sure," Avery stammered.

"Oh," T. J. said.

"There's always the local store," Sharon said. "Jen's tired of filling in."

"It'd be great to have you back," Jen added.

"You'd go back to Evangeline's?" The look on T. J.'s face had shifted into a full frown.

"I don't—"

"Sorry." T. J. held up his hand. "I didn't mean to butt in. I'd better get to work."

Sharon and Jen leaned forward, their attention shifting from T. J. to Avery.

The dairy case hummed behind them.

"Nice meeting you." T. J. ran his fingers under the collar of his shirt and almost sprinted toward the door.

"My, my." Sharon picked up her pie and licked a glob of chocolate off the side.

"Even if you won't leave town," Jen said, "will you take your old store back? Please?"

A dozen thoughts danced through Avery's mind, but she couldn't keep her eyes off T. J. working out front. So she settled on the only thing she knew for sure.

"I'll pray about it."

Kathleen shuffled through the back door of the store, her black pants and dressy blouse a contrast to the jeans she usually favored. Her hair was in its unruly brown bob. Howie whined at her entrance.

"If it's Tuesday, I must have been turned down for another job," she said to Avery, who was sitting at the register. "Swoosh. They're looking for someone who's plugged into *digital.* That's code for someone right out of college."

"Any business would be fortunate to have you. They didn't deserve you." Avery looked back at the notebook. "I'm glad you didn't get that job."

"Thanks for taking it so hard," Kathleen said dryly. Stepping into the stockroom, she said something to the dog and came out with her apron on.

Avery didn't get up from the stool behind the counter. She

nibbled on the end of the pencil and tilted her head toward the rear of the store. "Don't worry. You'll find the right job at the right time."

"I hate it when you do that."

"What?"

"Quoting my own words is against the rules of friendship."

"Oh, okay. Got it." Avery straightened. "Sorry you didn't get the job."

Kathleen's eyes widened. "Is that the calculator?" She looked past Avery. "When did you do that?"

A slow smile came to Avery's lips. "Which *that* are you talking about? The new products T. J. brought by to expand the Louisiana corner? Or maybe you're referring to the new— hand-lettered, might I add—menu?"

"I've only been gone since lunchtime."

Avery gnawed on her pencil. "*I* got a job offer this afternoon."

"Oh, that makes me feel better. Thanks for sharing. From *whom*?"

"The Fashion Group fashionistas paid me a call."

"While I was out interviewing? That's just wrong." Kathleen's shoulders slumped. "So you're leaving me?"

Avery tapped her temple with her index finger. "I've been *thinking*." She moved the calculator and notebook from her lap and stood. "We're on to something here."

Drawing back, Kathleen put her hands on her hips. "You're on something all right, but I haven't figured out what."

"Something weird's happening—"

"I can see that."

Avery moved to the chair and patted the stool. "Sit on your throne, and let me explain."

"Tell me you didn't take a job." Kathleen plopped down.

"We know sales are improving, right? And profits are better?"

"I keep the books," Kathleen grumbled. "I don't need a lesson in accounting. Did you take the job?"

Avery tossed her a grin. "It just doesn't seem that appealing."

Chapter 32

$\mathcal{T}$he woman, seventy if she was a day, waltzed into the store, a guy with a camera on her heels.

"We'd like to look around," she said before Avery, polishing the produce, could speak. Wearing a long putty-colored linen smock, leggings, and a pair of running shoes, she had sunglasses atop her gray hair and a pair of owlish spectacles perched low on her nose. Her thin build and pointed nose gave her the look of an unhappy greyhound.

The photographer, dressed in black jeans and a black turtle-neck, inhaled and headed their way. "Do you have any biscuits left?"

"I'm sorry. We sold out early today. People were extra hungry for a Wednesday." Kathleen smiled and set down her half-eaten dish of red beans and rice, leftovers from the lunch special.

"I was about to practice my beignets," Avery interjected. "If you have a minute—"

"Louis," the older woman snapped from the back corner. "What do you think of the light in here?"

The guy looked from Avery to the woman and back at Kathleen. "Do you put powdered sugar on them?"

"What's a beignet without powdered sugar?" Avery said.

"I'll take 'em—and would it be all right if I snapped a few photos?"

"No problem," Avery said, inviting a small frown from Kathleen.

"Louis!"

"On my way." He adjusted his lens as he sauntered across the store.

"Practicing *beignets*?" Kathleen whispered. "Did you decide that before or after the door opened?" She stared at the pair poking around the store. "I'm not showing off for some snooty stranger."

"Help me out here." Avery waved a whisk. "I've never made beignets on my own."

"No whisk, no gain, I suppose." Kathleen grinned. "That lady is way too scrawny to be your guinea pig."

"You don't know who she is, do you?"

Kathleen put her finger to the corner of her mouth. "Hmm. Oh, that's right. She used to drop by the manufacturing plant from time to time."

Avery threw her a dirty look and glanced back at where the woman was fingering a pottery spoon rest. "She's studying one of the items from the New Wine mission. Wouldn't it be cool if we could sell more of those?"

Shooting her a glare, Kathleen picked up a wooden spoon but didn't move toward the mixing bowls. "You're turning into some kind of merchant missionary, aren't you?"

"This could be a big break for Martha and Bill—and for us,"

she said through clenched lips, trying to hear what the visitors were talking about.

"Beignets it is." Kathleen waved the spoon. "And who do I have the pleasure of cooking for?"

Avery was in motion in the kitchen, one eye on the store. "That's Dixie Wilder-Ferguson."

"Why didn't you say so?" Kathleen rolled her eyes. "Never heard of her."

"She's the Queen of the South, columnist for *Best of the South* magazine and host of the TV show. Plus, she has a whole series of coffee-table books on southern life."

"Quit fooling around, and heat up the grease," Kathleen said. "Grab the powdered sugar while I mix up the batter." Pulling out a stainless-steel bowl, she grabbed the flour in a fluid move. "We've about used all the flour. Probably need to make another store run."

Avery reached for a large yellow crock bowl—like something from a grandmother's pantry—from a shelf over the sink and replaced the stainless-steel bowl, the flour landing perfectly in place.

"So now we're doing beignets and synchronized cooking?"

"It'll photograph better," Avery whispered.

A smile flickered across Kathleen's lips, and she inspected Avery from head to toe. "Get us both a clean apron while you're at it."

Avery started toward the stockroom, and Kathleen spoke again in a hushed voice. "Take your hair down, and put on lipstick too. You need some color."

"Aye, aye, Captain." She couldn't hold back a grin.

Howie, asleep on the cot, raised his head and flopped over onto his back. "Not now, pal. We've got company."

By the time Avery returned to the counter, a batch of

beignets floated in the hot grease. "Don't take them out until they're golden brown. And let them cool, but not too much, before you roll them in the powdered sugar," Kathleen said.

"Can't beignets be your deal?" Avery scanned the room for their guests. "I'm still trying to get the hang of fried pies."

"Miss!" Dixie held up one of the small figurines her father had sent to sell. "Are these imported?" Her sharp nose wrinkled.

"Yes, ma'am. They provide scholarships for children in Haiti."

Dixie made a tsking sound. "When I mentioned I was coming to Samford, my sorority sister told me about your store, said everything was regional." She turned to the photographer. "Let's get on over to the art gallery."

"They're all hand-carved."

"That's admirable, but not what I had in mind."

The two were headed to the door when Kathleen ladled the beignets onto paper towels spread on the old wood counter. "Sir!" Avery called out. "Don't forget your beignets."

"Louis." Dixie's tone was scolding, but the photographer was already loping back to the counter.

Avery swallowed. "Ma'am, would you like a sample?"

The photographer threw Dixie a pleading look, and she sighed. "Came all this way. Might as well."

"If you'll have a seat at our bistro table, Mrs. Broussard will bring them to you," Kathleen said in a syrupy voice. She looked over at Avery. "Smile," she said through clenched teeth. "You know how to handle her type."

Avery pasted on her biggest smile and yanked out paper doilies she had bought at the Dollar Store. After arranging them on one of the old café plates from a shelf in the back, she glided toward the two. "Would you like coffee?"

"Made in Shreveport," Kathleen jumped in. "Roasted and ground by a woman entrepreneur."

Avery bit back a smile. Kathleen always came through in a pinch.

"I'll have coffee if it won't be too much trouble," Louis said.

"No trouble at all." Avery looked for something other than paper cups to serve the coffee in.

"These just came out of the dishwasher." Kathleen stuck two of the mission's handmade pottery mugs in her hand.

"Excellent." Even if they didn't have a dishwasher.

The columnist's back straightened, and she pulled an old-fashioned reporter's notebook out of her canvas purse, then paused to take a bite of a beignet.

"In fact," Avery continued, "many of our lines help those in need, at the local New Wine mission and an orphanage in Haiti."

Kathleen gave her the *okay* sign and bit back a grin.

Dixie's thin lips almost disappeared, but she didn't lay the beignet down. "I'm interested in the best of the south, not an import store."

She and Evangeline would make quite a pair.

"Our menu is entirely southern," Kathleen said. "In fact, we're working on a cookbook with a combination of recipes from the owners and some of our own."

We are? Avery mouthed, but Kathleen's gaze had dropped to the floor. She looked alarmed.

"Excellent beignets." The photographer blew powdered sugar all over his shirt.

"If you don't mind—" Dixie said.

From behind the counter, Kathleen made a moan of dismay and lunged toward the back of the store.

What in the world?

Avery's gaze flew to the stockroom door, which stood ajar. She had been in such a hurry, she had not shut it firmly.

For Howie, Kathleen's movement signified a game of chase, and he yelped and flew around the counter, then skidded down the aisle of canned and paper goods.

"Howie," Avery said in a low, stern voice. "Stay." Which led him to run to her, barking with his aren't-I-a-smart-boy? bark.

The magazine spread was evaporating before her eyes—squeezed out by worthy Haitian art and a spoiled dog.

"Oh, aren't you a cutie?" Dixie cooed, leaning over. Her haughty mask softened, and she made kissing noises. Howie, never one to miss a snack, licked a stray spot of sugar off the woman's face and put his paws up in her lap.

The photographer wiped his hands on his pants, leaving white prints, and grabbed his camera. He snapped photographs as though he had caught Brad Pitt and Angelina Jolie in the midst of their wedding vows.

Kathleen gasped and Avery froze.

"Fantastic, Dixie," he murmured, moving from his chair to squat beside the woman. "Just a few more. We can do an online photo gallery from these."

"We don't usually let him—" Avery started, but Kathleen gave a quick shake of her head.

Dixie stood, giggled like a teenager as Howie jumped around her.

"I think you've got a fan," Avery said. Kathleen stifled a chuckle.

"I write about the south." She paused long enough for Avery's heart to drop. "I like the personality of your store."

"Oh, we know who you are, ma'am." Kathleen nudged Avery

closer to Dixie. "My friend wanted Magnolia Market to have the homey feel of country stores of the rural south. Avery's a big fan of your work. Avery Broussard."

Dixie scribbled in big bubble writing in her notebook. "How did you come to be business partners?"

"I ran into Kathleen one day."

Kathleen guffawed. "And we decided to enjoy life for a change."

"We're not the owners," Avery added. "We're filling in, building on the foundation laid by a fine couple. Would you like to see their photograph?" She pointed to the black-and-white picture of Martha and Bill standing behind the old wooden counter, the cash register drawer open on their first day in business.

"My goodness, it looks the same." Dixie paused. "Only cleaner."

"Thank you." Avery nodded.

Kathleen appeared at her back, holding two small dishes of red beans and rice. "Would it be too much trouble for y'all to taste these for me?" She made a clucking noise. "I'm trying to decide if they're too spicy."

Enough with the Martha Stewart act, Kathleen.

The market's beans and rice, made with Gabriela's spice mix, were the best Avery had ever eaten, including down in Lafayette. With cheap ingredients, they were a high-profit item. Customers raved about them.

"I suppose we have time for a bite," Dixie said, while Louis took a sample.

Dixie didn't smile when she handed back the dish and fork, but as she bent to pet Howie again, she spoke. "The seasoning in that dish is unusual." She paused long enough for Avery's nerves to surge. "I'd like to print your recipe."

"We're launching a line of those seasonings," Avery blurted

out. "They're made by a young local woman. She wants to go to cooking school."

"You people certainly have a lot of projects going." Dixie scribbled something in her notebook and glanced at her Cartier watch.

"We're never short on ideas," Kathleen said. "Just capital."

"We need help." Avery's face grew warm with the proclamation.

A frown flew onto the columnist's face. "I'm not involved in the business side of things."

"How'd you get your start?"

Kathleen stifled a gasp at Avery's blunt question, and the photographer's eyes widened. Even Howie seemed to recognize something had shifted, giving a sharp bark.

Dixie looked at the dog again before meeting Avery's gaze. "Like you two. A friend introduced me to the right people, gave me a hand." She nodded for the photographer to open the door for her. "I suppose," she said, her nose once more tipped up, "you might contact the magazine. It has a push to support businesswomen, and they might have a scholarship for your spice girl."

Without a wave, she got in the car, pointing to the gallery as they drove away.

"So that's the Queen of the South." Kathleen grabbed Howie by the face and kissed him on the mouth. "And we are her loyal subjects."

Avery burst out laughing. "Oh, Queen Dixie, would you like to sample our poor, pitiful beans and rice?"

"How about a beignet?" Kathleen mocked, tears streaming down her face. "And did you know we're planning to write a cookbook?"

Howie jumped up and started running around the store.

While Kathleen chased the dog, Avery lettered a sign about the girls at the orphanage in Haiti and added a donation box next to the "imported" items.

"Did she actually say 'spice girl'?" Kathleen asked.

"Can you believe that woman?" Avery wiped the powdered sugar off the bistro table. "But I'm going to find Gabriela a scholarship and help her get started."

Chapter 33

$\mathcal{A}$very lugged two flats of early strawberries from the car, inhaling their earthy smell.

Between the Thursday breakfast and lunch crowds, she had dashed over to the Cypress Parish Cooperative Extension office to pick up the berries, sold as a fund-raiser for the 4-H club.

"We should have ordered more of those." Kathleen took one flat from her. "I could make great jelly with these."

"Are we going to add homemade jam to our product line?" Avery teased.

"Maybe we should. I could make chowchow too, if you can find us a deal on homegrown tomatoes."

"Are you serious?"

"Halfway."

"Bud probably knows someone in Sweet Olive who'll have tomatoes this summer." Avery set the strawberries on the shelf by the sink and pulled out her notebook. "That might help another local vendor."

Kathleen held up a pint-size green basket of berries and

looked back at Avery. "Are you the same woman who crashed into me in a snit over a biscuit?"

Avery let out a peal of laughter, her heart lighter than it had been in months. Arranging a few pints of strawberries in what had developed into the fresh produce section, she glanced up as a carload of attractive young women pulled near the front of the store.

Dressed in bright-colored jeans and gauzy shirts, they entered the market in a swirl of laughter and conversation.

"Ladies who lunch," Kathleen murmured, moving over to the grill.

Avery had known it was bound to happen, but the sight of a cluster of her former customers made her feel off balance, like running into a group of church friends in a nightclub.

"Good morning." Maybe her smile didn't look as forced as it felt. "May I help you?"

"We're browsing," one said, flitting toward the Louisiana corner without looking at her.

"Avery?" Another of the women approached the counter. "So this is where you ran off to!"

"Hi, Lynette. Good to see you."

"You look great. How *are* you?"

Avery looked down at her apron, glad she had worn her favorite shirt and slacks. "I'm fine."

"I miss you so much at Evangeline's. The new girls should ask you to give them lessons." She glanced around. "Although you probably don't have time now that you're *famous*."

"I hope you haven't run out of biscuits because I spent an extra thirty minutes at the gym so I can have one," the wife of a prominent obstetrician said. "I'm Shelley Dixon."

Avery knew who she was. She'd whispered loudly in the boutique that Avery was the woman who couldn't hold on to her husband. That memory didn't bother Avery today. "How'd that dress work for your Christmas party?"

"It was a big hit. I can't believe you remember that." Her pale pink lips made a moue of disapproval. "They don't have many cute outfits at the boutique these days. It seems kind of... flat."

"Ooh, girls, look at these fresh Louisiana strawberries, and so early in the season," one of the other women said. "The grocery store still has the ones from California."

"The lunch group is going to be so jealous that we got here first." Shelley drifted toward the berries.

"If the food's as good as the Queen of the South says," Lynette said, "we can bring them here next time."

Perplexed, Avery looked at her. "So you know Dixie Wilder-Ferguson?"

"I wish. Maybe you can introduce me."

Shelley giggled, migrating back with a basket of berries and a package of homemade peanut brittle that a local church had brought in to sell. "We're on a birthday outing today. I happened to see Dixie's tweet as we were leaving the house."

"Her tweet?" Kathleen moved from the grill, where she had been conspicuously silent. She said the word *tweet* as though it were an illegal drug.

Shelley nodded, looking past Kathleen. "Is Howie here today?"

"Howie?" Again Kathleen's voice was bemused.

"What an adorable mascot," Lynette said.

"Mascot?" Avery said.

"Dixie linked to the pictures of your shop," Lynette said. "The World's Only Biscuit Boutique and right here in Samford!

We would have driven to New Orleans or Dallas for something this fun."

"She named your handmade Louisiana items a Southern Top Pick of the Week. Those mugs will make the perfect hostess gifts for my niece's bridal shower," Shelley said.

"Is this all you have?" The other woman held up a royal blue mug.

"We're getting more," Avery said. *If we can stay in business.* "I could take your number and drop them by your house."

"We deliver?" Kathleen murmured from behind her.

"We do now," Avery said between her teeth.

"Look at this jewelry." Shelley bent to read Avery's new sign. "This is so sweet. These help orphans in Haiti." She slipped a bracelet on her arm. "Wouldn't this be a precious graduation gift?"

By the time the quartet left, they had cleared out the mug inventory, decimated the Haitian jewelry, and announced plans to bring their lunch bunch in for gumbo. By closing time, the Samford mission crafts were sold-out, crumbs remained of the daily specials, and Avery and Kathleen were trying to get online to see what Dixie had posted.

Chapter 34

𝒯.𝒥. and Bud stepped off the elevator Thursday afternoon and walked down the spotless corridor. A tree decorated with purple, green, and gold ornaments stood by the nurse's station, and a woman in scrubs was typing on a laptop on a rolling cart.

"Do you think Bill's found a buyer?" T. J. asked, the silence making him whisper.

"I suspect he's trying to figure out how to care for Martha and run the store at the same time. I sure can't see him letting that place be torn down."

A nurse stepped out from behind a counter as they approached, several strands of Mardi Gras beads around her neck. "Martha and Bill are in the sunroom." She dropped a string of beads around Bud's neck, then slipped a strand around T. J.'s neck and winked. "We're having a Mardi Gras party today."

As they walked off, Bud shook his head. "Oh, to be a young man again. She practically throws the beads at me and all but asks you out while putting yours on."

T. J. rolled his eyes, took the beads off, and stuffed them in his pocket. "You're almost as bad—no, make that worse—than my mother about matchmaking. And you're fifty-seven, for heaven's sake. Quit acting like you just rolled into town in your wagon."

"I don't always see eye to eye with Minnie, but I'd like to see you settle down." He stopped walking. "Have you talked to Avery this week?"

T. J. stuffed his hands in his pockets. "Could you have told me you were going to meddle before I agreed to go into business with you?"

"With that attitude, I'll take that as a no."

"Between our other jobs and the mission, I have a lot going on."

"If you're as interested in Avery as you seem to be, you shouldn't be too busy for her." Bud's voice was patient. "You've known her how long now? A month? Isn't it time you asked her on a date?"

"If you're so keen on her, why don't *you* ask her out?"

"I've got my eye on Ginny Guidry." Bud winked. "But if she won't have me, maybe I will."

T. J. shot him a grin. "Don't even think about it. I'll talk to Avery as soon as I can."

Martha sat in a wheelchair by the window, eating a piece of King Cake, a remnant of the Mardi Gras party.

"I got the baby." Bill held up the tiny plastic doll. "Martha says I have to host the next party, and I ain't in a partying mood."

"Cheerful as ever, I see." Bud bypassed Bill to kiss Martha on the cheek.

"He's relieved I'm out of bed," Martha said in a weak voice, "but he won't let on."

T. J. shook hands with Bill, his gaze moving to a man of about forty who had risen to his feet nearby.

"This is my nephew, Greg Vaughan. He's helping us decide what to do about the store."

"Greggie owns a used-car dealership outside of Little Rock."

T. J. bit the inside of his cheek, trying not to laugh at the childish nickname Martha used. He imagined Greggie in shorts and kneesocks.

"Late-model vehicles," Greg said. "I can't stay in Samford much longer."

"It was thoughtful of you to come down at all," Bud said, his tone wry.

Wearing a pair of jeans, starched and creased, and a V-neck sweater over a shirt, Greg looked like an aging version of the preppy boys T. J. had gone to school with. His loafers were leather with tassels, and his hair made a weird loop on his forehead.

T. J., who gave people the benefit of the doubt, disliked him instantly.

"I want an immediate update on the repairs. I'll authorize enough renovation to keep the buyer on the hook."

Greg's manner reminded T. J. of Willie when he got a piece of particularly good meat, although that wasn't a fair comparison for Willie.

"It's a little late for that," Bud said in a sharp tone he seldom used. "The new front was *authorized* by Bill, and T. J.'s almost finished with it." He grinned at Martha. "You're going to be pleased."

"Oh." A smile came to Martha's cracked lips.

"Ain't going to happen. Tell them, Uncle Bill."

"Greg's found us a good buyer." Bill's voice was unusually subdued. "The fellow plans to tear down the old building and use the lot. He wants to close the deal by early next week."

"But the changes to the front are almost finished." T. J. felt like someone had set off a Roman candle in his gut. "And business has picked up considerably."

"I want to make that Broussard woman pay and get Uncle Bill and Aunt Martha out of the grocery business. Now."

"Her name's Avery, and she's the only thing that has kept Magnolia Market going," T. J. said.

"Now, Greg, calm down," Bill said. "That gal's done more in a month than Martha and I were able to do in a year. And she sends food, keeps me posted on sales. Always dropping something off for Martha. Hasn't even taken a salary."

"Avery's a fine young woman," Bud said, looking at T. J.

Greg turned toward Bill. "Don't give her too much credit after all the trouble she caused." He leaned closer and patted Martha's hand. "We'll get this taken care of and get you situated in a nice spot."

"Our condo in Hot Springs?" she asked.

"Or something every bit as nice. Once these two tell us what our building's worth with the repairs."

"Ross Broussard would be better for that," Bud said abruptly.

"Oh, right, the CPA's son." Greg's smile gleamed, annoying T. J. further. "Is Creswell Broussard Sr. as loaded as he looks? He sees that whole corner going light industry."

"I so hoped we'd find someone who wanted to keep Magnolia Market open," Martha said. "I love that place."

"How many times do we have to talk about this? Those old

stores are worthless. People don't shop at places like that any-more." Greg glanced at Bill. "We're lucky I found a buyer. That store could sit vacant like that church across the street. Then where would you be?"

T. J. wanted to knock the smug look off his face.

"You have to look out for yourself, Uncle Bill, because no one else is going to."

"Ironic," T. J. murmured.

"You're right. Martha and I will sell." Bill put his arm around her and gave her shoulder a squeeze with such tenderness that T. J. had to clear his throat. "I'll take care of it."

Walking to the parking lot, Bud looked at T. J. "Didn't think much of Greg, did you?"

"He reminds me of Cres."

"It'd be a shame to see that old store go, wouldn't it?"

"To quote Greggie, it ain't gonna happen."

C⁓

Avery jabbed her finger at the paper after she digested the finan-cial information in front of her.

"Look at this. Our revenue isn't coming from traditional things: bread, milk. It's coming from things we've added."

"That's hard to believe." Kathleen glanced from the paper to the glass case. "Biscuit sales have increased 30 percent since we added the Biscuit of the Day."

"Your fried pies are raking in the dough—pun very much intended—and that honey from that farmer out in Sweet Olive sold out. Sold out!"

Kathleen cocked her head. "So this is what you look like when you're happy."

"And that's not all. Look at this." Avery flipped to the back page of the notebook and shoved it forward.

"Hmm. This is either the mailing list for your fancy boutique or the guest list to a Mardi Gras ball."

"You're close." Avery reached for the notebook. "When I started here, I jotted down the names of customers, to help me remember. That first week it was mostly regulars, people like you who worked, or used to work, in the neighborhood. But look at this." She slid her finger to the bottom of the second column of names. "After week one, our customers shifted, widened. Thanks to the godsend of Dixie's visit and word of mouth, we kept the regulars, but we've added—"

"The see-and-be-seen crowd." Kathleen walked to the register and punched a button. The drawer flew open, and she reached beneath the tray of cash and pulled out a sheaf of old-fashioned ledger sheets. "I found these in the back of the safe." She thrust the pages at Avery.

A neat list of months and years chronicled the expenses, revenue, and net profits the store had made for fifty years. "This goes back to the beginning." Avery flipped through. "Wow, this place was a cash cow."

"Keep going."

At the back was a new page, a computer graph, a black line climbing and then plunging, with a minuscule jump in recent months.

Avery chewed on her lip.

"These"—Kathleen pointed—"these are our sales."

"So we've turned the corner?"

"It's not much time but the numbers are solid."

Avery grabbed Kathleen's hands, the ledger sheets between them. "Do you know what this means?"

"That you're way more organized than I gave you credit for?"

"Our offer to Bill can work."

"I'm listening." Kathleen's face was impassive.

"Don't you think we're creating something special here? That we might be part of something bigger?"

"If it would save me from another job interview where a kid younger than my daughter tells me I don't have the right skill set, it'd sound downright magical."

"Think about those numbers from the early years. We could make a lot of money."

"Whoa," Kathleen said. "The world's changed a lot. People go to big grocery stores or discount places. Our sales are increasing but not fast enough."

Avery's gaze dropped to the chart.

"Not for what Bill would want for a down payment and not with Greg nipping at our heels. We'd need more cash to keep it open, and it'd take months—maybe years—before it could support both of us."

"I'm going to figure out a way." Avery hesitated. "I've lost too much in my life. I'm not going to lose this."

"I'm in."

Avery stuck the sales figures back in the register but kept the overview. "Kathleen, my friend, we're going to fill a niche on this corner. One biscuit at a time."

Chapter 35

*H*owie growled, soft at first and then louder, straining on the leash.

Avery paused, the key in the lock of the store's back door. "You sound serious, fellow." She looked around. Hers was the only car in the alley, and she hadn't noticed anything amiss when she drove past the front.

Everything looked pretty much as it had for the month she had been opening the market.

But Howie never made threatening sounds. Pushing the door open, her heart beating faster than usual, she sniffed. A trace of men's cologne, similar to what Cres had worn, hung in the air. Howie nosed around the small hallway, his growl intensifying, until he jerked at the leash and dashed fully into the store.

"Howie! Wait!"

"What in the world?" Greg jumped up on the counter next to the register, Avery's notebook in his right hand. Howie leaped up, looking like he might fly onto the counter at any moment. "What's that mutt doing in here?"

"I was wondering the same thing." Walking to the back door, Avery flipped on every light in the store. "You are getting mud on my clean counter." She picked up Howie's leash. "Good boy." She patted his head, the motion calming her trembling fingers.

Howie quit growling but stood on alert, his tail still, his ears sticking up. His gaze never left Greg.

Glancing down at his shoes, caked in red Louisiana clay, Greg sneered. "Uncle Bill says you are trying to talk him into passing on the deal I brokered." He still stood on the counter, looming over her. "I'm inspecting the area. Assessing our worth."

"At five o'clock in the morning?" Her eyes narrowed. "Give me my notebook."

He stuck it behind him, like an overgrown bully playing a game of keep-away. "I parked over at that vacant church. They could use some landscaping." He stomped his foot, throwing more mud onto the counter and floor.

"Get out." She took a step closer. Howie moved with her, growling once.

"You're the one who will be leaving." Sweat popped out on his brow. "That old coot may be softening, but I am still in control."

He held up the notebook, as though offering it to her. But when she reached for it, he snatched it back.

All of her store information was in that notebook in detail. Ideas, profit margins, suppliers—and at least a dozen original recipes. "That's my property. I may not own the store yet, but that belongs to me."

He flipped through the pages. "You ought to be ashamed of yourself, stealing from poor old people."

She was tempted to let Howie loose. "You're the one trying to take their money."

He tapped on a page. "This biscuit recipe belonged to my aunt, which makes it my family property. If you want to keep using it, you'll have to pay me." He smirked. "Or I'll file a cease-and-desist claim against you."

She glanced at the clock. "File whatever you want to file, but I've got to make biscuits if we're going to open on time."

Drawing a deep breath, she tugged on Howie's leash and started around the counter. Not usually allowed back there, Howie gave a quick bark and sniffed, sticking his nose up under the sink.

"I'll be going." Greg hopped over the counter to the other side, then headed for the front door. "I have to prepare to meet with my attorney." He waved the notebook in the air. "This will come in handy."

But before he could exit, the door flew open. "Avery? I saw the lights—" T. J. stopped as Greg attempted to walk past him, then looked to the back when Howie gave a quick, happy bark. "What's going on here?"

Superman himself would not have been more welcome at the moment. T. J. wore sweatpants and a T-shirt that showed off his broad shoulders. His brown hair was a damp mess.

Greg appeared quite the wimp next to him. "I came by to check on my property." He inched toward the door.

T. J. blocked his exit, throwing him a glare that caused a flicker of fear to run across Greg's sweaty face. "Did he hurt you?" T. J. growled.

"No. I found him going through our things."

She took a step toward them, but T. J. gave his head a quick shake. "I want my notebook back," she said.

Greg took one step, and T. J. shoved him against the door, pinning his arms behind him.

"If you don't release me this instant, I'll have you arrested for assault. She doesn't own this place yet."

"Give her the notebook."

"Everything in here is going to belong to me anyway." Greg sneered. "Your little girlfriend will not get away with stealing my property."

T. J. threw her a questioning look.

"I told you," she said. "Kathleen and I made an offer to buy the store."

The corner of T. J.'s mouth quirked upward. "I'm more interested in the girlfriend comment."

She blushed.

"Give me a freakin' break," Greg said.

"Avery, call the police."

"You'll be the one behind bars," Greg said, but he sailed the notebook across the room. It landed on top of the fountain-drink machine, where it teetered for a moment before sliding to the floor.

"You obnoxious—" T. J. squeezed him tighter.

"I'll have her evicted." Greg's lip curled under. "She has no signatures, and I'm family. I have more right to this than she does."

T. J. looked back at Avery, Greg still pinned to the door like a moth in a science project.

Unexpectedly, a smile came to her mouth. Cres had never defended her with such fervor in all the time they were together. "Just let him go, T. J. He's not worth our trouble."

T. J. did not relax his grip.

"I've been wanting to tell Bill about the money Greg's stolen." She looked over at the cash register drawer standing ajar. "How pathetic a man is that?"

Howie dashed from around the counter, leash sliding across the floor, and sank his teeth into Greg's leg. While T. J. grabbed the dog, moving slowly to do so, Avery retrieved her notebook.

Walking to where Greg sat on the floor, she ripped a page out, wadded it up, and threw it at him. "Here's your ancestral biscuit recipe. Turns out my mother's was much better."

c—

Avery pulled out the big metal bowl, her hands still shaking.

T. J. leaned against the counter, wishing he could walk around the counter and hold her until she calmed down. Or longer.

"Are you sure we should have called the police?" Avery threw him an agitated look.

"Absolutely," Jazz said. "You should have notified us sooner that someone has been entering the premises after hours." She patted T. J. on the arm. "Thank goodness you noticed the lights."

"That was a blessing." Avery added flour without a measuring cup in sight. "But Greg was right. Bill hasn't committed yet. It's like a bad replay of the boutique sale."

"You have to fight for this," T. J. said, enticed by the way she made biscuits.

She tossed in a pinch of baking soda and salt. Her hair was pulled up in a knot on her head, and when she brushed a stray piece from her face, she left a dusting of flour.

Darn, she was pretty.

And stubborn.

His heart had just about stopped when he noticed the store lights blazing and saw the man inside.

"What will happen with the report Greg filed?" Avery asked, not looking up from the lump of dough.

"It's a gray area since he claims to have been acting on the owner's behalf." Jazz looked toward the storeroom. "You may be cited for that dog bite, but I kind of doubt it."

"I guess we should leave him at home," Avery said.

"No way!" T. J.'s exclamation drew a raised eyebrow from Jazz. "No telling what Greg would have done to Avery if Howie hadn't been here."

"And you." Jazz stared at the pinches of dough lining the baking sheet. "I wish I could stay for one of those, but I'd better go."

"Stop by later. I'll save you one. Today we have green-onion sausage from that plant in Stonewall."

"Count on it." Jazz walked a couple of steps toward the door and turned. "You going to stay for a while, T. J.?"

"You're kidding, right?"

Jazz gave him a smile. "You're in good hands, Avery."

The screen door slammed behind her, the room quiet.

"So," he said.

She looked at him, a question in her eyes.

"We need to talk."

"Before I open?"

His head moved up and down slowly.

She bit her bottom lip. "Have a seat, and I'll get you a glass of tea."

Sitting at the fancy little table she had arranged in the corner, T. J. drew in a deep breath.

"It's almost time for the breakfast rush." She lowered herself to the edge of the dainty chair. "Are you going to lecture me about being careful?"

"No." The word was abrupt. "This may not be the best time or place, but I can't put this off any longer." He reached out and touched her hand. "I want you to trust me."

"I do trust you."

"I was on the wild side when I was a teenager—and through college. I liked gambling—the horses, cards, casinos in Shreveport, sporting events." He shrugged. "I figured I'd give my mother something worth being upset about."

"T. J. . . ."

"I don't want there to be any secrets between us, Avery." His attention was focused on her. "Bud helped me figure out that I should do more with my life. But when I figured it out, I wanted to get as far away as I could."

"The job in Seattle?"

"It was either there or Anchorage." He twisted his lips. "A little over a year ago, my parents had some trouble. I knew it was time for me to come home, to prove to them—and myself—I was a man to count on." He held a long breath. "The incident involved your in-laws."

"I know." She set her fingers over his mouth. "Let's agree to trust each other and go from there."

He put his hand up to hers. "Are you sure?"

When she nodded, he placed a kiss on her palm.

"I've never even been on a date with you, but . . ." He hesitated. "Avery, I'm crazy about you."

She smiled. "Does this mean you're about to ask me out?"

"Oh yes." He threw her that wicked grin, the one that crinkled the skin around his eyes. The one that made her heart beat faster every time.

Chapter 36

_K_athleen adjusted the burner on the fifty-year-old stove, down, then up again. "I haven't been this nervous since I gave birth."

"I think it might actually happen." Avery inhaled. "If it doesn't, I'm eating every one of those meat pies."

"Not without me you aren't." Kathleen added more of Gabriela's seasoning to the beef. "Hopefully we'll be eating to celebrate, though, not to drown our sorrows."

"Greg wants his hands on that money pretty bad. He won't like the new plan."

"It doesn't matter what he likes."

Avery shrugged. "One way or the other, it'll work out."

"I hate it when people say that." Kathleen put one hand on her hip.

"It will. Our purchase had better go through, though I officially turned down the Fashion Group."

Kathleen stirred faster. "Things are coming together."

Avery filled the sink with hot, soapy water. "I still don't know how this place will support two of us, so I said I might be available for seasonal work." She winked. "Just in case."

Kathleen looked toward the front of the store. "Ugh."

Avery turned, her sight blocked by a shelf. "What?"

"You might want to dry off those dishpan hands. We appear to have a gentleman caller."

"The beloved nephew?"

"Nope."

"Don't tell me it's Creswell," Avery said. "Because if it is, I may stick my head under the faucet and drown myself."

"Not the father-in-law. But by the looks of that car, it's either a lawyer or a great customer."

"I'm praying for the latter."

"I'd bet on the former."

"Oh, good grief." Avery dried her hands on an embroidered towel, another new product from a woman at Kathleen's church. "It's Slattery Richmond."

"The oil guy?"

"The oil-and-gas *lawyer*—and one of Creswell's cronies."

Big and blustery, Slattery had played football for LSU with Scooter and had spent recent years as an attorney on the fringes of the law himself. His daughter had had a brief summertime fling with Cres when they were both lifeguards at the country club.

Slattery jerked the screen door open so hard that it flew back against the wall, then charged into the store, a leather satchel in hand. He wore khaki slacks and a short-sleeved golf shirt, despite the weather. Saturday casual, no doubt.

"He's not here for the meat pies," Kathleen murmured. "Get over here."

"Do you think Bill hired him to handle the sale?" Avery whispered.

"Hello, ladies." He looked around the store before sauntering to the counter. "Got any fresh coffee?"

"You're in luck, Slattery. We just brewed a pot."

"Do you take anything in it?" Kathleen asked, her face revealing her annoyance as she meandered toward the self-serve pot.

"Sugar and milk's for sissies." His gaze followed Kathleen for a second, then he turned back and set his briefcase on the counter. "So this is where you've been keeping yourself, Avery. A little different from that dress store where my wife and daughter spend so much money."

Avery looked at him, unafraid.

"And this must be Mrs. Manning," he said as Kathleen reappeared with the coffee. He pulled a money clip out of his pocket and handed her a five-dollar bill. "Keep the change."

"Will there be anything else?" Avery asked.

"As a matter of fact, I have a little something for you." He reached into his pocket and drew out a pair of reading glasses, perching them on his florid nose. Then he patted his slacks, as though looking for something. "Oh, right. It's in here."

He snapped open the case, then pulled out a manila envelope.

He extended his hand, the envelope brushing against Avery's apron.

"Don't take it," Kathleen said.

Slattery shot her an amused look. "Been watching too much *Law & Order*, Miz Manning?"

Kathleen's mouth tightened and she slipped the five back across the counter. "The coffee's on the house. Now if you'll excuse us ..."

Slattery peered at them over the edge of the cup. "Strong. Just like I like it." And with a deft hand, he picked up the money and strolled to the door. "You ladies have a nice day."

Avery lowered a hand to the envelope, but Kathleen swatted it away. "How I miss my nice, calm job at the plant. Maybe we need a lawyer."

"We can't afford one." Avery glanced at the parking lot, where Slattery was talking on his cell phone. "He makes more in an hour than we take in all day."

Kathleen's mouth turned down. "Didn't you have any lawyer friends in that circle you married into?"

"You just met him. And then there's Marsh, but he's helping the Sweet Olive gallery." Avery grabbed the envelope from Kathleen, then ripped it open. A piece of linen letterhead fell to the counter. She fingered the stationery and frowned.

"Greg has filed for legal guardianship of his aunt and uncle. There's some sort of seal here." She read on. "We're no longer permitted to communicate with Bill or Martha."

"Bill's got a better memory than I do!" Kathleen snatched the letter from her hand. "We can fight it. That can't be what's best for Martha and Bill." Kathleen rubbed the seal. "It isn't even official. I'm a notary—used it in my old job. This is fake." She stabbed at the paper with her index finger and let loose a wild laugh. "This is nothing more than a threatening letter. They can't stop us without Bill's permission or a court order."

"Are you sure?"

"One hundred percent. I have my seal at home. Those sneaky liars."

"Could Greg be acting in their best interest? Do you suppose we should meet with all of them?"

The door jingled again, and Kathleen's gaze flew up. "Davis, thank goodness. Maybe you can talk my partner here out of throwing me back into the unemployment line."

"Is there a snag?"

"Dear sweet Greggie wants his aunt and uncle declared mentally incompetent." Kathleen shook her head.

"He's pushing Bill to take a lump-sum offer for the property, instead of our lease-to-own deal." Avery sighed. "Martha's unable to make a business decision, but Bill—"

"I've dealt with Bill for years," Davis said. "He doesn't get around as well as he used to, but his mind's as sharp as mine."

"Greg ought to be ashamed of himself for treating family like that," Kathleen said. "I'm telling you, Avery. We can't let Greg beat us."

"I won't roll over the way I did on the boutique. We'll get Magnolia Market."

Kathleen glanced at the clock. "I need to make a phone call. I'm taking Howie for a walk."

Avery, lips pursed, watched her head out the back door. What was she up to? Was the hassle with the market too much? Or was there trouble with her daughter?

Davis still stood at the counter, sipping on a cup of coffee.

"Bet you wished you'd gone straight to work today," Avery said.

"Are you kidding?" His mouth quirked into a half smile. "I've paid good money for movies that aren't half as good as the show at this place."

"I don't know what's wrong with her. We're keyed up about our offer, but she's been jumping up every few minutes."

He shrugged. "She's probably nervous."

"I suppose." Avery sighed and pointed to the parking lot. "Just what we need. Another visitor in a fancy car."

"I'd better get going." Davis snapped his fingers. "One of my customers said you should look into one of those local foundation grants. Some of them help small businesses trying to fix up neighborhoods."

"Oh, Davis! That's a great idea," Avery called as he walked away. "Thanks for your encouragement. And for protecting me from your aunt."

He was still laughing when he reached the door, then paused to hold it open for the approaching woman. "Hi. Welcome to the loony bin."

"Davis!" Avery chuckled, but he seemed focused on the customer. Thora Fairfield.

A curious smile crossed Thora's face when she looked up at Davis. She wore a pair of jeans and a blue-and-white striped long-sleeved T-shirt under a red-denim jacket. She had aged well. And she didn't belong here, as she hadn't belonged in the midst of Avery's marriage.

But Davis didn't seem to share that sentiment. When she walked past him, he turned and opened his eyes wide, throwing Avery an "okay?" sign. For a second, she thought he was going to follow her into the store.

Thora looked around the market and headed for the counter. "No wonder the asking price has gone up. This place looks great."

Avery stood by the register. "Don't let the mighty Creswell hear that. He's not patient with people who disagree with him."

"So I've learned."

It was hard not to stare at Thora's solemn face, to wonder why Cres had chosen her. But that was a waste of effort now. "I'm guessing you aren't here for lunch," she said instead.

Thora inhaled. "It smells good, but no." She kept looking around.

Avery scooted from around the counter, going face-to-face

with the woman who stood about six inches shorter than she did. They stood for a split second, then Thora spoke.

"I want to apologize."

Avery studied her, expecting a rush of victory. But the words didn't bring the expected satisfaction. She had moved on.

But she couldn't make it quite that easy, so she assumed the look she gave when customers picked over baked goods and didn't make a purchase. She didn't speak.

"I made a terrible mistake in getting involved with Cres." Thora chewed on her bottom lip. "And I've been a coward. I should have called you when he died."

The refrigerator case hummed, and Avery didn't blink.

"I was a kid when I first went out with Cres."

Enough is enough. "Got it. You were young and stupid. Weren't we all?"

"Will you forgive me?"

Avery shrugged. "I suppose."

"You're supposed to make this harder. Make me squirm."

Avery exhaled. "Did you really have to come here?"

Thora touched the base of her neck, the white-gold bracelet sliding almost to her elbow.

Avery reached out and tapped it. "Why do you still wear this?"

"I don't know." She took a step back. "I guess it's a tangible reminder of a day when things seemed happier."

"A child isn't tangible enough?"

Thora took another step back. "So you did see Beau last week."

Beau. He not only has a face, he has a name.

"That's why you came here today, isn't it?"

"Partly," Thora said. "I beg you not to say anything. I'll do whatever you ask."

"Don't his grandparents have a right to know?"

"Yes." She met Avery's gaze. "But I'm afraid they'll try to control his life the way they did Cres's. I couldn't bear it."

"So you went to work for Creswell? That's logical."

"I want to get to know them, maybe see if time does heal. I even saw Evangeline socially once." Thora gave a quick shake of her head. "Not the right approach."

"What about your son's uncle? Any child would be blessed to have Ross in his life. He still hurts over Cres, and Beau might help him move on."

"I regret that the most," Thora said, "other than what I did to you."

"A baby's a mighty big secret to keep in a small town."

"I live in Shreveport, and Beau stays with his grandparents while I'm at work." She fidgeted with the bracelet. "He's never been to Samford, and we're staying in more after . . . after we ran into you that night."

"Doesn't sound like much of a life."

"Anywhere with Beau is good." The love on Thora's face was almost dazzling. "I'm amazed every day that something so pure could have come out of the ugliest thing I've ever done."

"It's your decision," Avery said after a moment. "I won't tell."

The same words she had said to Creswell Sr.

The back door to the store opened, and Howie gave a welcoming bark before darting into the storeroom. "We're b-a-a-a-ck," Kathleen called out and then stopped. "I didn't know we had a customer. Need any help?"

"She's not a customer."

Kathleen raised her eyebrows.

"This is Thora Fairfield."

"I see." Kathleen shot Avery a quick look, her expression furious. She stopped by the register. "I'll handle things here if you want to . . . I don't know. Talk in private? Run her over with your car?"

Thora surrendered a tiny smile. "I came to apologize."

"You're like one of those sports stars," Kathleen scoffed. "The ones who beg forgiveness because they got caught."

"Avery, could you and I have this conversation alone?" Thora's voice rose.

"Afraid not. Kathleen and I are a team."

Kathleen nodded. "Let me guess. You didn't know Cres and Avery were engaged when you started going out."

"I didn't!"

"And our wedding conveniently skipped your mind too? Because as I recall, you were there wearing one of your red dresses. And obviously you kept seeing him." Avery glanced at Kathleen. "Her son's name is Beau."

"Cute."

Thora's face flushed. "When I was in law school, Cres came to New Orleans on business."

"He did that a lot," Avery said.

"My boyfriend had dumped me—"

"How convenient," Kathleen muttered.

"I agreed to have dinner. He told me you were separated."

"Do you want to listen to this, Avery?" Kathleen frowned.

Thora continued before Avery could answer. "I knew it was a mistake before the evening was over. We had words, and he left." She looked down at her hands. "An hour later he was killed."

Avery's eyes widened. All these years she had begrudged Thora sharing her husband's last moments. "You weren't there?"

She shook her head, her lips pursed. "I was at my apartment when Creswell called."

"Of course." Avery's stomach flopped.

"Now that you've tossed your burden on my friend's shoulders, how about leaving?" Kathleen said. "We're expecting paying customers."

"You're fortunate to have a friend like her, Avery. I won't come here again."

"That's a good idea." Avery nodded. "But, for what it's worth, I've forgiven you."

"A real good idea," Kathleen said. "Have a nice day."

Thora walked through the door, then paused by the new trash can on the edge of the parking lot. She slipped the bracelet from her wrist, dropped it in, got in her car, then drove off.

Avery flinched and headed for the door.

"Where are you going?" Kathleen yelled.

"Do you know how many children in Haiti that bracelet can help?"

Chapter 37

*O*n Monday, Martha peered out the back window of the Brown Beast as though released from prison. Getting her in the car had been a chore, but seeing her in the rearview mirror, Avery was glad she had made the effort.

"I wish spring would get here." Martha's voice was shaky.

"It won't be long now." Avery gave a small laugh. "A little more daylight would sure make those early mornings easier."

"Running the store is hard, isn't it? But you meet the nicest people."

"You certainly do." Customers were eager for someone to listen. Avery had discovered how much she enjoyed being on the other end of a conversation.

"We may need to stay open later this summer, Bill," Martha said. "Customers stay out later when it's light outside."

Avery shot a look into the backseat and then at Bill, who had insisted on sitting up front. "You've changed your mind?"

"Don't worry," Martha said. "We'll keep you on, won't we, Bill?"

"I'll think about it." He looked at Avery and lowered his voice. "She's not herself since that heart attack." He tapped his temple.

"That hospital stay really took it out of her. Sometimes she's perfect, and then she gets confused. She can't remember that you made an offer."

"I didn't realize ..."

"Comes with getting old, I reckon. The doctors say she might have a touch of dementia. Most folks don't notice." Bill cleared his throat. "But I still don't know why you wanted to give us a danged tour."

"I don't want you to have regrets."

"Do I need to take an ad out in the newspaper? I've told you, Kathleen, Bud, T. J., Greg ... My regret is not becoming a city employee like my brother. Steady paycheck and health insurance. Good hours. Martha could've been an art teacher, and we might have found a way to have a baby. Even adopted." He rubbed his chin. "She's good with kids and a good artist. We made a mistake when we bought the market."

Something twisted in Avery's stomach. *Are we making a mistake? Is this a bad idea?*

"Magnolia Market was not a mistake," Martha said. "We had a lot of good years there."

"Thanks for sharing it with me," Avery said.

"You've been a big help this past month." Bill wiped at his eyes.

Avery noticed the signs of his fatigue. He had lost weight, and the wrinkles on his face reminded her of the hound dog on a childhood cartoon.

"Let's go on." He coughed. "Might as well get a last look at the old place."

"Did you know we're moving to Hot Springs?" Martha asked. "With both of us getting old, we're going to—" She stopped. "What's it called, Bill?"

"Assisted living. Someone else will do all the work for a change."

"Greggie's taking care of things," Martha said. "He's such a good boy."

Bill let out a sigh. "Greg's a greedy con man," he said in a low, angry voice. "He tried to put us in a nursing home in Samford."

"I've always loved this part of town," Martha said as they approached the light at Trumpet and Vine. "It has such character."

She beamed as Avery pulled the station wagon into the parking lot. "You didn't tell me we put up a new sign."

"Remember, sweetheart? Bud carved it." Bill swiped at his eyes again and turned to look out the other window. "Martha drew that magnolia logo when we first bought the store."

A lump grew in Avery's throat. "It's lovely."

"Pull up there." He gestured to the front door. "But keep your foot on the brake."

"I'm still not quite sure how—"

Martha chuckled. "That's not the first time this store's been run into—"

"Martha," Bill said, "stop your yapping."

"You said you were going to tell her."

"I said 'one of these days.' That's not today." He opened the car door before Avery put the car into Park and used his cane to lift himself. "Let's get this over with. I want to get home in time to watch the news."

Helping Martha out of the car took both of them. "Put your hand on my arm, and take it slow. Avery's got your walker."

"I'll take your other arm," Avery said, but Martha shook her head, not speaking.

"Pork chop, you're not having a spell, are you?" Bill murmured.

Pork chop?

"No, Crawdaddy. I'm taking it all in." She patted Bill's hand. "It looks almost like it did when we first bought it."

Bill covered her hand with his, in the crook of his arm. "You were a young filly. Told me I'd better treat you right or you'd go back to your mama and daddy."

"I did a time or two, didn't I?" Martha's weak chuckle had turned into a full laugh. "But you always wooed me back."

Avery picked at her fingernails, a habit she had given up in high school. This was as uncomfortable as her bridal shower at the country club.

"I hope you don't expect me to carry you over that threshold, Martha, because I don't have that in me."

"Phooey," Martha said. "You could do it in a New York minute, but I don't want you down in your back."

Bill gave a laugh. "Let's go see what Miss Fancy-pants has done to the place."

Avery bolted to the door and held the screen while pushing open the main door. "Kathleen, we're here."

"Howdy, everybody." Greg stepped out of the back. "Took y'all long enough." He eyed Avery. "Store was locked up when I got here with a note on the door. Some kind of shop help this one is!"

Avery frowned and dug the beat-up cell phone out of her purse. Sure enough, there was a text message: JOB-INTERVIEW EMERGENCY. HORRIBLE TIMING. STORE LOCKED. BACK SOON. SOOOO SORRY. XOXO KM.

Greg walked over to kiss Martha on the cheek and shake hands with Bill.

"I told you not to come here again." Bill guided Martha to the old desk chair behind the counter.

Greg ambled to the soft-drink cooler. "You're making a big mistake. Creswell Broussard is willing to beat any other offer."

Greg glanced at Avery. "This is a prime piece of real estate, and you're tying it up for years in some lame lease deal."

Avery halted in front of the counter and started to speak. But then she closed her mouth. With Bill and Martha in their old seats, she felt like she had walked into someone's living room without knocking.

Bill's eyes were focused on Martha, who braced herself against the counter as she rose. She could have been meeting an old friend after a long separation. She waddled out from behind the counter, holding onto it as she moved. "Everything's so clean. It smells good too."

"You left things in great shape," Avery said. "You and Bill built a good business here."

"Is this where we shop, Bill?" Martha stopped to rub her hand on the glass.

"No, dear, this is our store."

"Oh, that's right." With excruciating slowness, she made her way back to where Bill stood.

Avery fought back tears as Bill eased Martha into the old desk chair, but then he opened the cash register and thumbed through the money. "Doesn't look like my nephew has been in the till this time."

Greg's eyes widened. "You'd better deposit those. You don't want that kind of cash lying around."

Bill shook his head and placed the money back into the drawer, then closed it with a ding. "This is Avery's store now."

"So you own this place?" Martha looked across the counter at Avery. "I can tell you love it."

"Very much." Avery swallowed, while Greg moved closer to the register.

JUDY CHRISTIE

"Creswell Broussard is willing to beat Avery's offer. It would be an outright sale—none of this lease-to-own rigmarole. You could get your hands on more money sooner."

Bill sat on his stool, the place he sat the first time Avery had ever seen him. He picked up his big ring of keys from the counter, rubbing the door key with his fingers. "Don't you mean *you* could get your hands on more money sooner?"

Greg scowled.

Martha put her hand up on the brass keys of the cash register. "This nice lady is going to buy it." She gave Avery a bright smile. "She works for us. Have you met her, Greggie?"

"She's a good one." Bill put his hand on Martha's shoulder. "Pork chop, you ready to go home?"

Martha stood, clinging to Bill's arm. "I'll be ready as soon as I make the biscuits."

"I'll take care of those, Martha," Avery said, her voice soft. And she dashed her hand at the tears that trickled down her cheek.

Chapter 38

*M*ay I help—?" Avery stopped midquestion.

Kathleen beamed as Avery's flushed *we're-out-of-biscuits-already?* look disappeared. If Prince William and his wife, Kate, had walked through that door, Avery could not have looked more astonished—or thrilled.

"Surprise!" Kathleen said.

But Avery was already running—*how did she do that in those heels?*—into her father's arms. "Daddy? What? How?" And then she quit talking and settled into his arms, tears pouring down her face.

"Happy birthday a month late, baby girl." Morris sniffed. And he hugged her again, causing tears to pop into Kathleen's eyes. "You look wonderful—and so happy." He wiped his eyes.

When Morris Theriot had exited the airplane, Kathleen was certain she had made a mistake. Expecting an old preacher with stooped shoulders and gray hair, she nearly walked past the man striding off with the gait of an athlete.

Wearing a pair of jeans, a pressed shirt, and cowboy boots, he looked more like a gentleman farmer than the pastors she knew. His wire-frame glasses added a professorial touch.

But the Bible in his hands was the first giveaway, the symbol they had agreed on when they talked yesterday morning. And he had Avery's kind blue eyes.

They reached in for an awkward handshake-turned-hug, and he had pulled her close. "Kathleen, what a pleasure to meet you. You'll never know what you've meant to my daughter." His deep voice sent a tingle down her spine. "You helped her through a difficult time."

"She's meant every bit as much to me. You raised her right." She looked into his eyes. "I'm thankful she went ahead and told you everything."

He reached out and squeezed her hand. "God sent you to her. I'll never know how to repay you."

About her age, Morris had sandy hair, a shade darker than Avery's. He tossed his oversize piece of luggage into the trunk, as though it were a handbag, and opened the car door for her. "I brought another load of crafts."

The way his eyes lit up when he saw his daughter was one of the most attractive things Kathleen had ever seen.

"I don't know what to say." Avery pulled him close again, her ponytail swinging back and forth. "How in the world did you get here?"

"Your friend Kathleen worked it out."

"Leftover frequent-flyer miles. They were going to expire anyway." Kathleen smiled. "Davis pitched in a few too."

"That's the nicest, best, most wonderful thing ever—" Avery stopped. "Your hair. It's red again!"

Kathleen put her hand up to the spiky strands. "I was ready for a change. And this time I'll stick with it."

"I love it! Daddy, don't you love it?"

Morris looked at her, a quirk to his mouth. "I've always liked redheads."

"So your wife was a redhead?" Kathleen asked.

"She had brownish hair, darker than Avery's." He shook his head. "But my first love, way back in sixth grade, had red hair. She was a firecracker."

"Kathleen is too." Avery glanced from her father to her friend.

"I can tell." He grinned.

"She's the best, Dad."

Kathleen put her hands on her hips. "You threw me for a loop, child, when you decided to pick up Martha and Bill. I was calling all over the place for someone to mind the store."

"And then you were gone. I had to ask Camille to keep an eye on things when I took them home." Avery's eyes flew open wide. "I forgot to tell you! Bill left the final paperwork for us to sign. Marsh is stopping by later to take care of it. And he's going to let us pay his fee in fried pies."

Kathleen let out her big laugh. "Hooray!"

"Praise the Lord," Morris said.

"Group hug!" Avery said. The three of them hugged, Kathleen and Avery jumping up and down.

"Is everything okay?" T. J. stepped through the door, tool belt slung around his hips.

Avery laughed. "Everything's perfect." She grabbed her father by the hand. "This is my father, Morris Theriot. Daddy, this is T. J. Aillet." Exuberant, she gave T. J. a quick hug.

He extended his hand, and Morris shook it slowly.

Kathleen knew that assessing look. She had seen Wayne use it on Lindsey's boyfriends.

"Good to meet you, son. Avery's spent quite a bit of our phone time lately talking about you."

"Dad!"

T. J. threw her that potent grin. "She's a special woman."

"You two have so much in common, Daddy. I told you about New Wine, T. J.'s mission on the other side of town, and they're doing some of the things you're doing in Haiti. And, T. J., my dad's pretty handy with a hammer and nail too."

"Morris is a great storyteller also," Kathleen said. "You should hear all he's got going on. The story about young Angel just about made me pull over by the side of the road and weep."

Avery moved to stand near her dad. "Did something happen to Angel?"

Morris nodded. "Her mother's sister has asked her to move in with them. They will have to stretch to make it work, but we're all thrilled."

"And Angel?"

"She loved the shoes you sent but is worried you won't visit her if she leaves the orphanage."

"Oh, Daddy, you know I will. Be sure to tell her I'll always visit."

T. J. looked at Kathleen out of the corner of his eye and winked.

Seeing him light up every time he looked at Avery added a sparkle to the market. And the strain of the past month—probably from the past few years—had melted from Avery's eyes.

"You, you tricky thing." She turned to Kathleen. "You said you went on a job interview."

"I did. Before I went to the airport."

"Oh," Avery said. "And you were turned down for a thirty-year-old who has three young children to support?"

Kathleen raised her eyebrows. "I got an offer."

"What?"

"My old boss is starting a small manufacturing business. He needs me part-time."

"Didn't he move to Minnesota?"

"Not for long. It isn't the best corporate strategy to transfer someone to Minnesota in January. His wife and kids never moved, and he hated it up there." She raised an eyebrow. "So he came back. He's begging me to work for him—can't afford me full-time, though."

A smile crept onto Avery's face. "How would this work?"

"I'm thinking we keep our fifty-fifty investment, and you run it full-time. I fill in." She shrugged. "We'll figure out the rest."

"Sounds like a plan to me."

"I have more news," Kathleen said. "I was telling your father about Lindsey in one of our e-mails, and he suggested I call her."

"I've been telling you that for a couple of weeks."

"I know, but he's got a parent's perspective. But that's not the good part. I worked up my nerve and invited her for a visit."

"Oh, Kathleen, that's fantastic."

"She sounded glad to hear from me and said she's been thinking about going back to school. I told her you and I would love to have her live with us." Kathleen gave a tentative smile. "We'll see."

The bell on the door jingled, and one of their regular customers stepped in, smiling. "Hey, Avery, what's the special today?"

"Jambalaya, and it's good."

"Everything's good." T. J. eyed Avery.

"Could I get four orders?" The woman glanced at a slip of paper. "Any bread pudding today?"

"I can help you," Kathleen called. "Morris, want to see what it looks like in the command center?"

"Great idea," Avery said. "Would you mind, Dad?"

"It would be my pleasure."

Avery swatted Kathleen on the rear end and winked. "How about you, T. J.? The special?"

"Wouldn't miss it. And then I'm going to hang your new awning. You were right about the stripes. They look awesome, and the company got it back in record time."

The sight of Avery's sparkling eyes and big smile made Kathleen want to yell with sheer joy. Who would have expected their string of awfulness to wind up so happily?

She shifted her attention to Morris and recalled the Bible verse taped to her bathroom mirror. "Weeping may stay for the night, but rejoicing comes in the morning." Kathleen gave in to the moment and let out a jubilant whoop.

⌒

Avery pulled the Brown Beast into the bank parking lot that afternoon before closing time and brushed flour off her jeans. Maybe she should have dressed—no, she liked this look. Too bad she hadn't borrowed Camille's cowboy boots.

With a Magnolia Market canvas tote thrown over her shoulder, she strolled toward the lobby. Through the glass, Scooter watched, his face expressionless. At the last moment, he stepped forward and held the door. "They're expecting you."

Avery nodded and headed toward the elevator, an odd calm settling on her as she approached the office.

Evangeline sat in the chair Avery had used on her last visit.

Was that only a month ago? Creswell was on the phone in Scooter's desk chair, turned toward the window.

A bolt of unexpected anger zinged through her but disappeared almost as quickly as it appeared. Avery could not erase the past, but she had moved beyond life in the Broussard family.

Her gaze met Creswell's in the window's reflection, and he stared at her for a second before ending the call and turning. Evangeline shifted at the same time, her attention going first to Avery's jeans and then to the empty ring finger.

Avery had sealed her wedding band in an envelope to send to a Shreveport thrift shop benefiting an animal shelter, then headed to the post office. But in the end she circled back and asked Kathleen to drop the anonymous package in a mailbox for her.

Evangeline wore a suit Avery had not seen before, nothing from earlier boutique collections. A gold brooch, a gift from Cres and Avery, graced the lapel. The choice was encouraging.

"Thank you for meeting with me." Avery walked to the chair next to Evangeline.

Evangeline was more rigid than the coatrack at the boutique. "May I?"

Evangeline's nod was so slight it was almost imperceptible, but Avery lowered herself into the chair with ease.

"You missed your deadline. Let's get this over with." Creswell's gaze shifted from right to left, anywhere but Avery's face.

"You've come to your senses?" Evangeline asked.

"Yes."

"Finally. When will you be leaving?"

"I won't leave. And I expect you to withdraw your offer for the market—and any other property at the corner of Trumpet and Vine."

Evangeline made an inelegant snort. "Why would we do that?"

Creswell fidgeted with a monogrammed cuff link.

Standing, Avery held up her fingers. "One: The money is mine. I expect it and the rest of the money from my savings account. Two: Razing the corner will hurt Samford, a town that has made you wealthy, in ways that can never be repaired. And three—" She paused, even though it was clear she had Creswell's attention.

"You're so naive," Evangeline said.

"Let her finish." Creswell sounded like a parent chiding a child.

The inflection, so similar to Cres's when Avery displeased him, caused a rush of sympathy—and relief—that a new part of life had begun.

"It's past time we put everything—and I do mean everything— behind us."

"Cash the check." Creswell's voice was low. "Buy that ridiculous grocery store. But don't ever contact us again."

Avery bit her cheek to keep from smiling.

"You're not going to let her win," Evangeline snapped. "Everyone in town will talk about us."

"Sounds like another excuse for you to run away to the beach house."

Evangeline's mouth opened, even as her eyes narrowed at her husband's words.

"Scooter's waiting downstairs." Creswell waved toward the door. "See him on your way out."

Avery walked out of the office, then hesitated and walked back toward Evangeline. "There's one more thing." It was time to let go of the last of her shackles.

Sweat popped out on Creswell's forehead.

Avery reached into her tote bag and pulled out her heavy

white-gold bracelet. Placing it in Evangeline's hand, she closed her fingers around the cool metal, their two hands clasped together for a moment.

"Cres loved you very much." She turned on her heel and walked away.

Chapter 39

Avery straightened the new Haitian crafts her father had brought and lit three vanilla candles, one on each table and one on the counter.

Their scent mingled with leftover smells of lunch and coffee—and the étouffée she had fixed for dinner. Only the dim light over the register was on. After all, she wouldn't want to confuse the customers.

The bells on the front door jingled, and a smile lit her face. A man, more than six feet tall, stood on the threshold, the person she had been expecting.

He looked over at the big round clock on the wall behind the counter and wrinkled his nose. "Did I get my wires crossed?"

"This is Magnolia Market. What address were you looking for?"

"I'm T. J. Aillet, and I'm looking for Avery Broussard."

"You found her," she said softly, and he moved to gather her in a hug.

He glanced down at her feet. "I want you to know you're the only person whose shoes I've ever noticed."

She laughed, and he kissed her, running his fingers through her hair.

"Ahem."

Did the bell on the door jingle?

"Ross!" Avery jumped back, her face flooding with heat.

Ross Broussard stood inside, his face unreadable. "When I asked you to check on Avery, T. J., looks like you took it seriously."

Even in February, he was tan, every golden hair in place. With his dress slacks, starched shirt, and blue-striped tie, he could have been about to sign a big real-estate deal or preach at a wedding. But his eyes looked tired, and his mouth was tight.

"Best favor I ever did for anyone." T. J.'s eyes were wary. "When'd you get back?"

"This afternoon." The veins in his neck stuck out. "Marsh said I'd probably find the two of you here. Congratulations on signing the papers, Avery—and whatever else is going on."

"I was going to call you, man," T. J. said, "but things have been crazy."

Ross looked at the candlelit table. "So that's what you call it when you start fooling around with my brother's wife?"

"Ross." His name was mixed with a gasp as it left Avery's mouth.

"Uncalled for." T. J. stepped forward, his fists clenched. "Avery doesn't deserve that."

"Wait, T. J." She put her hand on his arm. "Ross, I should have told you we were getting ... close, but it's brand-new. And I didn't want to hurt you."

"You hurt me by not calling me back and avoiding me whenever possible." He crossed his arms. "You were my sister-in-law for five years. Doesn't that mean something?"

"Yes, it does." Her voice was so quiet that the hum of the

cooler almost obscured it. "I loved Cres, but it didn't work out and now he's gone."

T. J. opened his mouth, but Avery squeezed his arm.

"I want your blessing to move on, Ross." She sniffed. "I want us to be friends and to make new memories."

Ross cleared his throat. "I wish my brother had made different decisions, but he wasn't all bad."

"No, he wasn't." She moved toward him and gave him a quick embrace before stepping back to T. J.'s side. "I'll never forget the good. But I'm putting the bad behind me. Starting over."

He narrowed his eyes, looking toward T. J. "This caught me off guard."

"Me too." She gripped T. J.'s hand. "But I'm thankful. For so much, I'm thankful. Finally."

"I never intended this to happen," T. J. said.

"You'd better not hurt her." Ross's voice was rough.

"I promise you I won't."

Ross looked around, drawing a deep breath. "Am I interrupting a romantic dinner?"

"Not exactly," Avery said.

"Sorta," T. J. said.

Avery looked from one man to the other. "My father surprised me today, and we're having a family celebration." She could hardly wait to see her dad's face when she slipped him the money from the Broussard check. It would go a long way to help Angel's aunt raise her.

"How about joining us?" T. J. asked.

Ross looked first at Avery and then at T. J. "I don't think so, but the store looks great." He picked up a praline and studied it. "This corner changed in a hurry."

"I'm working with Camille and the gallery to bring Trumpet and Vine back to life. We're applying for a grant. There's hope here."

"Avery's serious," T. J. said. "She's considering running for city council."

Ross's eyes widened. "I guess you've decided to get out from behind the counter." He gave a slight smile.

"I guess I have."

"Well . . ." Ross shuffled his loafers on the floor. "I promised the folks I'd have dinner with them at the Samford Club. We'll visit another time."

When Ross walked through the door, the screen creaked. The sight of his back left a hollow feeling in her stomach.

But then she turned to T. J., and her heart felt as if it might pop.

"Are you okay?" He drew her up against his chest.

She nodded, rubbing her cheek against his shirt. "I'm good."

T. J. pulled back. "I brought you a belated birthday gift." He pulled a small package from his jacket pocket. "Bud made it."

Her hands trembling, she pulled out a carving of a dog. "It's Fearless," she gasped.

"Does it look like him? I asked Bud to make his ears extra pointy."

"It's exactly like him." Tears blurred her eyes.

T. J. bent to kiss her, and she leaned in, one high heel off the floor.

As they pulled apart, slowly, she opened her eyes a slit and looked over at the biscuit case.

New mercies. God's compassions never fail.

The traffic signal flashed through the display window, and Avery snuggled against T. J. New mercies were ahead.

New mercies were here.

At this corner.

Her future beckoned. A store of her own. Kathleen's friendship. A chance to help others.

And this man, solid and warm.

With delight, she lifted her face to meet his lips once more.

Discussion Questions

1. An unexpected calamity rattles Avery Broussard and sets in motion a variety of changes in her life. How does she handle it, and what might you have done differently? Have you ever had an accident, illness, or tragedy that resulted in change? What advice might you offer to someone in the midst of such a situation?

2. Magnolia Market brings an assortment of people together to help one another, sometimes reluctantly. How do the characters learn from each other? Who in your life has lent a helping hand when you needed it? Is there someone you know who might need your help now?

3. In what ways are people in Samford contradictions? Are they good and bad? In your experience, are people what they seem on the surface? Why or why not?

4. Before the novel opens, Avery withdraws from friends and family for a year. Why does she do this? Have you ever had a time when you retreated from the world? How might you help someone hurting in such a way?

5. Avery and T. J. are young adults, growing and making a difference in their community. But they also need coaching, mentoring, and wisdom. Who helps on their journeys? How do they respond? Who in your life has played such a role? Is there someone who might benefit from your guidance?

6. What do you think of the importance of family in this story? What are the good aspects of family? What troubles you about these families?

7. Avery and Kathleen come from different corners of Samford and don't seem to have much in common. What draws them together? Do you have people you are close to who are different? What binds you together? How do you benefit from these relationships?

8. Avery's father is a missionary in Haiti. While Morris does wonderful work with an orphanage there, he is away from his daughter during a time of sorrow. Do you think he makes the right choices? Has your work or calling ever taken you away from those you love?

9. The betrayal by Avery's husband is one of the hard issues this story addresses. How did Avery deal with this trauma? Have you ever made a major life decision that did not go the way you planned? How did you handle it?

10. Avery and Kathleen need a fresh start. In what ways do they go about it? What part does faith play in their stories?

11. Magnolia Market is located at the intersection of Trumpet and Vine, where lives intersect. Where in your life do you connect with others? How might a group help build community?

12. Avery makes decisions—large and small—that affect

others. What are some examples? What is their impact? Are there people in your life who make a difference in the world around them? How do they do it?

13. At times T. J. and Avery have trouble trusting each other. What is at the root of their suspicion? How do they handle their struggles? Have you ever had a tough time trusting someone else? What advice about trust might you give someone?

14. What inspires Avery to make changes in her life? What steps does she take, and how do they turn out? Have you ever made a major change? What did you learn from it? How might you coach someone about to embark on a fresh start?

15. The market itself becomes a character in this novel, and regional food plays a major role in its personality. What draws people to the market? What does Avery learn from her work behind the counter? Do you have a favorite market or place to eat? What is the specialty in the area where you grew up?

Kathleen's Easy Pralines

1 large package vanilla pudding mix (not instant)
1 cup sugar
½ cup brown sugar
½ cup evaporated milk (not condensed)
1 tsp. margarine
1 cup chopped pecans

Combine pudding, sugars, and milk in boiler. (Double boiler can be used but isn't necessary.) Cook over medium heat, stirring until sugar dissolves. Cook until mixture reaches full boil and then boil for 2 to 3 minutes (until good soft-ball stage*). Remove from heat. Add margarine and nuts. Beat candy until it thickens. Drop by spoonfuls onto waxed paper. Let set until firm.

A tip from Sarah, who shared this recipe: "The key to making these pralines is knowing when to start spooning them onto the waxed paper. They harden pretty fast. Don't beat too long. (It's easy to beat them too long thinking they won't harden.)"

* Soft-ball stage is when the mixture forms a soft ball when dropped in cold water. Keep a little dish of cold water by the stove and test the mixture every few minutes (getting fresh water each time). The longer it cooks, the firmer it will be in cold water. A variety of factors can affect how quickly pralines harden, but don't be afraid to give this recipe a try.

Quick Mini Binis (Beignets)

1 cup self-rising flour
⅛ tsp. salt
Dash of nutmeg
2 T. honey
½ cup buttermilk
Vegetable oil—enough to make a minimum of 2 inches in
    your frying pan
1 cup powdered sugar (have measured in a heatproof dish,
    ready to receive hot mini binis)

Measure all ingredients.
Pour oil into the pan and begin to heat.
Mix flour, salt, and nutmeg in a bowl. Add honey and buttermilk and stir until combined.

When oil is at the proper frying temperature (360° F), drop the batter in batches (I use a small cookie scoop) into the hot oil. Do not crowd with too many at a time, as this will decrease the temperature and allow for oil absorption. Continuously monitor temperature, turning the mini binis as they brown.

When golden brown on all sides, remove from the oil and place into dish containing the powdered sugar. Coat, then plate the cooked mini binis.

Continue cooking in batches until all batter is used. Yield 12 mini binis, 4 servings.

—From Cindy Gleason Johnson http://southernfaire.blogspot
.com/2013/04/quick-mini-binis.html. Used with permission.

With Gratitude

What fun it has been to gather again at the corner of Trumpet and Vine—and what a debt I owe to many, including my home state of Louisiana that provides flavor to write about.

A special thanks to:

My agent Janet Grant, editor Julee Schwarzburg, and the entire team at HarperCollins Christian Publishing. What a blessing it is to have such help on this adventure.

To friends and readers who step up in numerous ways, from phone calls and letters to blackberry cobblers, including Ginger Hamilton, Carol Lovelady, and Kathie Rowell; Karen Enriquez, who helps with my Spanish language questions; the creative Mary Dark, who inspired the name New Wine; Cindy Gleason Johnson, who shared her mini beignet recipes; Sarah Leachman with her Ashland recipes; and a host of other authors, including Carla Stewart, Kellie Gilbert, Lisa Wingate, Liz Talley, and Lenora Worth, who enrich my life in ways too numerous to list; and to my family, the Paces and the Christies.

And always to my husband, Paul.

About the Author

*J*udy Christie writes fiction with a Louisiana flavor. She is the author of the Green series of novels including Gone to Green. A fan of primitive antiques and porch swings, she blogs from her green kitchen couch at www.judychristie.com. She and her husband live in northern Louisiana.

The self-help books lied: fresh
starts aren't nearly as glamorous
as they appear. And love isn't
any easier the second time around.

AVAILABLE IN PRINT AND E-BOOK.